"*LET'S GO LET'S GO LET'S GO* is sharp and [   ] sticky aspects of having flesh. This coll[   ] outsiders of different shades, of people [   ] their realities with secret and burning questions. There are really tender portraits of yearning, of the unsteady but pre-, cious entanglements of both platonic and romantic love. It's careful and soberly rendered, and it was a pleasure to read."

—RAVEN LEILANI,
author of *Luster*

"Perfectly askew, the stories in *LET'S GO LET'S GO LET'S GO* thrum with restless questioning and acute longing, shot through with a tart, knowing sense of humor. It seemed to vibrate in my hands as I read it." **—LING MA,**
author of *Bliss Montage*

"Cleo Qian's *LET'S GO LET'S GO LET'S GO* is an uncanny Asian American fantasia where fringe artist collectives, melancholy K-pop stars, anxious piano prodigies, disembodied digital ghosts, and lovelorn alchemists converge. Deeply psychological, these stories confront the bizarre horrors of modern life, finding surprising beauty and supernatural catharsis. I'll be thinking about these characters for a long, long time."

—JEAN CHEN HO,
author of *Fiona and Jane*

"Mischievous and hypnotizing, *LET'S GO LET'S GO LET'S GO* takes us to manifold narrative realms where stories self-proliferate and artificial simulations often hijack and replace reality. Formally complex and emotionally potent, this is a collection I'll return to again and again." **—YAN GE,**
author of *Strange Beasts of China*

"In *LET'S GO LET'S GO LET'S GO*, Qian devastates like the best photographs from our youth, making us long for what's lost while never losing sight of what is necessary for survival. The stories remind you that what you observe is already gone, and make you want to pay closer attention to what is already passing into memory." —**KYLE DILLON HERTZ**, author of *The Lookback Window*

LET'S GO LET'S GO LET'S GO

stories

CLEO QIAN

TIN HOUSE / PORTLAND, OREGON

Copyright © 2023 by Cleo Qian

First US Edition 2023
Printed in the United States of America

Manufacturing by Lake Book Manufacturing
Interior design by Beth Steidle

Library of Congress Cataloging-in-Publication Data

Names: Qian, Cleo, 1993– author.
Title: Let's go let's go let's go : stories / Cleo Qian.
Other titles: Let us go let us go let us go
Description: First US edition. | Portland, Oregon : Tin House, 2023.
Identifiers: LCCN 2023006439 | ISBN 9781953534927 (paperback) |
ISBN 9781959030003 (ebook)
Subjects: LCGFT: Short stories.
Classification: LCC PS3617.I36 L48 2023 | DDC 813/.6—dc23/eng/20230217
LC record available at https://lccn.loc.gov/2023006439

Tin House
2617 NW Thurman Street, Portland, OR 97210
www.tinhouse.com

DISTRIBUTED BY W. W. NORTON & COMPANY

1 2 3 4 5 6 7 8 9 0

For the ones who want to escape

Yes, I am a person so ordinary that I cannot be more ordinary, so plain I cannot be plainer, a girl like all the other girls. I like to eat snacks, I like to have fun, and I like to look pretty. So from being ordinary and plain I will make my start.

—FROM CHUNMING'S DIARY,
IN LESLIE T. CHANG'S *FACTORY GIRLS*

I still heard a terrible whining noise in my head. It stayed with me for a long time. I knew what it meant. Emergency, emergency . . . Being a girl was beginning to feel more and more dangerous.

—CATHERINE LIU,
ORIENTAL GIRLS DESIRE ROMANCE

TABLE OF CONTENTS

CHICKEN. FILM. YOUTH.

It was hard to articulate the point at which we switched from wanting to get older to feeling like we could stand to be a little bit younger. Perhaps there had never been a point when we *really* felt like we wanted to be older, only to have the things we thought being older entailed: freedom, money, privacy, love. But it had always been true that if we were a little bit younger, a little bit fresher, then we'd be a little bit better.

It was raining in LA, a slurry of wet in a city never designed for it. Water poured down from rooftops and pooled in inconvenient potholes. Aggressive Porsche 718s and equally aggressive Honda CR-Vs competed on right turns, raising miniature tsunamis over the sidewalks. Sitting by the windows of Mr. Kang's chicken restaurant, we watched the rain drizzle over the billboards and blinking lights advertising the other stores in the strip mall: the Thai restaurant, the shaved-ice café, the boba-and-crepe shop, the Tofu House, and the aspirational artisanal grocery store with the twenty-six-dollar charcuterie plates. The rain made the strip mall look muted, pretty, the neon lights taking on a fairy-tale aura as they blurred through the pane.

"Half-and-half spicy sauce and soy garlic," Mr. Kang called out.

"Grab some radish, too," Dake reminded me as I pushed my chair back. When I put the tray on the table, he said, "This chicken looks amazing."

The fried chicken, unveiled from its styrofoam lid, glistened with a honeyed texture. Underneath its sprinkling of white sesame seeds, the skin of the chicken pieces beckoned with its coy, crisp, perfectly golden color. In an unusual move that had given this restaurant its write-up in the *Times*, the chicken was layered with a hearty handful of cut fruit: avocado, raspberries, blueberries, and a few slices of jalapeño. When we bit in, the meat was warm, moist, and tender. Eileen *mmm*ed. The glazed fruit added a startlingly light contrast to the meat.

Jessica sucked on her iced water. The rest of us all had beers. Jessica was a killjoy who cared about calories. And something about how alcohol caused skin aging? When she was a kid, she had entered into beauty pageants. She wore little tiaras, had skin so bright and glowing it was like her face was a spotlight. Now she was still pretty, but she wasn't a pageant winner. She was a dental hygienist. She wore fuzzy cardigans and circle lenses. Every year she spent hundreds, if not thousands, on skincare, makeup, and lash extensions to keep her three thousand Instagram followers and trickle of occasionally fraudulent sponsorship offers, but hey, what else could she do? She was no longer twenty-two. She was twenty-eight.

We were all twenty-eight, or just about to turn twenty-nine. There were four of us: Dake, Jessica, Eileen, and me. Dake and I were high school friends. We met in LA, or more precisely, Long Beach, where we went to the California Institute of Mathematics and Science, which is a magnet school for cutthroat bitches and overachievers. It's the kind of place where if you aren't already taking college-level calculus when you're in eighth grade, you're behind. When I transferred in, Dake and I bonded over our mutual relative inferiority.

Senior prom, there had been a "let's go as friends" date, an awkward kiss, emotional fallout, and then we stopped speaking—until the summer he was interning at Snapchat, I was interning at the LA Department of Cultural Affairs, we got lunch, and things were okay again. Sometimes I look at him and wonder a little what we would be like together, but for the most part, I leave it alone.

"Luna, tell me about you and Billy," Eileen said to me.

"God, I can't believe you're dating someone named *Billy.*" Dake's sardonic tone made me bristle with a slight frisson of irritation.

"I know, I know," I said, trying to shrug it off. Billy was new. I'd run into him in a Trader Joe's. My cart had stiff wheels. He had two towering stacks of canned San Marzano tomatoes and cannellini beans in his arms. An accidental nudge and they all came tumbling down. One can bounced off the naked toenail of my big toe. "I'm so sorry," I gasped, as my toe throbbed. "I'm so sorry," he gasped. He ran to find an employee to get a Band-Aid for the toe. There were no other injuries.

"Has it been awkward, you know, dating white?" Eileen probed.

"It's been okay so far, but there are some moments where I'm like, oh, you don't come from the same place I do. Like when we got mochi ice cream and he didn't eat the mochi skin. He took it off and just ate the ice cream."

I was Billy's second Asian girlfriend, but he had dated a couple of white girls and one Latinx girl and didn't watch anime, so I was fairly confident he didn't have yellow fever. Aside from one ill-begotten crush on a white boy named Andrew in high school, my exes, including Kevin, a chemistry-major-now-turned-Twitch-streamer from college, Aaron, a photographer I'd met in New York, and Minji, the on-again off-again DJ ex-girlfriend I'd been entangled with in LA, had all been of East Asian ancestry.

"That could be you being classist," Jessica pointed out, annoyingly. "Mochi ice cream is kind of bougie."

"I guess that's true." I tried to concede.

It was fun to be in a relationship again, to have someone around to watch TV and do shrooms with while laughing at the dumb things people on reality shows said. With Billy, I felt safe, even a little bored. There were nights when I forgot to think about him. There were nights when, sitting next to him, I sensed that in one year, two years, even four years, I might wake up and find that all that time had passed and I was still with him, and that would not be the worst thing. This feeling terrified me.

I changed the subject. "To Eileen," I said, cracking open a new can of Hite and raising it into the air. Ostensibly, we were gathered to celebrate Eileen's promotion to senior marketing manager at the wellness app she'd worked at for three years.

"Oh my god, thank you," Eileen groaned. "It's been five years, three apartments, four terrible roommates, and a broken-down car, but I can finally upgrade to living alone now! Thank the LORD."

Eileen was from Manhattan, and before she moved to LA, had never touched a steering wheel. Back at Barnard, we were mainly party friends: we'd meet up to pregame with shots at someone's apartment before going out to dance sloppily with blurry strangers or text misbegotten matches from Tinder. We lost touch until I burned out on New York and moved back to California two years ago. Now she had a Class C license, a Prius, and a new job title; I was working at a nonprofit and had private healthcare for the first time in years; and our friends were being promoted to middle management and getting engaged.

The rain trickled outside. The restaurant felt private. The only other group was sitting all the way at the other end, next to a couple of pulpy movie posters with titles I didn't know. The beer, the smell of oil, the hot food and lights made me feel woozy, dreamy. Our conversation revolved around the people we knew. Jessica had three wedding invitations for summer. Eileen's cousin's start-up had just IPOed. Our college friend Melissa had finished her PhD. Minji, my ex, had scored a sponsorship from The North Face. And my cousin Vicky had just proposed to her girlfriend and won funding to lead a major new research project, something on a boat, in Puerto Rico.

"Rachel and Danny just bought a house," Dake said.

"Oh my god, *what*? In *LA*? Where?"

"*And* they got a dog," he continued.

"How did they afford a house?" Jessica demanded. "What neighborhood is it? Is it, like, a real house, or is it, like, a condo? This does *not* sound like a good idea. She was *just* thinking of breaking up with him in November!"

Dake shrugged. He worked at Facebook and probably had enough money of his own to buy a house, but was embarrassed about it. "I mean, everything's easier with two people."

"Are they going to get engaged, or what?" Eileen popped a radish cube into her mouth.

"Danny told me he's planning on asking soon." Dake's Adam's apple bobbed as he finished his Hite. Jessica rolled her eyes.

"One of my coworkers is going to Taiwan to freeze her eggs," I offered.

"Oh my god! Isn't that really expensive? How old is she?"

"She's doing it in Taiwan because it's way cheaper there. She's in her midthirties," I said, but already I felt guilty for spilling someone else's secret. My coworker was a divorcée. Her ex-husband had always hesitated about kids and now she felt like she had waited too long for him to make up his mind. But in my mind, thirty and twenty-eight were basically the same, and people I knew might have to make similar decisions soon.

What about all our potential? Where had it gone?

*

"NO MORE ORDERS!" Mr. Kang shouted into the phone, and we all jumped. He slipped his phone into his apron with the energy of someone slamming down a landline.

"Should we get going?" Dake eyed Mr. Kang, whose eyebrows gave him a murderous intensity. The other group got up and bussed their trays to the trash can.

"We should be fine." Jessica checked her phone. "It closes at nine. Ten minutes."

"Where are we going after this? Jessica, do you have to go back?"

"No, Henry is out with his other friends tonight." Henry was Jessica's long-term college boyfriend. He was such a fixture that no one even thought about him anymore, like the streetlamp you walk under on the way to your friend's house. I honestly thought he was cute; he had a quiet attention that would switch on to you like a lightbulb when he listened to you, intense and consuming. He didn't hang out with us often. I wondered who his other friends were.

No one had asked if I was busy. No one was used to me being in a relationship yet. Billy wanted to come over tonight; we would probably watch a movie, go to sleep, and take our bikes to Frogtown in the morning, but it had been a while since the four of us had gotten together and now I didn't want to leave.

Specifically, it was still a novelty to be hanging out with Jessica again. Not even a full year after Eileen introduced us, our fallout had culminated with me calling her a selfish, only-child bitch and her snorting that I was a codependent Negative Nancy with the impulsivity of a twelve-year-old. Eileen and Dake had shuttled back and forth between us like the children of divorced parents. Only a few months ago, when Jessica and I ran into each other at an acquaintance's birthday party, had we started talking again. In the group chat, we were a little too eager to laugh at each other's jokes. We didn't mention the rupture, but she had to be thinking about it, too.

Dake scrolled Yelp on his phone. Eileen gestured at the movie posters on the opposite wall. "The *Times* said the owner here used to be a movie director."

"Really?" Jessica turned to look at the posters. "So did he do those movies up there?"

I pulled up the article on my phone to check. A text message from Billy: *Hey, when are you going to be done?* I swiped left so the notification disappeared. "That's wild. How did he start running a fried chicken restaurant?"

"You wanna know?"

We looked up, and Mr. Kang was standing next to our table. No one had heard him come up. His shirtsleeves were rolled, his shoulders straining the seams. His arms were crossed and his forearms looked like what I imagined Popeye's would after he had eaten his spinach.

"Uhh . . ." We blinked awkwardly at the owner. We were the only customers left in the restaurant. The sound of rain intensified; the view through the window grew blurrier.

"Sorry, what?" Dake said.

"You want to know how I went from directing movies at the beginning of the Korean wave to running a chicken restaurant at the edge of K-town?" Mr. Kang asked again, thunderously.

"Um . . . the chicken is really good," Eileen said timidly.

He slapped his thighs. "You're absolutely right! My fried chicken is in-CREDIBLE! The best in LA! You won't find better! So. You want to know the secret? You wanna know how I got here?"

He abruptly picked up the tray with our styrofoam container on it. The chicken had been picked clean, only the bones were left.

"Let's go in the back," he said, and we followed.

*

The back of the restaurant was a supply room. Next to a monumental steel fridge there was another door. Mr. Kang opened it, and instead of the door leading to a plumbing closet or private bathroom, it led into a movie theater.

Mr. Kang shuffled around while we clumped together at the entryway. The theater had a soft red carpet, a single leather reclining chair, reclining chair, and a ghostly white screen that covered an entire wall with a projector mounted across from it. He turned on the projector, which whirred alive and beamed a blue light onto the screen.

"Sit down," he boomed. "You don't want to watch the movie standing up. You want beer? I'll get you more. On the house."

Dake looked at me; I looked back and shrugged. Jessica raised her eyebrows. "Not for me," she said delicately.

"That would be great," I said over her, annoyed. "Thanks."

Brass music played from a speaker installed in some upper corner. *Kang Original Productions* flashed on the screen. "I have lived an ordinary life," Mr. Kang said, but the voice came from the speakers. It was a voice-over, his own. The voice faded. The sound stopped. The screen cut to a student sitting at a window in a classroom full of children in dark uniforms. He was young, a boy with a blunt nose and curly hair. Mr. Kang?

The real Mr. Kang reappeared, shoving a cold can into my hand. I startled. Up close, his face was haunted and bluish under the light of the projector.

"Sit down, kids," he grunted. He sank into the recliner. The rest of us found our way to the floor.

In front of us, the setting of Mr. Kang's life—if this was his life—spun out on the reel. The camera panned across a landscape. We saw a soggy town, surrounded by hills, which the boy frequently looked beyond, as though longing to escape. His mother, a hairdresser, a woman of constant sighs, sweeping up black scraps of hair from the floor. His father, behind the flickering sign of a pawnshop, sitting at a counter in a room filled with the detritus of once-loved items. Lighting played in advanced, subtle ways: shadows articulated into sheaths of cut hair, soft darkness resolved into unfurnished rooms in the shade of gloomy hills. Had he done this all by himself? A piano, startlingly clear, played four chords in a minor progression. The lens settled again on the student, the young Kang.

*

The boy Kang passed through school. He was a solitary child, silent around classmates, bored at home. After class, he read movie

magazines and browsed the DVD rental store. Then college came. He
went to Seoul. He attended parties, smoked cigarettes, learned how
to get drunk. Kissed a girl at one party, lost his virginity at another.
At the university film club, he met an upperclassman who liked him,
treated him to a dinner out. The upperclassman brought his girlfriend, also in the film club, a pretty girl with long, silky black hair.
She started hanging out with Kang occasionally, complaining about
something her boyfriend had said, and let him put a hand on her
shoulder while she teared up.

In the evenings, the boy Kang worked at an Internet café where
drunk patrons pressed in on him with haunted faces. He wrote movie
reviews for a small-time paper, saved up enough to get his own camera.
One day, he was working at the Internet café, trying to write his script
while manning the desk. A client came in, a tall man in a black pea-
coat, with amazing amounts of gel in his hair. The man looked around.
He asked about rates. He sat down at one of the computers, clicked
around for a bit, and came back. Asked Kang what he was working on.

"You want to make movies?" the client asked. "What's your story
about?"

He pulled up a folding chair and listened to the script idea. The
man offered some pointers, gave some advice on structuring scenes,
then the boy Kang realized who he was. "You're Park Myungjae," he
said, naming the famous director of one of the year's most popular
indie films, which had even been shown at Cannes. It was a big deal
for a Korean director's films to be shown at Cannes, and he had been
the pride of the nation.

The famous director began telling Kang his own story. He said
that when he was young, his parents had a family friend who came
over often, whom he called "uncle." "Uncle" was a rich man, a singer,
with a beautiful bass voice, powerful, rich, full of intimations of grandeur: the grandeur of life, of love, of country and patriotism and
religion and God. Nobles, prime ministers, and presidents sought to

have him sing for them. The broken-hearted gave him lyrics to sing to their beloveds. It was said that at some funerals, his voice could briefly bring back the souls of the dead.

One night, when it was only Park and this "uncle" sitting together, the "uncle" drunk on wine, he started telling young Park that he had grown up with a great knack for imitation. He was talented at mimicking the sounds, mannerisms, quirks of his peers. Sometimes he made people laugh; sometimes he made people angry.

He was especially good at mimicking voices. If his face wasn't visible, he could easily fool others into believing that he was someone else: a parent, a teacher, a celebrity. He discovered he could use his talents by playing pranks on the phone, pretending to be other people. "I'm the secretary at your husband's law firm," he might whisper, or "I'm the janitor, I saw the vice president come in the other night . . ." Eventually his community turned against him, suspicion spread through all his friends, no one could trust what their lover or father or friends had said or not said.

When he grew up, the "uncle" continued, he left his small hometown and moved to the big city. He did the usual things to get by—waiting tables, construction work, a little thieving, a little lying. Then someone approached him. A rich man, not so far in age from him, but a different class, the son of a wealthy family. He wanted the young man to use his talent of imitation and talk to a woman over the phone. One of his lovers. In fact, the rich man had a multitude of lovers, both men and women, and he hired the young man to stay on the phone with them, murmuring sweet nothings to keep them in check.

The mimic spent hours on the phone, soothing the lovers with honeyed messages to keep them from finding out about one another, to make himself available to them when the rich man wasn't. It was his full-time job. He would let himself into the rich man's home and cradle the phone to his ear, twining the wire around his finger as he talked, hours and hours of talking while lounging in those opulent rooms. And the longer he spent with this man's voice, this man's identity, the more he loved being him. He loved the deep voice he used, the melodic tones, the lovers sighing on the phone. And sometimes, in another room far away in the house, he would hear the rich man singing in his beautiful bass voice . . .

"And then?" the young Park asked.

"The rich man died not long after that," the "uncle" stated. "Totally unexpectedly. And I became a singer."

Later, when Park asked his parents if they knew about the singer's story and where he came from, they laughed at his wild imagination. The "uncle" never spoke of it again; Park began to doubt he ever had heard this story. He watched carefully, but the singer never slipped up, the voice he had in front of the family seemed so wholly his own, he was so confident and in control of it, the voice occupied his lungs and throat so naturally, as though perfectly molded.

And Park started to wonder if there really ever had been a rich man, a rich man with a beautiful voice who had mysteriously died . . .

His whole career, Park Myungjae told Kang in the Internet café, he had been haunted by this family friend's story, which he wasn't even sure if he had really heard, or if he had dreamed it up. The uncertainty dogged him. He distanced himself from his family and cut off ties with his past. All his movies were stories of slipping identities; his films were famous for his moody, saturated style, which evoked the surreal logic of dreams.

The director left the Internet café. Kang grew older. He went on to work jobs in small offices with red-faced bosses, drink heavily in barbecue restaurants, make short films on the side, and scrape together enough money for his first full-length film, five years later. He cast the girl with shiny hair as the lead. She was still dating the same boyfriend. Kang's first feature was screened in small local festivals and panned everywhere.

The years passed, Kang was thirty-two, no longer a boy. He pitched another script. He got together a skeleton crew and the same girl. He wanted to film a cerebral, intellectual erotic thriller. Two people in a room, a lot of raw dialogue. The girl, married by now, agreed. The actor he had chosen was an everyman, could be anyone, could be Kang.

Kang recalled Park Myungjae, the famous director he'd met in the Internet café, the story of the family friend, the usurped voice, the telephone, the lovers. Kang's film made extensive use of voices, darkness, husky whispers over phone lines. One night, he called the girl to the set alone. He was waiting in the director's chair. The set was a cheap apartment they had rented for two weeks. The shiny-haired girl, now not really a girl anymore, knew what he finally wanted to claim. They had sex, the camera off the entire time. "How is your marriage going?" he asked at the end. She snuggled close to him. "It's going great," she said sincerely. "My husband and I love each other so much."

When the erotic thriller came out, Kang scanned newspapers and websites for reactions. There was only one review. The story, the critic said, was banal and predictable. Kang's sophomore attempt showed no subtlety, vision, eye for framing, or originality, which his first film also did not possess. The review finished off by saying that the actress from both of Kang's films was wooden and unconvincing.

The girl Kang had loved all those years had stopped speaking to him. The last thing she said was she had finally gotten pregnant.

Meanwhile, Park Myungjae, the famous director from the Internet café so many years ago, had gone on to make one more major film, critically lauded, completely different from any of his previous movies, a straightforward historical realist drama. Then he quietly died of a cancer he had told no one he had. Kang found the obituary in the newspaper at work.

He left the office early and went back to his apartment and started calling friends on the phone. College friends, coworkers, acquaintances, people he had met over the years. "How have you been?" he said. "Are you free tonight?" On the other side of the line, murmurs of surprise, soft demurrals, many calls that went unanswered. He went through his address book to call number after number, but there weren't so many people on that list, and finally, he hung up, no one was around, that was it.

Kang went out to walk along a bridge overlooking the Han River. It was night. He contemplated the dark water. He thought of jumping in. He thought of the hills he'd escaped from. He lit a cigarette. He thought of Park, the famous director, and the family friend, the singer who may or may not have stolen someone else's identity, may or may not have killed a wealthy man.

Kang finished the cigarette and walked until morning. He went back to his apartment, looked at his notebooks full of ideas, the half-finished scripts, the collection of DVDs he'd accumulated, all classics. He called in sick to work, spent a week in bed rewatching each DVD all the way through. Then he took them all on a bus to a remote countryside, three hours away, and found a field. In the field he covered the DVDs in gasoline and lit them all on fire.

On a piece of paper he wrote:

Youth! It will never come again. Youth! It will never come again. Youth! It will never come again. Youth! It will never come again. Youth! It will never come again.

He threw the paper onto the pile of burning DVDs. When he got back to his apartment, his boss had called to say he was fired. On TV, there was a cooking show teaching how to make fried chicken.

*

The amount of effort put into the thing was staggering. Almost obscene. The actors looked completely natural. The camerawork was so close-up on their faces it was claustrophobic. Sound came through crystal clear: the drip of water, the huffing exhaust of a bus. Dialogue—what there was of it—was spoken in quiet, almost mumbled tones. The movie spanned sets, scenes, locations over the decades. It must have cost a fortune to produce.

I twisted my neck to look up at Mr. Kang. On the enormous chair next to me, his wide face was like a stone's.

"Is this . . ." Eileen hesitated. "Did you make this all yourself?"

"It's really good," Jessica piped up.

Mr. Kang shrugged. The projector was now showing only a black screen. He stood, turned everything off. Some warmth in the room faded. Without speaking, we knew it was time for us to leave.

Outside, the rain had turned into a light drizzle. The strip mall was quiet, the silence almost harsh. All the other stores had closed. We stood on the sidewalk like children, waiting for direction on what to do.

Mr. Kang flipped off the restaurant lights. The laminate chairs and shiny metal counter fell into shadows. He came out and locked the doors. Without his apron and bandanna, he looked like a much different man. Angrier? Kinder? I couldn't say. Ignoring us, he started walking away. When he fished car keys out of his pocket, in the parking lot, the lights on an ordinary black Nissan Altima came on.

"Is there a title?" I blurted out to his back.

He stopped and turned. "No," he said. "I'm waiting for someone to help me think of one."

I remembered my phone in my pocket. I pulled it out to see a swarm of messages from Billy. *Where ARE you? / Did you drop off the face of the earth? / It's late, are you home yet should I still come over? / Okaaay, it's late and I'm going to stay here, thanks for this really fucking excellent communication*

A car pulled up—smooth and silver, a silken little Audi. Jessica waved. Henry stopped near the sidewalk, got out and stood next to me, and greeted us.

"Luna, it's been a while," he said, smiling at me. "I was worried about you all when Jessica texted me."

"That crazy owner just left," Jessica stage-whispered, jerking her chin to indicate the departing Nissan. "I seriously thought he was going to axe murder us . . ."

Eileen made a noise of agreement. "That video was so shitty. Do you think he makes his other customers watch it? No one wrote about this on Yelp."

I looked at Jessica's smug and scornful mouth and Eileen's nervous face, lit by her phone as her fingers tapped quickly. I could feel Dake's eyes on me from behind. He hadn't said anything since we left the theater. I thought he might feel it, too, the shared, gaping emotion the movie had aroused in me. I didn't want to look at him, so intimate was this feeling.

"Anyone need a ride?" Henry asked affably.

"I'm good," Eileen said. "I parked in the lot."

"You should come with us," Jessica said to me. "We'll drop you off on the way."

"Thanks," I said. The prosaic conversation of the real world rubbed at my skin painfully. Henry smiled at me, a sudden warm pin-prick, like the kindling of a lighter. Memories flashed through me, feelings rather than images. The confused high school kiss with Dake, the volatile crying jags over my DJ ex, the lackadaisical warmth of the photographer I'd dated in New York, my long-ago fight with my college best friend, Melissa. So many nights and so many feelings, so many times my heart felt gnawed raw as a bone.

Against the neon sign of Mr. Kang's chicken restaurant, Jessica's face looked baby-fresh and soft, not so different from when I first met her. How sad I'd been when we stopped talking, and now she was back. Our lives were turning into what lives they would be. Everyone was looking at me. On an old phone, I thought, a young man was whispering in the voices of other people. Youth, it would never come again. I stepped up, tilted my face, kissed Henry squarely on the mouth.

MONITOR WORLD

She died in the game, and saw him looking at her.

That summer, she always spent her lunch outside of the hangar. She ate in her car, or squatted in the shade of the fence, dribbling bottled water into the dirt. There was a game she played on her phone, shooting zombies. Across the parking lot, a hundred or so meters away, was a pilot school, with a flat roof and a smoky glass door. She never saw a single airplane take off from the tarmac. At lunch or at five thirty, when she was coming out at the end of the day, she would see the man standing on the deck in front of the school. He wore aviator glasses and had a cigarette. She never saw his eyes, but she knew he was looking at her.

He had short, bristly black hair, and wore a crisp white shirt with an embroidered insignia and pressed dark pants, even in the heat. He must have been someone at the school; he must have been a pilot. If she looked him in the face, he didn't turn away. Not his mouth, not his body, nothing about his posture ever changed, and particularly not the angle of those impenetrable black lenses, which were always directed at her face.

That summer she was twenty-five. Her boss was a guy with a plane and a hangar. She spent from 9:00 a.m. to 5:30 p.m. in the hangar, which had a steel-framed ceiling like an enormous tent. Her boss's plane was partitioned from where she and her coworkers sat by a makeshift wall, and he had rigged up electric fans around the space to alleviate the dead air. She and two others, one twenty-one, one twenty-two, worked on shiny new iMac computers with little labels with their initials: *N.R.* for her, *A.M.* for the twenty-one-year-old, *K.L.* for the twenty-two. They edited web copy. The web copy read as suspiciously scripted, sent in by cheap ghostwriters from non-English-speaking countries. They posted the articles on websites with too many hyphens in the URLs, then shared the links on social media websites under fake profiles they made up in the dozens. In the hangar, their screens were visible at all times. There was no privacy. N. hated being the oldest worker there.

All around them was arid desert. Beyond the pilot school there was a diner, where some early mornings N. got coffee and listened to the TV news. The local news was full of stories of pedophiles and abducted children, bus drivers who were keeping women locked up in their basements for years. Listening to it, you could easily be convinced the world was dark and unnavigable, and danger could swallow you up on any street corner.

The waitress at the diner was like a character from a Lucia Berlin story. She had brown hair bleached gold by sunlight and bronzed, spotted skin. She knew N. by sight; she acted motherly toward her. When N. sat down at the counter, the waitress poured her coffee first, moving protectively through the weather-beaten men wearing the same dark glasses as the aviator who watched her.

At twenty-five, N. believed herself pretty enough to be looked at, and too old to be mothered. Before that, she had been awkward. In high school, her cropped hair puffed out unevenly and her eyeliner ran because of her flat, oily eyelids. Her acne had persisted even after her breasts and hips failed to fill out. Her skin was permanently sundarkened from laps she ran around the football field. Since then, she had grown out her hair, found a skincare routine, and bought different eyeliner, but this last thing, the tan of her skin—despite the papaya soap she bought from the Vietnamese mart, the kojic acid soap she ordered from Japan via eBay—she had not managed to change.

*

The Cave had popped up in her sponsored ads. It had a dark pixel-art interface that looked decidedly retro, a callback to '90s anime predicting what the Internet would look like in the future. The motto was: *for lovers of the underground.* The chat function used avatar sprites, like something out of MapleStory, and everyone listed some kind of Internet handle instead of their real names, which made it feel a little more like an actual game, set in some digital alternate universe, and a little less depressing than real life.

N. uploaded two pictures into the app. Her username was dDdghost. On her profile, under *Occupation*, she'd written: *disembodied digital ghost.*

His name was agamemnon_the_king. His chat avatar had purple hair and green eyes. There was one picture, shot in black-and-white, which showed the serious, elegant face of a man with long hair looking directly into the camera. His *Age* was 31, his *Occupation* was *Theater*.

Hello, he wrote on the day that they matched.

What's up, she said. It was evening, she was in the kitchen, and over the island, the canyon sunset was falling through the window. Her mother had left a bowl wrapped in the refrigerator, which she was warming up for a meal.

Why is a nice girl like you in a place like this?

It was such an old-fashioned line, so casually derogatory, she was intrigued.

Looking for a prince, but a king could be better, she wrote.

You appreciate me more than my wife does, he said.

(That was a joke) sent a few moments, but not too quickly, after.

Her mother had bought this one-story house in a half-finished development deep in Poway the previous year. Bushes of wild yellow flowers dotted the trails along the neighborhood, and if she got close enough, she could hear the dry hum of bees. There weren't enough streetlights and night driving was dangerous. The long distance from the city center would have made it hard for N. to see her old friends, if she had had old friends, but she had not hung on to her friends anyway.

Her mother was an emergency room physician and was never home during normal hours. With her sister out of state, it was just the two of them there. Since N. had moved back, mother and daughter passed through the house like two users in an A/B test, with only the bowls of food N. left on the counter and the drip coffee she set to be ready at 4:00 p.m. as the tracks of each other's existence. It had been almost a year since Hillary lost the election, since the night people had cried walking the streets of New York, and nearly three months since N. had left graduate school and found a job off Craigslist editing web copy in an airplane hangar. She was giving half of each paycheck to her student loans.

In her bedroom at this home, which was not her childhood home, N. lay on the mattress with the red flower-patterned duvet she had had as a high schooler, folded her clothes into the white dresser she had once put her first bras into, and drew pictures on a Wacom tablet at the same desk where she'd studied for her AP Statistics exam. When it got dark, she lowered all the blinds and tried not to feel uneasy at being on the ground floor, alone in an empty house. When they first moved in, to reassure herself in the stillness, she had played the piano, which was not kept in tune. The notes filled the air in an eerie way, and putting her small hands out like that, when she was alone in the house, made her feel too vulnerable so she would quickly shut the lid. At night, the air was cool, and she would take out her graduate school sweaters, then huddle watching anime at her desk and telling herself she was going to shower and sleep, in just ten more minutes, fifteen . . .

She'd downloaded the Cave because she wanted something to happen.

A few hours after her last message of *lol*, just as she was getting ready to shower, agamemnon_the_king had written, *So what does a nice disembodied digital ghost like you do for fun?*

Haunt Tumblr, she wrote back, *play pranks on the audio tracks of YouTube videos, steal webpages and bring up 404 error codes.*

He said, *What a busy life. Do you ever come out to play in the real world?*

*

The King lived in a new apartment complex that was not quite downtown. It took her forty minutes to get there. Racing through the empty intersections and the stoplights blinking red and green, N. thought, *Am I really going? Is this really going to happen?*

She had never done this before: gone to the house of a man she had just met over the Internet on the very same night. Her car felt like a protected bubble of unreality from the outside world, she felt like she was in a video she could pause at any moment, she wasn't really inside her body.

It was much more plausible to think she was astral-projecting and her real body was somewhere else, in bed, sleeping. Her body was only dreaming that it was in the car and turning off the exit ramp and stepping on the brake and parallel parking in front of the address she'd gotten from agamemnon_the_king. Her body was only dreaming that she was texting him, *I'm outside!* and checking her reflection in the rearview mirror. Everything was a fiction, a fantasy imagined by that body still in pajamas lying in her bedroom . . .

Agamemnon_the_king walked out of the sliding glass doors. In Real Life, he was short. He had sloped shoulders, a long neck, deep bags under his eyes visible under the streetlight. Then she really was following him inside, up a silent, smooth elevator to a living room where there were stacks of heavy white books, a deep couch, framed pictures on the wall. He was a little bit uglier than she had thought he would be, and this was comforting and made the scene feel more like playacting.

The man offered her scarlet wine in a crystal glass, asked her if she was hungry, leaned over the kitchen island, pushed her lips open with the edge of the glass. The wine was dry and left a taste of salt on her tongue as she swallowed. This, the injection of her sense of taste, brought the scene more judderingly into reality for her. She was like Persephone, eating in the Underworld. He refilled his own glass, and something about his hooded eyes, how they monitored her, scared and thrilled her.

He didn't turn on any lights in the bedroom. There was more art on the walls, photos in large white frames, the shapes were fleshy, grotesque, erotic. The whole time she had been smiling, joking, performing. And still it felt like it wasn't really happening. She was in a cut scene that she had to see to the end. *This is real/This is not real*, she thought, like a coin toss. The man laid her on the bed, peeled off her sweater, ran a finger from her collarbone to her ankle, and said, "You are very lovely." Liquid pooled into her underwear, which he took off a moment later. When he put his fingers inside her, she thought, apropos of nothing, of the aviator, the dark sunglasses observing her under the omniscient and ravaging sun.

*

The next morning, N. drove to work from the man's house just after dawn. She had slept for perhaps three, four hours. At the diner, the Lucia Berlin waitress came over with the coffeepot.

"So early today," the waitress remarked. "Here you go, honey."

At work, she nodded sleepily over the lists of "10 ways to get the most out of your garden fertilizer" and "Try these top 5 anti-virus softwares for business professionals." She plucked at her sweater feverishly; should she take it off? She didn't want the others to notice she was wearing the same T-shirt. She could still feel the King's fingers in her. N.'s organs writhed and she squeezed her thighs together as tight as they would go.

"It won't let me make any more Facebook profiles," the twenty-one-year-old said suddenly.

"Let me see?" Their boss stood up.

"I'm getting the same issue," the twenty-two-year-old said from his desk.

N. looked at the article she was publishing on best-garden-hose-enthusiast.com. After she published it, she was supposed to share it on four different social media platforms under fake names. She opened the Gmail account she'd made under the name Linda Hallberg, contributor at best-garden-hose-enthusiast. "Your IP address has been blocked due to suspicious activity," Facebook informed her. Her boss went around the other side of the partition and began rummaging around.

"What about you?" the twenty-one-year-old asked N., but N., who had her earphones in, pretended she didn't hear.

"What are we going to do?" the twenty-one-year-old asked.

"I think he's going to scramble our IP address," the twenty-two-year-old said.

"How?"

The twenty-two-year-old shrugged. "I dunno, I just hear that's what people do."

And meanwhile, N. thought, gazing at the Facebook email, no one knew what she had done last night. The sex had been good—so good that remembering it now her legs went weak and she wanted to drive back to the King's house and repeat everything they had done the previous night, again, right this instant. She thought of the boys she had slept with before, the awkwardness, the self-consciousness, how the sex had at best been *almost* enjoyable but never quite. How distant and unreal they felt now. She had come out of the night and left the King's house alive.

Her boss came back and started fiddling with another device. When he bent down, the sweat along his hairline glistened under the artificial light like a lick of slime. It couldn't be good for them, working in this heat day after day even with the fans on. N. stared at the shiny skin on his forehead.

The air felt stifling, the writhing in her stomach intensified—was it the thought of the sex? She fanned herself with one hand, the lights above seemed too bright, the twenty-two-year-old asked, "Everything all right?" She nodded and scooted her chair back to be directly in front of a fan. She was fine, it was just, she felt, quite, very hot—

And then she was stumbling out to the parking lot and the twenty-two-year-old was following her, asking if she could drive home okay, N. was waving him off, in the car she checked the rearview mirror and saw that her skin was pallid, damp; she pulled out of the lot in a reckless swerve; through the rear window she could see the aviator, who had come out to the deck, who was staring at her car under his black sunglasses, standing at the porch of the pilot school. His gaze made her stomach churn more, she stopped the car for a second with an abrupt shuddering of the brakes. She wanted to step out, speak to him, but then she saw his foot move—was he going to walk toward her? Her foot swiveled to the accelerator and she was out on the street; she managed, barely, not to hit the car in front of her changing lanes off the freeway; and in her mother's house in the half-abandoned neighborhood, she was tugging off her sweater and heading to the toilet and lifting the lid and vomiting out an egg-colored bile—but why? She didn't feel ill, no, it was *good* what she felt, tingling all over, from her belly to her toes, yet still—she lifted water into her mouth from the bathroom sink, flushed the toilet, realized she had to pee, pulled down her pants, sat down, and saw the smear of blood on the underwear she hadn't changed from last night: Oh. She had started her period.

*

In graduate school she made an animated short titled CHECK THIS BOX TO VERIFY YOU ARE NOT A ROBOT. It starts with a tiny girl with an electrical outlet in her back waking up in an empty bedroom. The girl, the room, everything is sketched out with rough lines and no color. The scene expands, the girl's bedroom is actually an enormous control room with a spread of computers, a huge monitor, and a thick coaxial cable dangling on the floor. The girl plugs herself in and the monitor turns on.

Her avatar pops up on the monitor's screen, reborn into a new world, and *this* world is fully realized, it has color, shape, dimension, music, cotton candy trees. But before long blocks of gray creep in, there are shadows in strange forms on the floors of the tree houses, the background music turns ominous, the screen flickers, pixelates, squares of gray dot the sky in binary patterns (cut to the physical body in the colorless world, comatose and plugged in, twitching), and finally, once the dreamy pink world has degraded into a sketchy, draft version just like the world outside, the avatar onscreen enters a computer room with a monitor. In *this* computer room, there is a new character, a man with a mask's fixed smile. His speech scrolls across the bottom of the screen, *welcome, isn't it beautiful here?, this place, it's so lovely, I could just stay here forever, sit and watch the world go by without me. This place, it's so lovely, I could just stay here forever. Isn't it beautiful here? To sit and watch the world without you.* And the monitor in this onscreen computer room, the monitor-inside-the-monitor world, turns on, there is another world in there, full of color. The color starts to bleed out over the edges of the screen, greens and oranges and yellows, pumpkins, a road, the man turns to look, the girl's avatar sees the man has no back, he is all face and nothing behind it, he is completely depthless, a straight line, and the world in the second monitor expands out and intrudes more into the first . . .

N. was thinking of expanding it into a video game. The girl's avatar would hop through a series of monitors within monitors and explore their associated worlds, meeting strange figures (once people?) who talked in long strings of zeroes and ones or Wingdings. Vaguely, she was trying to decide how she wanted the story to end—what if there was an option for the avatar to remain in the monitors forever? Maybe it was easier to stay even in those decaying empty places than to emerge into the Real World. Maybe all the characters the girl encountered had once been Real People who decided to move into the Monitor Worlds for good.

She thought that the physical girl plugged into the computers probably had some trauma at the back of her life (why else would she avoid her actual life so hard?), but N. wasn't very interested in the "why" of things, only the "what." And more and more, she liked staying in the imagination of the Monitor Worlds, creating tableaus of different worlds and color palettes, then ruining them all with a few mouse clicks . . .

The second time she met the King was on a Thursday. He called her over late, 11:00 p.m., and she once again fell into the comforting sense that they were playacting. Nothing that happened this far into night could be real, including their meetings, which felt clandestine for no reason. He greeted her with a flourless chocolate loaf cake, sprinkled with powdered sugar, and she wondered what he was overcompensating for. On his couch, which was expensive, deep, and very comfortable, he massaged her calves. He had a very strong grip. "Do you do sports?" she asked. He said he had a black belt in judo. She felt the thrill of *being cared for* in *a dangerous situation*.

He had a shelf of DVDs behind the couch. For movies, there were names she didn't know, like *10 to Midnight*, *Death Wish II*, *Basket Case*, *Cat People*. For music, there were CDs: The Police, Depeche Mode. N. picked up a DVD and looked at the cover: garish and pulpy. "I don't know any of these," she said.

"They're from the '80s. Classics."

The photos on his wall were of naked bodies arranged in strange poses against a brutalist landscape of a stark black house. The bodies were thin, pale, long-legged, firm, arranged in strange poses. The pictures were not sexy—something about them was very cold.

"What are these? Porn?"

The King laughed. "They're by a Japanese photographer. He's famous."

"They're kind of creepy." Nothing was real, which made her bold. "Are you creepy?"

"I like them. Everyone seems like they could turn violent in just a second."

That was what it was, N. thought. The feeling she got from him. Of not knowing whether the next moment would be safe. What was so alluring about being in his company: he rubbed her legs and she didn't know what he would do next.

The King slid his hands up her thighs.

During the night he started snoring with the deep, throaty rumble of an old man. This punctured the film of unreality and N. wanted to leave. She shifted restlessly around on the bed. One of the small photographs by the Japanese photographer hung on the wall. In the background was a tiny woman in a ballet pose who seemed about to take off. Swallowing the foreground, a man facing her; his posture, the adamant line of his legs and shoulders, was threatening.

*

On Saturday she was watching TV on the couch when her phone pinged.

Still recovering from the scratches you gave me, the King said.

The intrusion of the King into her weekend morning was unwelcome.

Lol, she typed, though she didn't find it very funny.

He followed up shortly: *What are you up to?*

I'm staying home today, not feeling well

Oh no, what's the matter

Stomach issues

Where do you live? I can bring some soup

N. paused. Below her stomach, she felt her intestines knotting together again. Was he being caring, or was this crossing a line? Instinctively, she didn't want the King to know where she lived. Even if she didn't live with her mother she wouldn't have wanted him to know.

She closed her eyes, her mind brimming with feverish images: the dark highway, the white sugar on the chocolate cake, the airplane hangar, her reflection swimming in the black coffee in the diner . . .

"Did you eat lunch yet?" Her mother's voice floated into the miasma.

Oh. N. opened her eyes and saw her mother there, looking tired. It felt like a long time since she'd seen her.

"Sorry, Mom, I forgot to start the coffee."

Her mother moved to the couch and put a hand on N.'s forehead. "What's wrong? Are you feeling sick?" Her hand was cool and dry.

"My stomach's been a little funny."

Her mother brought her hands down and squeezed N.'s feet, hard.

"Eek!" She squirmed. "Mom, it's okay, I already took some ibuprofen."

But the grip on her feet relaxed her. Her mother said, "I'll make you some ginger tea."

N. watched her set a small pot on the stove. Her mother was short, thin, and pale, with sensible short hair and a competent, no-nonsense manner, and even watching her bent over the cutting board, N. felt protective of her.

"How's the hospital?" she asked.

"We had a sad case last night. This guy brought a girl in with bruises all over her neck and face. He said she'd fainted."

A whispery feeling ran up N.'s skin. "Did he hit her?"

"She said she 'fell' because she had 'low blood sugar' and kept asking, 'Can my boyfriend stay?'" Her mother sighed. "I asked if I could speak to her alone, but she didn't let him leave."

"At least he brought her in?"

"These abusers do all sorts of things," her mother said. "You girls have to be careful."

She brought the mug to N. and smoothed her daughter's hair gently, rhythmically. When N. brought the cup to her mouth, the smell of ginger was spicy, pungent, traveling through her nostrils up to her brain, where she imagined it lighting a tiny fire.

*

The King started texting her more through the weekdays.

Think I might need someone to help mount some shelves, haha, have you heard that one?

Did you eat lunch yet today?

How's work?

3 PM slump

I get headaches when it's hot like this

It's so dry I have a nosebleed

At lunch, N. checked her messages sitting in her car outside the hangar. She tried to identify what she was feeling and it was repulsion. She didn't like that the King was trying to talk to her more now; it was needy, and made their encounters less flimsy, less transactional.

In the side mirror, she saw the door to the pilot school swing open. The aviator came out and lit a cigarette. It was hot, but there was no trace of sweat on the starched white shirt. N.'s cell phone pinged again.

Are you busy tonight? the King asked.

This would be the last time, N. decided. The King was getting boring. The fear she had so viscerally felt had been replaced by a kind of pity.

When she went over it was raining, and only 6:00 p.m. In the cool gray light of his living room, the man looked sagged and tired. He brought her a small cup, she brought it to her mouth, took a large gulp, and then almost gagged, because it was unexpectedly wine, perhaps the same red wine he had given her the first night.

Having alcohol without having eaten, N. felt herself growing languid. Turning her eyes onto the man in the early evening light, she saw the bags under his eyes were puffy, and there were even a few gray hairs at his temple.

"What've you been doing all day?" she asked.

"Watching this old reality show, it's called *To Catch a Predator.* Have you heard of it?"

"No." N. hesitated. "True crime?"

"Yeah. These pedophiles, it's so funny." The man laughed, a short, ugly laugh. Had he always had those jowls? "Some of them say the craziest shit. My favorite one—"

Later, in bed, after sex that felt, for the first time, perfunctory and disappointing, he told her he had started writing a play.

"What's it about?"

"Charles Manson."

"The cult guy?"

"He just died, you know."

"He was still alive? I don't even know when all that stuff happened."

The man chuckled. "He was misunderstood. There were a lot of ways in which he was a genius. And charismatic. The guy was a leader! But everyone only remembers the one thing."

N. kept her voice very measured. "But he was a murderer, right?"

"He didn't actually kill anyone himself. It was his followers. The young women."

Suddenly, the King lunged at her stomach and tickled her. "Girls can be scary!" His voice turned high-pitched, incongruously childish. N. wanted to ease away from his circling hand.

"So what's the new thing about the play?" She tried to change the subject. "Like how is it different from what actually happened?"

"I'm thinking of having all the parts played by children. Twelve and under."

"Like, Charles Manson and all the women and everything are just going to be kids?"

"Don't you think it would be cute? All *Lord of the Flies*. Inherent brutality of humanity, and all that."

His voice had turned crueler, talking about the children. She didn't like the way he sounded. She imagined a young kid on stage artlessly acting out an orgy. She felt tense, her hands tingled.

"I'm going home," she said a moment later. She sounded very natural. "Gotta make dinner."

"You sure?" He smiled. "You're welcome to sleep here if you want, you know."

"I want to sleep in my own bed."

"What is your bed like?"

N. turned her head. "That's a weird question."

"I'm curious how you live," the King said, also sitting up and kissing her on the cheek. "All right, I'll walk you out."

＊

"Shit," she said, outside his apartment. She tried the key again and again. "It's not starting."

"I have jumper cables," the King said. "Don't worry."

While she waited for him to come back, she wondered if she should call her mother.

But nothing has happened, she told herself. He hadn't said anything that she could point to as obviously sketchy.

She remembered the excitement she'd felt the first time meeting him. He had been an unknown, and she had felt the rush of getting away with something. There was the way he'd looked at her over the food he gave her that night. His eyes, hooded, intent, obviously monitoring to see how much she drank.

(The casual way he put his hand on the back of her head when she was giving him oral. There was no pushing, but there was the suggestion that if he wanted to, he *could*.)

No one knew she was here.

"I've got them," the King's voice came through the window from behind her.

*

He insisted on following her in his car.

"No, no," N. said, shaking her head. "It's fine. I'm just going home, it's a long drive, don't worry." Then she bit her tongue, wishing she'd said she was expected somewhere else.

"I'll just go along with you a little bit to make sure there's no problems. What if your car dies again?"

"I have triple A," she lied.

"Don't worry," the King laughed, standing very close to the car door. Under the streetlight, his teeth were not very even. "I'm parked right behind you. I'm not busy. It's not any trouble."

"You really don't have to." N. shrunk away, then, because she was still alone with him, she gave an excuse. "I live with my parents, so . . ."

He didn't seem surprised. "I won't come in," he promised. "I won't even stop. I'll just see you park and make sure everything's good, and drive right off."

He won't take no for an answer. On the drive home, her arms were locked in so closely to her body she could feel the tightness in her inner elbows. In the rearview mirror she saw the King in a Chevy

Tahoe, pursuing close behind her. There was heavy traffic. She tried to subtly lose his car, but every time she changed lanes, he reappeared, on her left, one or two lanes to the side, then directly behind her, skimming along confidently. He was wearing black sunglasses so she couldn't see his eyes. As though he knew she was looking at him in her rearview mirror, he suddenly grinned.

I am never going to see him again, she thought.

The world seemed too real now.

N. pulled off the 163 early. She was near Clairemont. The exit was near a plaza with a frozen yogurt chain and a yoga franchise. She remembered coming here once, to volunteer at a senior home or something. N. swallowed hard. The Tahoe pressed behind her.

She kept driving, trying not to look around too much or go too slowly. She saw a turn-in with a stone sign and pivoted. There was a parking garage. Some neat shrubs outside. Without looking at the numbers, she pulled into a random opening. In the second between the death of the engine and her seat belt shriveling, a black hole opened inside her lungs.

She opened the door. His car was idling behind hers. She prayed whoever belonged in the actual spot didn't show up.

"Well"—the King rolled his window down and looked at her without taking the sunglasses off—"everything looks good?"

"Yup." N. forced herself to smile.

"Nice little neighborhood."

"Yeah."

The King looked around and said, "No one's here. Come here a sec."

Unwillingly, N. approached the car.

He pulled her face up and kissed her on the lips. "See you next time." *God, his lips are dry*, she thought. *And too thick.* Disgust ran down her esophagus and she had to stop herself from wiping her mouth.

"Next time," she said easily, and with enormous, invisible effort, lifted the corners of her mouth. She brought her hand up and waved.

Surely he wasn't going to wait to see her unlock a door and go into one of the houses?

No, thank God, he wasn't. The King rolled his window back up and smiled his unpleasant smile at her again. He pressed the gas on his car, looped around the roundabout, and exited the neighborhood.

By the time N. got back to her real home, it was dark. She'd waited for ten minutes in the parking garage, hiding in the back seat of her car with the lights turned off, in case the King for whatever reason decided to come back. Then she'd driven aimlessly for nearly two hours, going the wrong direction on purpose, before pulling into a gas station, filling up, and at last setting her route to home.

From the moment she'd peeled from the curb in front of the King's apartment until now, she had not let herself think or feel too much. Now, her head felt hot and her heart strangled inside her airless, black hole torso. She put a hand on the wall to steady herself. Then she turned on every single light in the house and went around pulling down the blinds one by one, avoiding looking at her reflections in the dark panes or at anything in the windows beyond, because—because what? In her bedroom, she locked the door.

Why are you feeling so scared? she told herself. *There's nothing to be scared of.*

She forced herself to shower and pull on her favorite sweater. She pulled out her phone and got into bed. She started playing the usual video game. Her avatar ran around a dirt field shooting little pixie zombies who turned dark green, then purple when they were hit in the brain. The soundtrack was a cheerful piano medley.

Gradually, N. felt sleepiness overtake her. She became aware she was hungry, too, because she hadn't eaten. Her eyes grew heavy on the pillow. *I don't have to decide right now,* she thought, *what I feel.*

Also, nothing happened, she thought. *Maybe I was just being paranoid.*

She drifted off with the sound on her computer still going and all the lights in her room still on. Perhaps because of that, or because her sweater made her too hot, her dreams were fitful, and all through the night she couldn't quite tell if she were fully asleep or half-awake.

*

Her stomach hurt.

In the bathroom, no vomit came out.

When she walked outside, there were a lot fewer bees than there'd been in the middle of summer.

*

Nothing had happened.

*

Nothing had happened.

*

She typed his name into Google. First name + city + theater. First name + city + the name of a university hoodie she had seen in his closet. A reverse image search of his profile photo from the Cave.

Nothing. The invisibility of his presence on the Internet cemented how little she knew about him. An air of doubt had crept into her searching: that she had ever met him, driven to his house, that she had lain on her back in a dark room with pale photographs on the walls . . .

First name + Charles Manson. First name + Japanese photographer. No hits.

35

*

She blocked the King's number. She started avoiding her phone, started turning the radio on when she was driving, started driving faster, started looking out for a black Chevy Tahoe. She started eating her lunch inside the hangar, started leaving work later, started not wanting to be alone, started wanting witnesses. He wouldn't be able to find her, he hadn't come to her house. They only knew each other's first names. The fear she had felt only in his apartment, only when she had wanted to feel it, was oozing through the cracks in her bedroom walls and made her afraid when driving at night.

A week later it was just her and the twenty-two-year-old in the hangar. Their boss had left for lunch. Their mouse clicks echoed into the silence. She couldn't focus on the horticulturalist-tips-for-single -moms.com article. Coiled claustrophobia threatened to pop every blood vessel in her body.

Stealthily, breaking the rule she had set for herself, seeing the twenty-two-year-old immersed in a YouTube video that clearly was not about his assigned topic for best-mixed-martial-arts-gear.net, she opened a private browser and continued searching for the King online. She typed in his first name + his phone number. His first name had an unusual spelling.

"Hey," the twenty-two-year-old said into the dead air of the hangar. "Did you bring lunch? Or do you wanna go out and get something?"

"Mmmm," she non-answered.

And there—in an online directory that was the first result on the search engine—were three results.

Something.

She clicked on the page. The directory was like an online Yellow Pages. There were full names, addresses, phone numbers, even dates of birth. All this information just available with some swipes on the keyboard. The first two results were for people with misspellings of the first name, and who lived too far away. And the last result on the page was the name of the man who must be the King.

The street address was the one she had driven to.

He was a real person.

The date of birth listed was 1975.

She felt her intestines again, like snakes. Pressure ballooned inside her head.

N. logged onto Facebook. She was still using the Linda Hallberg fake account. She typed the full name she had found into the search bar. There was one in Arizona, one in Colorado, one in Hong Kong, and there, the sixth one in the list. The Facebook profile with the same black-and-white photo from the Cave. In the information box, the name of the city they lived in. The name of a liberal arts college in Vermont. And a graduation year—1997—

She counted backward in her head. He must have been at least a decade older than he had said.

She pushed her chair back. "Yes, let's go get lunch," she said to the twenty-two-year-old. Though it had been a long pause. Though it was too late to respond.

The twenty-two-year-old, whose name was Kevin, looked at her, a little surprised. *As well he might*, she thought, because she had been unsociable for more than two months.

He turned out to be gracious. "Cool. The diner?"

N. took them the four-minute drive in her car. The aviator was standing outside the door of the pilot school, smoking. In the diner, the TV news played a story about a woman who had escaped her father's cult. The Lucia Berlin waitress brought them glasses of iced water. "Hi, honey," she said to N. "This your coworker?"

Kevin was short, baby-faced, and very, very normal. He was originally from Texas, he'd studied business merchandising. He speculated on their boss, their jobs, how much longer it could possibly last. "I mean, it's not like we're making money, but what are you gonna do when he runs out of cash?"

"Oh. I didn't think about that." N. could barely chew on her burrito. Out of habit, she had asked for a black coffee.

"You were in New York, right?" Kevin went on. "But your family's here?"

"My mom's here," N. said. "My sister's in college. Northwestern."

"Your younger sister?"

"Her name's Maya." They hadn't talked in months. "She's studying accounting."

"Nora and Maya," Kevin mused. "Do your names sort of match on purpose?" When she shrugged, he said, "Must be nice to have a sister. I'm an only child. My parents moved us here like a year ago. I don't know any people here."

What people? N. thought. *People with real lives? I don't know anyone with a real life.*

"I don't either," she said. "I was seeing someone for a bit. I just stopped."

"I'm sorry to hear that." Kevin stopped, then asked, since she was clearly waiting for him to, "Any particular reason, or . . . ?"

"Well—" N. hesitated. "I started feeling like there were some things that didn't add up . . . Like some of the things he said . . ."

The thoughts congealed inside her. The King, *Age: 31, Occupation: Theater.* If he was born in 1975, he was forty-two years old. Some of the things he'd said about her body, which she'd found so flattering and old-fashioned. Now she thought he might have said them because she was young. How had she let him touch her? What signs had she missed? And what signs had she seen, and let go? Had he done this before? The first night, hadn't he been so confident, so relaxed? How many young women had he seduced? What kind of man . . .

"I mean, he didn't do anything wrong?" she said, half question. "Technically. Except . . ."

"No, no," Kevin leaned forward, shaking his head. He had very pale fine eyelashes in that baby face. "Trust your intuition. You're feeling like you can't trust what he says, that you've been lied to—no matter what, that's not a good way to be entering a relationship." He crooked a smile. "I'm sure your mom would want you to be careful."

Suddenly N. wanted to cry. In the rush of everything that had happened since she moved home, she'd forgotten—she was someone's daughter, a beloved daughter, and her mother would be sad if she were hurt.

In the car on the way back to the hangar, they were silent. In a loop in her mind, N. recalled the times the King had touched her. She felt disgusted, also—she had let herself enjoy it. She couldn't lie to herself and say that she hadn't liked it, at least in the beginning. How horrible that she had let herself be touched by him those times, had been so *eager,* even—

"I've never actually seen a plane take off from here," Kevin mused, looking out the window, where the roof of the pilot school was coming into view.

The thought of the aviator being there, with his dark glasses, watching her, infuriated her. She turned into the parking lot, there was the chain-link fence. In the rearview mirror she saw the pressed pants, the white shirt, still there.

"That man is always fucking creeping on me."

Kevin turned his neck. "Who? That person standing over there?"

N. turned the wheel sharply. "He's always looking at me when I'm out here," she said, or thought she said, but her organs were writhing again and that fever-dream miasma—black coffee, sunglasses, TV news, pale bodies, black house, chocolate loaf cake, a cup of wine— was crowding over her thoughts. She thought of the girl wandering inside the Monitor Worlds. She wanted the body to wake up. She wanted the body to feel safe. What had she been doing all this time? Her hands tightened on the wheel.

CLANG—and then N. was coming to herself, Kevin was yelping, "Oh my GOD, what are you *doing!*," and the car was stopped, she saw that she had rolled into the chain-link fence, her engine was still running, Kevin was unbuckling his seat belt and opening the door, and the aviator was walking over, taking off his sunglasses, a light voice she had never heard was saying, "Are you okay?"

N. opened her mouth to yell something at the aviator, something like *back off* or *get away from me!* But no words came, only a choke of surprise. Coming up to her window, framed by the blue sky, concerned and kindly and no longer hidden by sunglasses—was the innocent and naked face of a young woman.

ZEROES:ONES

It was early fall when I arrived in Suzhou. The leaves were turning, the crowds at the classical gardens were getting thinner, and at the university language center, where I worked as a writing tutor, there was only one other fellow, a Princeton graduate named Marcus. He was a typical white-man-in-China, well-spoken, well-educated, well-read, and well-intentioned. I automatically disliked him on principle, not least because his Mandarin was better than mine. The only other person we worked with, our boss, was in his midthirties, with a coarse bird's nest of dark hair that spiraled away from his forehead in a most appealing way and a clear treble voice that always sounded sad and somewhat distracted.

The university gave me an apartment, a long, bright studio within walking distance of the school. It had no gas burner to cook on. I stockpiled bread from the convenience store and drank tea by the floor-to-ceiling window in the mornings.

As far as Chinese cities go, Suzhou was considered new tier 1, which is a step below tier 1, the ranking of the biggest metropolises like Beijing and Shanghai. It was a city of whispering water and stone gardens, multilevel department stores, mopeds, and convenience stores with faded signs. My view of the city was lazy and gray, with chain stores and clusters of orange bicycles and laundry airing on balconies underneath an always cloudy sky. Which is to say, it was not a familiar view, and I never forgot I was a stranger to this city.

Our first week at the job, my boss took us to a Korean fried chicken restaurant near campus. It was still warm enough to sit outside. He ordered beers and paid for the food, then leaned back in his chair, smoking a cigarette whose thin trail dissipated into the air. His conversation branched off rapidly. He was a prodigious reader of various ephemera: he talked about the restoration of Yipu Garden, the cloud forest conservatory in Singapore, the work with fiber optics one of the campus labs was doing, and all the while he didn't touch his food. His English was energetic if not entirely fluid. The focus of his attention was intense when it landed, but distractible and erratic. Marcus joined him in smoking and I leaned away from the smell.

But in truth, I didn't mind the smoking. I liked listening to that low flow of words and barely connected ideas under the nicotine haze perfuming the evening air, which I inhaled along with a glorious feeling of invisibility. As I listened to him speak, I thought of Melissa, in faraway Stockholm, who was also a great talker. Earlier, she'd posted an Instagram photo of a bright, leafy café lunch with a glimpse of the torso of her boyfriend. She would have had much to say about everything, about my apartment, Marcus, my boss, the fact that I was actually in China, and I remembered that she had visited Suzhou when she was young. I thought of texting her, but even after the three of us parted ways after the meal, I didn't.

*

Before I moved there, I often said I had a lot of thoughts about China. This was shorthand for covering up the truth that I had views on China that were contradictory and made me uncomfortable. Some of those thoughts were:

- China was the motherland. The ancestral home. It was the vast, sprawling, welcoming land where I, despite the facts of my birthplace, passport, education, and the country where I had spent the overwhelmingly large proportion of my life, was truly "from."
- I did not understand China. I only half understood the culture and half understood the language.
- But I loved China. I had to love China, because it was where I was from and where I automatically and naturally belonged, unlike America.
- Besides which, America was evil.
- Not only was America evil, America was deeply, incredibly uncool. I had always felt that to be singled out as an American was very embarrassing.
- However (this I also did not like to admit to myself), China might also be evil.

But I couldn't bear to think that *my* country—and China was *my* country, despite everything—could be evil, and I exoticized it myself, polishing my dreams of my would-be life there like it was a fetish figurine to be worshipped and kept on a stone altar. I felt, no, I *believed*, that

- if I went there, that country both homeland and exotic, and understood it, then through this experience I would change and become a full person. I would nourish the half of me that had always been stunted, and by gaining the knowledge and full identity and sense of *enoughness* I had been denied the rest of my life, my full selfhood would be reclaimed.

The year I lived in China, Korean media was banned because of THAAD and Chinese military operations were advancing farther into the South China Sea. For two months, I made no friends. I went to bars and restaurants alone, but I found it hard to talk to anyone. I looked the same as everyone else in the restaurants; there was nothing to indicate I was an outsider or different, and thus my presence incited no curiosity. This was a comforting change from the constant alienation of my life in America, but it also worked against me.

Whenever I returned to my apartment, I sank into an unmovable lethargy. On social media, Melissa posted photos of cake in Vienna, train stations in Florence, the waterfront in Stockholm, always with the rangy shadow of Casper half in-frame. For our last two years at Barnard, she and I had been best friends. The whole past summer after graduation, while I was still in New York and she was just starting her teaching job in Europe, we talked every day, we called each other all the time. Until Casper came along. *They must be traveling Europe together*, I deduced; *he must be practically moved in with her by now.* Meanwhile, the most exploring I did was walking along the fruit stalls and cheap electronics stores in the two blocks around my apartment. I started tutoring on weekends at a college prep company where Marcus also part-timed. Under the terms of the fellowship this wasn't technically allowed, but the cash was hard to trace.

On days when I didn't want to go back to my empty studio, I would stay late at the language center and listen to my boss talk. He was always able to fill the silence and never asked about my personal life. Once, I stayed late designing a set of flyers. It was just the two of us there. He brought me a cup of tea in a paper cup. When I finally got up to leave, he thanked me for staying late and put a hand on top of my head. For a single moment, I thought about kissing him.

I fell in love often when I lived in Suzhou.

Not long after that, I went to a hair salon to get a cut and dye. The stylist, a young man with fluffed-up dyed hair and a quiet demeanor, was meticulous. I closed my eyes as he shampooed my hair, running warm water over my head. When he pressed his fingers along my scalp, firmly but ever so lightly, my heart quivered. Gentleness, any gentleness, touched me so easily then.

*

Most evenings, I ordered fried chicken from the same student hot spot near campus and took the food back to my studio, where I streamed Korean TV dramas and celebrity interviews with my VPN or played *Hakuoki: Demon of the Fleeting Blossom* until two in the morning. These were things I had done as a high schooler, and I was filled with the sickening and yet satisfying feeling of regression into immaturity.

The basic structure of *Hakuoki*, as with any *otome* game, is that you play a female character surrounded by five (or so) guys, and by the end of the game, one of them will be in love with you. The contexts differ—you could be playing a young woman captured by Shinsengumi samurai in the Edo period, a high school girl who time travels into the past and arrives at an archaeological dig, the first female student at a previously all-boys school, an older version of Alice in a Wonderland where the Mad Hatter, the Rabbit, and the Cheshire Cat are all hot guys—but the male archetypes are pretty universal. There is the hyperactive younger boy type, the cool "prince" type, the cold intellectual type, the hard-on-the-outside-soft-on-the-inside *tsundere* and his inverse, soft-on-the-outside-mean-on-the-inside *yandere*.

Choosing the right thing to say from a menu of options gave you romance points. You could play different routes depending on which character you wanted to fall in love with you, and you could replay the game over and over to get all the characters. Visually, I tended to go for the hot guy with glasses, especially if he had a touch of mischief to him. I was also weak for the tsundere type. The nice, gentle ones and the strong and silent ones didn't interest me, which maybe said something about my attachment style. In *Hakuoki*, I restarted the Okita route: the best swordsman of the Shinsengumi, cocky, smart-mouthed, mischievous, and coldhearted. When I had accumulated enough romance points, he would say coded things like, "It'd be troubling if you were scared of me."

Sometimes I also played the games in which you were a male character surrounded by females of various types who fell in love with you. Those tended to have sex scenes.

*

It was my idea to go dancing with Tenten and Marcus on the night I met Zero-One. Tenten, a Chinese girl two years older than me who had studied at George Washington University, taught math at the tutoring company with me and Marcus. She had lustrous skin and rosy cheeks, and fine-boned hands perfectly suited for music, of which she knew nothing.

I was feeling suddenly, acutely, restless, aware of the fact that I was wasting my time, that I was boring, that I was alone, that I would be twenty-two for only so long. That morning, Melissa had texted me a photo. I opened the message and saw a picture of a table decked out with food. She'd written: *How's China? We had a work potluck, I made cookies!*

She had posted the exact same photo on her Instagram the day before.

At the club, I didn't know how to move. I bobbed my head up and down and moved my shoulders a little bit and was embarrassed. Tenten plied me with drinks, trying to get me to loosen up. Two Brazilian girls came over with mojitos. Under their long, loosely glimmering brown hair they had sweet, young faces and wore sequined tops the size of handkerchiefs, showing flat, beautiful stomachs.

"What are you doing in Suzhou?" I wanted to know. It wasn't like this was a party city. People were looking at the two girls. They stuck out. Marcus, too, was singled out for his whiteness; I could see Chinese girls closing in on him at the bar. One of the Brazilian girls coughed, embarrassed, and said she'd been dating a guy in Shanghai but—

"He was an asshole," the friend said.

I looked at them more closely. "Are you guys underage?"

They admitted yes, they were. "I'm Luna," I introduced myself to them. The alcohol, three or four drinks in, was getting to me and the room was spinning. I had the beginnings of a headache. The two girls pulled me and Tenten out from the table to dance. Their hair fell sexily over their shoulders. They were good dancers, shimmying effortlessly, and they were also kind, putting their hands on my hips and trying to show me how to move. I tried, but my body wouldn't obey. Tenten held on to my hands and tried to shake the beat down my arms. "Luna!" she tried to cheer. "Come on!"

For a moment I saw myself as others would see me: tight around the mouth, with a stiff, awkward expression, someone who was repressed, controlled, with a nervous, people-pleasing smile. A hard and uncomfortable person. Who would want to be friends with someone like that? Who would love someone like that?

*

The next morning, I woke up with a nauseating hangover. My phone had several messages. I tossed it away without reading them, boiled water to drink, and washed my face in the sink. I looked in the mirror and felt like I could see what I'd look like when I got old.

It was Sunday. I had nowhere to go, nothing to do. After showering, I sat in front of the computer and played *Ef: A Fairy Tale of the Two*, one of the dating simulations in which you could play male characters going after female love interests. I ordered delivery from the restaurant my boss had taken us to: Korean fried chicken. It was a taste I never got tired of, the crunch of the skin and give of the meat, the tang of the seasoning made from soy sauce and gochujang and ginger and sesame seeds—a taste that never failed to make me feel happy, whole, even loved.

But that morning, when the chicken came, when I started eating, the meal grew heavy in my mouth. My chewing slowed. I wiped my hands with a napkin and dabbed at my mouth; inexplicably, tears leapt to the corners of my eyes. I'd eaten this far too often, all by myself. It only reminded me of all the other solitary, messy meals I'd had before.

I went to go wash my face and hands again. My phone buzzed and I picked it up automatically, seeing a WeChat notification.

____01100101: *Nice to meet you, America*

The contact was unfamiliar. The profile picture was of a jellyfish, the user ID all zeroes and ones, a string that could almost have been binary code: ____01100101.

___01100101: *You were very drunk*
Do you feel O.K. ?

I couldn't remember who he was, but we must have added each other at some point in the night, or how could he have my number?

I scrolled through my other texts. There was one from Marcus, one from Tenten, and then, below her name, Melissa's. She was going back to Wisconsin with her boyfriend for Christmas. Was I going home? She would "love"—her words—to catch up. Did I want to vidchat?

Her message was so casual, it made me angry. What was I supposed to say to that?

I closed out of her window and texted the Zero-One guy back: *I feel okay, thanks*

His reply was quick.

____01100101: *Have some water, eat something, don't be hungry*

I didn't feel like I could ask his name when I didn't know what I had told him. I had a dim memory of a man in a red shirt at the bar, then someone, maybe Marcus, maybe Tenten, pulling me away. Maybe he was one of those locals who wanted to practice English with me, which always made me feel slightly used. On the other hand, his messages were caring, even parental.

Me: *I'm eating right now*

____01100101: *hhh*

On the computer, I clicked through a confession scene. The girl led the boy to the school rooftop and they started having sex. The video game zoomed in on her face. The girl was all flushed anime face with squeaky moans. Was that what desire sounded like?

I paused on an image of her wet, half-closed eyes. Sex had never been like that for me. The last time I had had sex, I'd gone into Shanghai to go on a date with an Australian who was training to be a chef. I didn't know if I was actually attracted to him and tried to make up my mind all afternoon. He brought me back to the single room he had in a dingy dorm. Halfway through making out I decided I didn't want to be there and told him I was on my period, which was true, but he wanted to have sex anyway. So I lay on my back with my neck crooked and my head banging against the headboard because I was too high up on the bed. The smell of menstrual blood rose between us when he was done.

____01100101: *I'm playing basketball with some friends today*

I put my phone away and didn't respond. Some minutes later, it buzzed again.

____01100101: *It's Sunday, take it easy*

＊

After my next shift at the college prep center, Tenten and I went to Starbucks, where I paid my hard-earned tutoring dollars for an Americano that cost the same as it did in America, which was to say, very expensive for China. Tenten ordered peach tea and wore a white blouse.

I showed her Melissa's messages, which I had still not answered. I wasn't sure what to reply, and so had said nothing. But why did I have to respond, when I had nothing to say to her except "I'm angry"?

Tenten threw her long hair behind her shoulder. "Well, this is normal," she said. "You shouldn't take it so personally. If you got a boyfriend, you would talk to your friends less, too."

I looked at the window behind her neck. The smog was heavy outside, and I saw a lot of people wearing medical masks. Schoolgirls went up and down the street with their arms linked. Tenten's neck was very pretty, so soft-looking I yearned to lean against it. When we were out together, sometimes she liked to link elbows or put a hand around me and pat the side of my head, a gentleness I wished would last forever.

"I don't think I would," I said. "It's rude to dump a friend like that."

Tenten frowned, impatient, and I looked away. "It doesn't mean you're not important," she said. "But you can't blame people for living their lives. She fell in love. What *doesn't* change as we get older?"

*

In the weeks after the night at the club, Zero-One texted me periodically. They were short, easy messages, *how are you, how was work*. He still called me America. My answers were never long, but even so, I felt cared for, I looked forward to getting his check-ins. All I knew about him was that he worked in insurance, and mentioned James Bond movies. I imagined what kind of person he might be. Awkward? Tall? I got the feeling he was short. Maybe the kind of person who had been class president in school, good at taking care of others.

*

I didn't go home for the holidays, instead spending New Year's with my grandparents in Shanghai. Fireworks blasted the sky at midnight; I stayed inside, watching them on the television while my grandmother cracked sunflower seeds. We video-called my parents in Long Beach, they picked up from two separate devices and said my Chinese had improved. Melissa posted her New Year's resolutions on Facebook, and we didn't wish each other a happy new year. In *Hakuoki*, I was working my way through the Saito route—purple-haired and handsome, cool, calm, serious and collected. Unlike Okita, Saito had no sense of humor and never spoke unnecessarily. When I maneuvered my way into getting my first compliment from him, I felt a rush of euphoria.

The semester ended near the close of January. Marcus and I found ourselves busy with students asking us to help revise their papers, which often meant just writing them for them wholesale. My boss began disappearing for long stretches of time, and I didn't know what he was doing. After the new year, I grew more restless, anxious at the slow passage of hours. At work, I would get up to refill my teacup, sit down to work and drink from the cup, then get up again to find only five minutes had passed. Marcus was applying to other positions. He wanted to stay in China after our fellowship was over. I didn't know what I was going to do. If I didn't think of anything, I'd move back to New York.

One night, the university language center held an event and my boss and I were the last to leave the auditorium. I had stayed, though I didn't have to, to help fold all the chairs. At the door, my boss put his hand on my head a second time and said, "Good work, Luna," so casually it was almost cruel.

When I got home, I finally asked Zero-One to meet. His text messages had become a quiet rhythm in my life, though we had only progressed to *what did you eat today?* And *did you see the video with the little girl singing soprano?*

Still, it felt very natural for me to ask him, *Do you want to do something this weekend?* It felt equally natural when he said, *How's Sunday?* and suggested Pingjiang Lu, one of the historic streets near two of the classical gardens. When I examined my feelings, I felt calm, not nervous. The next day, when I was at the tutoring center, I told Tenten about him, the fact that I voiced his existence making him, at last, real. I bought new loafers, black, and a green wool skirt.

On Sunday, I put on lip stain and went to Pingjiang Lu. The open-window storefronts sold steamed cakes, dried tea, ice cream, candied hawthorn. I was early, and stopped inside a small shop for a crepe, where I ate it slowly, listening to music.

_____01100101: *On my way!*

We were meeting at a barbecue restaurant. When I arrived, I sat on the bench inside and checked my makeup with a compact. Now I did feel nervous. I was wearing a white beanie and had told him to look for it. What was he wearing? When I texted him asking, he didn't reply.

There wasn't much light in the restaurant, but it wasn't crowded. I kept turning my face to the door and then turning it away, so it wouldn't seem like I was watching for Zero-One when he arrived. The rich aroma of meat floated into the atrium and my stomach growled. The waitress, dressed in red, looked bored.

It took forty-five minutes and three unanswered text messages before I realized he wasn't coming.

I got to my feet and started walking. It was cold; it was still winter. I followed a side street winding along the river. On either side were lovely, classical houses strung with lights, casting subtle reflections into the water. Tendrils of tree leaves hung over white stone bridges.

Night darkened. I got hungrier and hungrier. My feet felt incredibly light. I walked back and forth along the long road, passing stores selling birdcages, postcards, English teacups, jade. The sightseers and families thinned out. The stores shuttered. Then I was one of the last people still on the street, and I sat on a stone bench next to the river, looking at the calligraphic graffiti scrawled on the white wall across.

I had the same feeling of disbelieving reality as the first night I had sat in that Korean fried chicken restaurant with Marcus and my boss, the two of them blowing smoke up into the sky. I was not sad. I felt, very simply, that this was the most obvious, inevitable outcome. Of course Zero-One hadn't shown up. What kind of person would have shown up? What kind of person would send texts every day to someone he had met once and knew nothing about, and what kind of person would answer?

I put my elbows on my knees and leaned my chin on my hands. I was aware that from the outside, my life looked pathetic. I stayed in with my games and my fantasies. I spent my time and emotions with people that were not real, literally or figuratively. I was embarrassed, yes, at the thought of how other people might perceive me if I admitted this. And yet it made me happy. No one knew the extent of my happiness, alone in my room, while I was building the romance points on one of the otome game routes, or when I was thinking about who the person behind Zero-One's texts might be. In those moments, I was happier than real life ever made me.

I opened up the last, unanswered message from Melissa and scrolled up. Past her last two texts, there were the short, defensive replies I had made and terse inquiries as we'd drifted apart, and before that, swelling like a wave, the texts grew thicker and thicker, gales of conversation, long paragraphs and bursts of short intense sentences, records of hours-long phone calls.

We had talked so much, we were always talking. I thought of her familiar voice, her flat affect, the droll way she said "Hey." I could summon all the evenings we'd spent in our regular place in K-town, the Korean fried chicken restaurant she had taken me to on that first day we'd hung out.

In Stockholm, it would be late afternoon. I opened up our chat window and called her.

The phone rang, and my memories fled downstream, flowing with the river. We'd met in a class on human rights, the only two Asians in the class. I vividly remembered the revelation of the meal we had together at the restaurant she'd chosen, the industrial lightbulbs, the wooden counters, the hard stools, the conversation, our fingers sticky with the chicken sauce. Of course I had loved her. We had spent so much time together, it couldn't have meant nothing.

But when Melissa did pick up, when she did say "Hello?" sounding startled, and a little guarded, I knew we were already far gone from that old place.

"Hey," I said, curling my fingers over the phone. "Um. What are you doing right now?"

Below me, the river quivered as though suppressing tears.

What could we say to each other from where we stood now? On either side of the line, what feelings were waiting to come out and greet us?

WING AND THE RADIO

Two hours before the concert, Cao Jinyi tapped her keycard against the door leading to the offices of the First Sichuan Radio Station and hurried down the stairs to the basement, where Manager Tian was plugged into the biggest monitor, headphones clamped over his bulbous, Buddha-long ears.

"Manager Tian," Jinyi said, "I just finalized the script. There's two personals I think we should air—"

"Sh, shh, shhh!" The manager pulled the knockoff Bose from his head and glared at her. "Can't you see I'm cleaning up this audio file?"

Jinyi saw the name Sunny Chen on his screen and felt a cloud form in her stomach. "What's that?"

Tian snorted. "You're so out of touch. This is Sunny Chen's newest interview. It was *all* over Weibo."

Jinyi was certain this was not true, at least not for the Weibo of the eighteen-to-thirty-year-old demographic. Her *mom* had a Sunny Chen CD.

"When did it happen?" she asked.

"Just a few days ago. She had another kid!" Tian said, clicking around. "We're going to play it first thing."

Jinyi thought of, and discarded, many remarks. Sarcasm had never landed with Tian, who also bristled at any disrespect, both real and imagined. She elected to adopt her most reasonable tone and say instead, "If so many people already heard it, why should we play it again? I think we should spend more time on the personals. The ones I got this time are *actually* interesting. Look, one of them is from a woman who thinks her husband is gay—"

"No, people *will* want to hear this interview again *because* it's popular!" Tian swiveled around to face Jinyi. "Listen, sweetheart, your little advice segment is cute. But if you ever want to get into the rooms upstairs, you're gonna need to hone your taste a bit. You need more than a couple dozen high schoolers listening to you give generic advice. You need stuff with appeal. *Appeal!*" He swung his arms above him for emphasis, gesturing toward Heaven, perhaps, which determined what had appeal, or, upstairs, toward Sichuan Radio and Television, which had the second say.

The First Sichuan Radio Station was, despite its name, not really the first. It was a one-floor operation housed in the basement of an office building in a small commercial area of Chengdu, the top seven floors of which were filled with the rooms of Sichuan's premier and far more well-known network, Sichuan Radio and Television. The First Sichuan Radio Station, a measly three-person operation that aired an episode on local radio only once a week and streamed to the rest of the country from its tiny WeChat channel, shared its production space with piles of tangled old cables, moldy TV scripts, and broken microphones cast off by the bigger network upstairs, like three ants scrambling over a rotting fruit pit fallen from an abundant tree.

Jinyi sighed and glanced at the clock: 7:00 p.m. In two hours she was going to be on air.

Unlike the glamorous, blow-dried news anchors of SRT who appeared nightly on TV, Jinyi was not what most people would consider pretty. She had shapeless, coarse black hair that was always falling into her face. Her mouth was wide and thin-lipped, and her small and squinty eyes were made smaller and squintier by the wire glasses she wore. Her complexion was pale, which was a plus, but oily, which was not.

But her real asset was her voice. It was smooth and resonant, neither too deep nor too high, and possessed of a particular warm, gentle quality so that even when she was speaking quickly it seemed as though she were lingering over each syllable. When she got into the sound booth and leaned into the microphone, her voice swelled with a depth and confidence that made it—in a word—*sexy*.

This voice was the pride and hope of her broadcasting school. She was from a poor family and a provincial village on the outskirts of Sichuan; when she moved to Chengdu, she'd worked at a textile factory to put herself through a late-night broadcasting school. Jinyi spoke proper Beijing Mandarin, with a beautiful standard pronunciation, and she even knew some English. Her role model was Terry Gross, from America's NPR, pirated episodes of which she'd listened to sneakily in the factory dorm. The broadcasting schoolmate who'd shared the episodes with her only had four, and so Jinyi had listened to those four episodes over and over again. She hadn't understood what was being said, but the cadences and clear, confident voice of Terry Gross all the way over in America's Philadelphia, Pennsylvania, had enthralled her.

After she graduated, she found her way into the offices of the First Sichuan Radio Station. She started as a tech. When the previous host got a better offer in Shenzhen and quit, Tian put Jinyi on his new program, *Magic Happy Hour*, at 9:00 p.m. Mondays through Saturdays. On *Magic Happy Hour*, she had a ten-minute segment as an agony aunt, reading stories of personal woe and dispensing the sagest advice she could muster with carefully rehearsed neutrality and aplomb. As Terry, she tried to channel the wisdom of the worldly American woman four decades her senior she'd named herself after.

Her signature opening, which she recited in English, went, *Good night, ladies and gentlemen. This is Magic Happy Hour, and this is your host, Terry*. On the first broadcast, she'd been too nervous and fumbled *good evening* with *good night* and so, for consistency's sake, had continued the same greeting for every episode thereafter.

But *Magic Happy Hour* was not doing so hot. Since the first episode, Manager Tian had insisted on making the show a misguided
grab bag of advertising and whatever content he could pull out of his
ass, always hoping one segment would land and make it big. He ripped
audio files from Internet forums, rehashed celebrity gossip, and, not
even occasionally, fabricated stories and fudged interviews. In one of
Jinyi's lowest moments, Tian had sat in the booth with her and pretended to be a hotshot businessman from Arkansas ("Where the heck
is *Arkansas*?" Jinyi had protested; "No one knows what Arkansas is!
No one will check!" Tian promised) who was going to invest in a
new cell phone factory in Chengdu and make everyone's lives better.
Thinking back to his garbled English mixed in with his Mandarin, to
say nothing of his ludicrous answers, Jinyi's neck burned. The Sunny
Chen interview wasn't as bad as all that. But it was still *embarrassing*.

"Manager Tian—" she tried again.

But the manager was no longer listening.

True to form, the final script for the night allotted ten minutes to
Jinyi's advice segment; forty to a grubby mix of weight loss commercials,
Sunny Chen's interview, and pirated audio files of her old songs from the
'90s; and ten minutes to a mash of local news and tabloid rumors.

"And finally," Jinyi read aloud, finishing out the news segment,
"as everyone in Chengdu knows, the immensely popular Hallyu star
Wing is performing tonight at Chengdu City Music Hall for his *Neon
Daylight* tour! This concert is the third stop on his East Asia tour.
Tickets have been sold out for months and fans have been camped
outside the hall for two days. *Neon Daylight* was a smash hit in eleven
different countries, and this is his second time touring China . . ."

After the broadcast was over, she tore off her headset and aggres-
sively banged open the door of the recording booth. The sound
mixer, a young man who had just started with them a few weeks ago,
looked startled. Jinyi attempted to brush past Manager Tian quickly.
She felt all the more annoyed because, even though she'd managed
to score one of the coveted Wing tickets, she'd been forced to scalp

it; Tian had refused to give her time off to see the show. The concert would be just ending, but maybe she could still get to the music hall in time to see him leaving.

Manager Tian blocked her at the entrance.

"Jinyi," he said, "you did good today, too."

"Thanks?" she said suspiciously.

He fumbled with his hands. "I know you're not happy that I didn't give you more time for your advice segment," he said. "But listen . . . I have some news . . ."

*

A few hours later that evening, Sun Wonseok, better known as "Wing," or by the affectionate Internet moniker the "Body Roll King," jingled into the bathroom in his suite at the Pagoda House. His reflection peered back at him from the mirror: bronze hair puffed up to three times its normal height, a lean body sheathed in a deep-V silvery suit trimmed with tassels and tiny mirrored disks clattering together like wind chimes.

Wing grinned, feral and proud. Traces of concert makeup still contoured his face. His head was swimming with triumph, and possibly the celebratory soju shots he'd taken after the concert with the staff. He was only three stops into his biggest Asia tour yet, and each concert was already sold out. Looking at his reflection, Wing gloated over the idea that this face, his face, was becoming as well-known as G-Dragon's. Okay, maybe not G-Dragon. But close.

His thoughts drifted. Yebin would have loved this outfit; she always had an eye for the extra details, and would have appreciated the tassels, the gold dust smattered on his eyelids. Well, why not? He straightened his spine and snapped a selfie. He sent it to her. *Chengdu tonight!* Now she'd see what she was missing.

Then there was nothing left to do but step out of his costume and into the shower. His silver suit puddled to the ground with a shy tinkle, and his skin, sticky with dried sweat, was suddenly exposed. The hot water coaxed the blood in his veins to quicken, and the woolly feeling in his brain dissolved. He wiped all the makeup off, washed the temporary dye out of his hair.

It was only an hour later, in his plush white bed, as he nursed a hot cup of fragrant Silver Needle white tea, that the loneliness set in. The room was silent, the TV blank, the windows dark. His crumpled suit lay in the laundry hamper. The clock on his phone read 1:00 a.m.

Under the anonymous hotel robe, Wing felt self-conscious, and very naked. His bed was cold and enormous.

*

Long before he was Wing the "Body Roll King," Sun Wonseok had been a run-of-the-mill kid from Busan. His father was a high school teacher and his mother's family owned a small restaurant. If he had never been discovered, he would probably have trudged through life as thousands of other Korean kids did, going to cram schools after class and aiming for a top university. But one of the regular patrons of his family's restaurant was a talent scout who saw the potential in the young Wonseok's softly angled double-lidded eyes, arcing eyebrows, slim nose bridge, and straight shoulders. He cajoled Wonseok's parents into letting him enter the boy in a local "Beautiful Kids" contest, and the rest was K-pop history. Wing got his fan-favorite moniker after a shirtless body roll in the music video of his first hit single, a shimmying move he conducted with his sculpted-from-stone six-pack.

Still, prior to *Neon Daylight*, Wing was B-list at best. His posters had sold, but his albums never broke the top charts. The only advertising sponsorships he got were for toothpaste brands and protein shakes. Then the Yoon sisters came along.

Yoon Soojin, a copyright lawyer, and Yoon Yeojin, an advertising writer, were surprising breakouts in the TV production world. They came from a high-achieving family with multiple executives across

Naver and Samsung; they'd both attended Seoul National. The sisters said they escaped the omnipresent pressure of their daily lives through the fantastical world of Korean dramas. The first script they cowrote, *Sour Plums*, was a melancholic, bittersweet coming-of-age story about tragic first love, which took South Korea by storm and catapulted its two main leads into household names.

Three years later, their sophomore drama, the highly anticipated *Neon Daylight*, was a significant turn from the somber *Sour Plums*. In *Neon Daylight*, an unlucky Korean high school girl, Cho Taeri, numb and grieving after her parents' funeral, walks into an underground live show. On the stage is a rock band she's never heard of. They're unbelievably good (and unbelievably hot.) The lead singer is named Léon, and after the show, Taeri wanders into a back alley and finds him making out with a fan. Only he's not making out with her—he's sucking her blood, because Léon is not just another grungy wannabe rocker from Hongdae, he's a three-hundred-year-old vampire, and he can't be exposed to daylight. (Thus the band's name.)

Wing played Léon. It was his first acting role, and it turned out the "Body Roll King" could act *and* sing *and* dance. The theme song from the soundtrack, a soulful ballad called "Lose You" with Wing's vocals, reached platinum as soon as it was released.

Neon Daylight was broadcast to eleven countries, and in a matter of months, Wing became an international star. Dior called begging to work with him; *Nylon* rushed to get him on the cover. Who wouldn't want to be him? And more to the point, who wouldn't want to be *with* him?

*

When she finally left the basement office, it was too late to bother going to the concert hall. Jinyi took a bus home, disappointment burning in her throat. The industrial pollution seemed to block the entire summer night sky out. She dully recalled Manager Tian's warning: advertisers were pulling out of *Magic Happy Hour*.

"We just don't get enough listeners," he'd said. "They've been threatening us for weeks. Unless we can raise the number . . ." The show would be shut down.

It was past midnight when Jinyi entered the cheap room she rented in an all-girls' dorm. She set down her bags, flopped belly-down on her bed, put her head in her pillow, and screamed, just once.

After a few moments, she got up, poured herself a mug of hot water, and put her dinner on the folding table: the day's last batch of *liangbanji* from the office canteen. She spooned cold rice from its plastic tub into a bowl and covered it with the fragrant cold chicken cuts, leaking red with chili oil, peppercorns, and crushed peanuts. She stuffed her mouth so full she could barely chew, and stared at the wall.

The only dredges of cheer in her room were the posters and brochures she'd put up: her graduation certificate from the Chengdu Broadcast Academy, a few postcards from Shanghai and Beijing, a reproduction of a *Coffee Prince* promotional poster. And taking center stage, in a real frame, was a poster of Wing from his "Amber Rain" release, the music video for which four years ago he'd taken off his shirt and cemented his nickname. She'd been a fan since his debut. When he announced that he was going to be in Chengdu for his *Neon Daylight* promotional tour, Jinyi was ecstatic. Like his other fans, she was in love with the songs Wing had sung for the drama's soundtrack, the moody ballads and gentle alt-rock songs a departure from his usual upbeat sound.

She finished eating with a sigh. Dutifully, she threw away the plastic food containers, washed her hands, and opened her laptop. Stories of family strife, arguments with friends, school fights, and boyfriend troubles spilled through her inbox. One email subject line caught her eye: "AM I JUST ANOTHER HOPELESS ROMANTIC?"

A high school girl had written:

Dear Terry,
    I live in Nanjing. There is a teacher at my school who I am very attracted to. He is handsome, intelligent, fair, and well-read.

He used to live abroad. I am graduating in a year and have had a crush on him all this time, but we never interacted besides in the classroom. Then, recently, he started running an English class after school and I volunteered to help him prepare. We've been spending more time together. Sometimes he lends me books. I feel like I have a chance with him! But I don't know what to do to find out if he thinks of me that way ...

Usually, she enjoyed the work of reading the emails, decoding what was promising and what wasn't, fitting together the puzzle pieces of what her next show would be. She waited for some flash of insight to come to her, some response to this dilemma that would shine a light on human nature and her own deep wisdom. There was nothing. Tonight, the emails might as well have been squiggles.

If *Magic Happy Hour* sank, she would have nowhere to go, and all her hard work would have been for nothing.

Defeated, she started scrolling through her chat groups, looking for pictures of the Wing concert. She watched a fancam of his dance number in an Elvis Presley–like silver suit—a questionable outfit choice, she thought.

Hot hot, one commenter said, with a flame emoji.

Guess his fans are really out for blood, someone else said.

Haha, good one.

Someone had posted a picture of herself holding a sign professing undying love for Wing and *Neon Daylight*. Jinyi tapped on the grainy picture. A normal-looking girl holding a big white sign with Korean characters written on it in brown ink. Something about her expression looked a little manic, but that was only normal. She had probably had the night of her life, watching Wing.

Jinyi put away her phone. She had to think of something to make the program survive. What could it be? Turning back to her computer, she flipped to the next email, uttering a silent prayer to Heaven and the gods of Appeal.

*

Wing woke up at seven, grabbed a banana, and went to the hotel gym. He ran through his sets of overhead squats, hamstring curls, push-ups, and jogging, ordered by his trainer to keep up his physique.

After he showered, he checked his phone. No response from Yebin.

Whatever. There were a million and one people out there who'd leap at the chance to talk to him, if he wanted, not to mention his adoring fans, who were already flooding the SNS sites with fancams.

He found his manager seated in the restaurant downstairs, and established himself with a glass of orange juice thick with pulp and an egg-white omelet with avocado, which he dug into while looking through Manager Jun's iPad at photos from the previous night's concert. Then Jun leaned closer and said, in a tone that made Wing's spine stiffen, "Listen, there's something you need to hear about."

Wing met his eyes with alarm.

"There was a . . . demonstration."

"What? What happened?"

"One of your fans posted a photo on your fan board." Jun pulled out his phone and tilted the screen so Wing could see. "Look."

He saw a poorly lit shot of a girl, fifteen or sixteen, with tousled black hair and a pale, angry-looking face, holding a white poster with some words scrawled on it. The characters were thin and messily written:

NEON DAYLIGHT TAKE MY SOUL!
WING-OPPA, I'M ETERNALLY YOURS!!

"This seems pretty normal?" Wing handed the phone back. He even smiled, preening a little. His fan board had blown up since his debut as Léon.

"No." Jun shook his head. "Look at the comments." He used his index finger to scroll down the screen. Wing read: *No way . . . is that?*, and *Didn't that hurt?!*, and *Cheers!!! What devotion!!*, and *What a great idea! Mind if I copy?*, and *Oh my god, you're crazy! Are you trying to curse him?!*

"I don't—"

Jun said, "It's blood."

A beat. Wing swore. "*Blood?*"

"This picture was posted around midnight yesterday and it's already attracted a lot of attention in Korea."

"What should I do? That's just—that's—" Wing had been stalked and harassed by obsessed fans, but no one had done anything like this before. He looked back at the grainy photo of the girl with the white poster and realized his palms were clammy. "Is it *her* blood?"

"It seems like it," Jun said clinically. He pinched his fingers to zoom into the photo and gestured at a patch of white on her inner arm that could have been gauze. "Of course, it seems that the blood was inspired because of your character in the show."

"Right. Yeah. Like *that* makes it totally fine." Wing groaned. "What should I do?"

"You'll need to issue a statement immediately," his manager said, already prepared. "I told the publicity team to have a draft ready for you to look over in a few hours. We'll put out something along the lines of, while of course you appreciate the devotion and care from your fans and the support you've received for *Neon Daylight*, you insist that fans take care of their own health and well-being and take care of their bodies."

Wing let his head droop down into his hands. He nodded slowly. That sounded right.

Jun got up from the breakfast table and clapped a hand on Wing's shoulder. He'd been with him ever since Wing was a fresh-faced newbie. He was the most reliable person in Wing's life. He was a mentor, protector, supporter, friend. It was a relationship closer than the one Wing had with his own father.

"Don't worry about it," Jun said, his voice softening. "It's not your fault. People get carried away."

But this didn't make Wing feel any better. As his manager stepped out of the dining room, he felt himself getting worked up. *This* stupid *girl!* he thought. She'd been all dramatic, and now *he* had to clean up her mess. It wasn't his fault that his name, his image were being used for whatever self-satisfied purposes people wanted, like these overzealous fangirls who felt like they had a right to *own* him, or the tabloid reporters who had followed him and Yebin around making up vicious lies about a relationship between him and the female costar who'd played Cho Taeri.

Why was any of this *his* responsibility?

Wing flipped back through the iPad. The photos of him on stage last night were bright and glorious; his gilded hair, his fingers curled around the microphone, his silhouette backlit by stage lights so it looked like he was floating in a golden halo. Just last night he had been invincible. Why did that triumph now feel so oddly like bitterness?

*

At the First Sichuan Radio Station, Manager Tian was, once again, unimpressed. Jinyi's two advice columns—the first using the email from the girl with the crush on her high school teacher and the second using a submission from a new housewife who didn't get along with her live-in mother-in-law—weren't scandalous enough.

"These are boring," he complained. "Anyone could have these problems."

"That's the point. They're *universal.* They're relatable." Jinyi had a shorter fuse than usual, after having stayed up until past three in the morning picking through emails that had all started sounding the same.

"Listen, we're looking at the bigger picture now, okay?" Tian snorted. His eyes glittered craftily. "We need something big. A *real* scoop. Why don't you get online and look for something juicy? What's being gossiped about on social media. Between the young people."

"Oh, sure." Jinyi leaned back in her seat chair and hunched away from Tian. She took out her phone and pulled up Weibo. The first video on her feed was a reaction video of cats being scared by cucumbers placed behind them. The cats' startled jumps were exaggerated with loud sound effects of protesting meows.

A few moments passed. Tian clicked around on his own computer. "Are you looking for new story ideas?" He spun a pen in his hands, drummed his fingers on the desk. "Or we could make up a more interesting advice column. A pregnant wife finds out her husband is cheating on her with her long-lost cousin who just reunited with the family after fifteen years."

"I think you should go into soap operas." Jinyi scrolled. A familiar-looking photo was coming up over and over again—a girl with a sign, this one written in Chinese characters, with another message of devotion to Wing. The picture had a lot of comments for what was a pretty low-quality photo. Jinyi thumbed through the reactions.

Then she realized what the sign was.

"Hey, Manager Tian," Jinyi said slowly. "Wing . . ."

"What wing?"

"You know, Wing. The one who had the concert last night." Was this it? The hot scoop? The sense for popular appeal that Tian said she needed to have? Jinyi shoved her phone at him. "A girl cut herself and wrote a sign in blood for him."

"What?" Tian took the phone and looked at the photo. The girl looked fourteen at most. "This is in blood?"

"Yeah. I saw a picture last night of a bloody sign from a Korean fan. And this is the second one. From China."

Did she regret telling him? Now it was too late.

"Oh, this is perfect!" Tian crowed. "So many ways to spin it. 'Popular Hallyu star reveals hidden fetish.' Or, 'Korean idol forces fans to compete in a gory display of devotion.' Sounds good, eh?"

"I don't—I mean, I don't know if we want to encourage this or spread it around," Jinyi said half-heartedly, still surprised at herself. "They're just confused fangirls. We don't want to give anyone else ideas."

"This is *just* what we needed. Oh, this'll be a PR disaster," Tian chortled. "We don't need to waste time. Take out your advice column, put in Wing."

＊

A round of vanilla press conferences and a VIP meet and greet later, and Wing was finished with Chengdu. It was 7:30 p.m. The sky was lit with the dredges of a setting rose-pink sun. Glassy blue and black skyscrapers cut into the hazy clouds. A strong wind blew through the power lines. He got into the back seat of the black SUV Jun was driving.

"Should we eat somewhere special?" Jun asked. "It's our last night."

"You pick," Wing yawned. "I don't care."

His mind drifted. Yebin still hadn't answered his text. Maybe she wouldn't reply at all. The thought embarrassed him, and heat crept up from under his skin. What the fuck was wrong with her? He wondered what she was doing right now, if she was avoiding the images of his face that must inevitably be all over the Internet.

He had first met Yebin when she subbed in for his main stylist. She was a quiet apprentice, starstruck and just starting out. A year later, he ran into her at a shoot for *Vogue Korea*. By then, she'd started taking on her own clients. On set, with her spiky red bob and studded three-inch heels, Yebin looked like a model herself. He remembered the tight black PU skirt she wore, under a blue-and-white blouse with folds like the top half of a *hanbok*, hanging off her thin shoulders like bat wings. He couldn't stop looking at her. On their second date, she kissed him first, her lips sticky with lip gloss.

But after he got the part for *Neon Daylight*, Yebin grew distant. He'd assumed it was only because of how busy he was, how quickly his life was changing. Then a gossip mag put out some unfounded rumors about Wing and the actress who played Cho Taeri—and Yebin tearfully dumped him.

"I know I can trust you," she'd sniffed in the dressing room. "But I can't do this anymore. All this sneaking around, being afraid of the media, of rumors, everyone breathing down your neck, trying to catch you at something."

"You worry too much" had been Wing's reply. He didn't understand her concern. The *Neon Daylight* dating scandal was the first he had had of this magnitude, but it came hand in hand with his ascent in the charts. This was simply what it meant to date a star. "You know I love you! Just stick by me. This will all blow over." He tried to embrace her.

But she'd gently pushed his arms back. A few days later, a new makeup artist started coming.

Wing couldn't think of those last few weeks working on *Neon Daylight* without bitterness. Yebin was his girlfriend; how could she not have supported him? He'd hoped his rising fame and the accolades being heaped on him would make Yebin regret the breakup. Surely she'd come back to him. Surely she'd reach out to him.

But she hadn't.

"Hotpot?" Jun suggested into the silence in the car.

"Let's go to karaoke," Wing said suddenly.

"Karaoke?" The manager jerked his head back at Wing. "You're kidding. You've got to rest your voice."

"I don't care," Wing snapped. "If you won't come with me, I'll just go by myself."

*

Jinyi went upstairs to use the fancy bathroom on the first floor. An older woman in heels glanced at her as she pulled up at the sinks. In the mirror, Jinyi's reflection was disheveled and shallow. She ran her hands under cold water. The other woman clacked out, the sound of her shoes decidedly judgmental. Jinyi sighed, all the fight gone out of her.

She wasn't sure what she should be feeling, or whether she should be disappointed in herself for giving up some kind of moral principle. Manager Tian was downstairs editing the script, playing up the Internet scandal for all it was worth. What was the big deal? Why should she feel depressed about this? After all, the fans, the bloody signs, *were* real news; she wasn't making up lies. Or was her guilt coming from some childish loyalty to a celebrity crush, to Wing, which, if that were the case, would also just show how really, stupidly childish she was?

She tried to look herself in the mirror and recite her usual spell. "Good night, ladies and gentlemen. This is *Magic Happy Hour*." But when she got to the "This is your host, Terry" part, she stopped.

Manager Tian wasn't wrong: She *was* naïve. Though she gave advice every night on this show, she didn't know what she was talking about. She was twenty-four years old, and she worked all the time. Her personal relationships were nonexistent. Her one real boyfriend had been a minor-level censor in the Ministry of Public Security. He had been fifteen years older than her, fat and nicotine-stained. She broke up with him because he was poor, and she was a poor girl who could not afford to marry a poor man. Though she'd dated him for a year and a half, she had not loved him, and he had not made her happy.

Jinyi felt like a failure. No, she *was* a failure. She had believed in some intrinsic quality in herself. She thought her voice, her beautiful voice, and her hard work and strong principles would be enough to make her successful. But now she saw herself for who she really was: a mouthpiece for sleazy, sensationalist content that exploited teenage girls.

"I'm not Terry," she said out loud to the mirror. A few tears broke out from the corners of her eyes. She was just Cao Jinyi, a name nobody knew or cared about.

*

Wing and Jun settled into a dark booth in a small karaoke studio in one of the outer commercial districts of Chengdu. The waiter came in and set the table with highballs, popcorn fried chicken, and fries. Suddenly enthusiastic, Jun flipped through the music catalog. "Oh, Wing, they have 'A Glass of Soju'!"

"Put it on." Wing settled back into the fake leather love seat and sipped at his highball. The whiskey trailed hot fingers down his throat.

Jun punched song IDs into the digital console. He was a karaoke fanatic. Once the music started, he belted away without any shame or compunction, even in the presence of celebrities. As the first song started playing and Jun picked up the microphone, Wing grabbed the tambourine lying in the corner of the booth and began rattling it in beat to the song.

It had been quite a while since he'd gone to karaoke. The tiny disco light spinning from the ceiling spattered green, blue, and red discs against the walls. *Ting, ting* went the tambourine.

*

Outside, a current pulsed through the air, into the city's power lines, radio towers, and electrical grid. Heading to the convenience store, Jinyi paused. She had felt an atmospheric crackle. Summer lightning? Was it going to rain?

She looked up, but the sky was clear.

*

"A Glass of Soju." "Up in the Clouds." Mika Nakashima's "Snow Flower," which Jun sang in a terrible falsetto. Wing carried him through the difficult "A Hundred-Year Love."

The disco light spun on. Wing ordered another round of highballs. Jun collapsed in the love seat. "You go." He motioned to Wing, gulping water. "I need a break."

But Wing just leaned back and stared at the screen. As he'd gotten drunker off the highballs, he'd lost his motivation to sing. There were no more songs in the queue. After Jun's last song, the TV display should have gone black and silent, but instead a synthesized set of violins began playing in harmony with power chords from an electric guitar. The words "Missing You" floated across the screen.

"You like F.T. Island? I didn't know that," Jun said, nibbling on a fry.

Wing stared at the screen, astonished. Before he could say that he hadn't put this song in, the manager was pushing the microphone into his hand and Wing stood up. He automatically started singing along. Quickly, the ballad crescendoed into its chorus, an eruption of emotion half an octave higher.

Jun cheered, rattling the tambourine. "Woo! Wing the King!"

Wing hardly registered him, caught up in a wave of nostalgia. It had been years since he had heard this song. Seven? Eight? His first girlfriend had loved F.T. Island. He remembered her sharing her earbuds with him after leaving a café one evening, walking back to the subway together, one of the rare moments they could meet between training and school. Yes—this was the song she'd played then.

"Why are you making me listen to F.T. Island?" he'd said, annoyed and a little jealous. This was before his debut, when his days were filled with the stress and pressure of looking up to the stars that had come before him.

"We never get to see each other. I'm telling you I'm *missing you*," his girlfriend had said, repeating the English title, sounding like an amateur actress awkwardly trying out lines.

Wing—no, not yet Wing, still just Sun Wonseok—was silent, unsure how to respond. They walked to the subway, both embarrassed. Before she got on the train, his girlfriend said in a more natural voice, "You'll be even more famous than F.T. Island, okay?" It had been late fall; she'd worn a blue duffel coat. They'd been so young.

The song ended. Before Wing could sit with his memories for too long, Shin Sungwoo's "The First Poem" flickered onto the screen.

"When did you add this?" he asked Jun, but his manager didn't seem to hear. The previous song had transported him back to his first love; this one took him back to the parties at his mother's restaurant when he was a child. This song was so old, his parents had sung it. On late nights after the customers had gone, he would watch his aunts and uncles and parents pour soju freely, pull out their old karaoke machine, and dance around like fools.

Embarrassing as he'd found it, he'd looked forward to his father stepping up to the karaoke machine. His father had a good voice, and when he crooned along with Shin Sungwoo, he shed his docile, scholarly demeanor and became someone else—a larger figure, even a romantic one. Wing admitted this was probably where his own talent came from. When was the last time he'd called his parents?

Jun teased him. "'The First Poem?' You're showing your age." Wing didn't answer. He felt fuzzy and exhilarated, as though bubbles of champagne were rising up in his consciousness.

＊

Jinyi settled into the sound booth. "Hey, where's Manager Tian?" she called to the sound mixer, noticing that Tian's usual seat was empty.

The sound mixer shrugged. "Stepped out."

She tried to summon up her old confidence and looked through the papers Tian had left. He'd written up the new segment, about Wing, full of phrases like "scandal rippling across Asia" and "dark face of Hallyu." She mouthed a few sentences to herself and any lingering, ambivalent desire to go on air dried up and died inside her like a slug put in salt. Dread settled in her stomach. Was she really going through with this?

These were teenage girls. They were people like her.

Wasn't there something else she could say about them?

Jinyi looked around. The show would be starting in half an hour, but Tian was miraculously not around.

"Hey, we're going to make some changes," she said to the sound mixer.

The young man raised his eyebrow. "Are you sure that's a good idea, Jinyi?"

She felt slightly giddy, or was it the lack of sleep catching up to her?

It didn't matter. *Magic Happy Hour* might be a nonexistent hour soon.

"Tian isn't here and he can't stop us," she said. "Besides, I'm the host. It's my show."

*

In the booth, Wing lost track of time. The song catalog lay untouched on the table. Jun's eyes were half-closed, his hand half-closed around an empty beer glass. He might even have been asleep. It was just Wing and the litany of musical memories. Without prompting, song after song rose onto the display. "Bus Stop," which he had used as a mood lifter all through his training days. "Arirang." "Time." Even a cover of the kid's song "Mountain Bunny."

His life before he'd become famous, which had receded into the blur of stage lights, came back into focus. His childhood house in Busan. His schoolmates, the neighbors and relatives who dropped by his parents' restaurant. The timid girlfriends of his youth.

Had it been an hour? Two? How long had they reserved the room for? The phone on the wall should have rung, the front desk should have asked if they wanted to extend their time. But this booth seemed to be in its own special space-time. Wing thought that if he looked for the door, it might have vanished and left just him and Jun boxed into this tiny dark room with the spinning disco light, songs from his memories arising one after another.

What's next? he asked the karaoke machine silently. Whatever glitch was going on, whatever trick was being played on him, he challenged it to give him everything it had. What else could this machine do? Could it rewind time, bring back what had been lost? Could it, for the three minutes it took to sing a song, make you as happy as you'd been when you first fell in love?

"Fly Me to the Moon" popped up on the screen. *Ah, of course.*

Yebin's favorite song. She played a little bit of piano, and one night in her apartment, early on in their relationship, she'd pulled her keyboard out and insisted on accompanying him as he stumbled through the lyrics he barely knew.

Strangely, this memory of her didn't sting.

He was remembering so much tonight.

*

Nine o'clock on the dot. The opening music for the program played and Jinyi stepped in after the hook. "Good night, ladies and gentlemen," she said, her voice automatically swelling. "This is *Magic Happy Hour*, and this is your host, Terry."

*

In the karaoke booth, the speakers crackled. A cheerful jingle, which he couldn't place, played. "*Good night, ladies and gentlemen,*" a resonant female voice said, speaking English. An American song?

"*This is Magic Happy Hour, and this is your host, Terry.*"

Terry? Was there a singer by that name? Wing frowned. The speaker sounded like she had an accent. She wasn't American. What was this? He stared at the karaoke console, completely befuddled.

The voice continued in a soft flurry of Mandarin. With his rudimentary understanding, he understood only a few snatches: "we are," "I am," "this girl," "thank you," "hope," "I feel . . ." The jingle played again. It sounded like a radio show. Was the machine malfunctioning, picking up some weird signals from outside? Were the random songs over? Was this whole experience just a coincidence, then, a coincidence made from a technical glitch combined with whiskey highballs on an empty stomach?

Wing was about to put down the microphone and wake Jun up. Then the most familiar chords drifted through the speakers.

Of all songs, this was the one he knew best, embedded into his very DNA. He had sung this song so many times that the words had become almost meaningless to him. The title "Lose You" flashed on the screen.

As though hypnotized, he stepped closer to the screen and brought the microphone back up to his lips. After the parade of nostalgia from his past, Wing now felt all the more viscerally the vast gulf between "Lose You" and the songs that had come before. For the first time since Jun brought it up that morning, he recalled the fan who had written him a note in her own blood, and suddenly felt guilty he hadn't worried about her more. Was she okay? Was she safe? Where was she now? Where, for that matter, were the other girls from the concert last night, some who had been so happy to see him they had been moved to tears? Were they at this very moment listening to music and dreaming, too?

A gentle regret tugged at him, for the boy he had been, for the parents he hadn't seen in too long, for Yebin, whom he'd loved too poorly to keep, for everything he'd given up without realizing on his way to the top.

He breathed in, and on his outward breath, let the first lyrics fill the room.

*

"Damn, Jinyi, you really went off," the sound mixer said in some awe after she took her headphones off.

"Thanks. Thanks?" Jinyi felt herself shaking off a trance. Oh god. That episode. For a brief moment, when she'd started reading the script she'd written helter-skelter, she had felt that panic-in-the-stomach feeling that someone feels at the top of a roller coaster, when too much momentum has gathered to stop. Her cheeks bloomed with embarrassment. "Was it okay?"

"It was *different*, for sure," the sound mixer said.

"Oh, no," Jinyi moaned. She'd been so cheesy! She grabbed her purse, ready to leave.

"Hang on, where are you going? Did you eat yet?" the sound mixer asked.

Before she could reply, Manager Tian pushed into the office. *Shit!* How much of the show had he heard? Before he could say anything, Jinyi struck first. "Where were you?" she challenged him.

"Huh? Is the show over?" Tian blinked.

Confused but not giving up her advantage, Jinyi played up her indignation. "Yeah! We had to do the whole thing without you!"

"My stupid watch told me it was still eight." Tian spoke slowly. He extended his wristwatch and frowned at it. The cheap digital display still blinked 8:00 p.m. "I'm sorry . . . I seem to have dozed off . . . Did everything go okay?"

"It was fine." *I hope.* Jinyi pushed open the door and the sound mixer followed her out.

During the last ten minutes of the show, Jinyi had changed her tone. "Listeners, friends," she'd said, speaking slowly, "I have something to confess tonight."

She'd read the news about the Wing fans who'd used blood to write their signs, then read the letter from the high school girl in Nanjing.

"I thought a lot about these girls. The ones who went way too far and actually hurt themselves, trying to get close to their idol. And this other girl, who wrote this letter, also wrapped up in her love for someone distant.

"On this show, people send me their questions and I try to help them find answers. I wanted to find something insightful to say, because that's what I'm supposed to do. But the truth is, I am just as lost, if not more so, than all of you. And when I read this girl's letter, when I saw the posters by those other girls online, I remembered that I am an inexperienced girl, just like these inexperienced girls. We're very similar. We all have intense desires, and feel confused about how to act on those desires. We don't know how to get the lives and the loves that we want.

"I grew up in a tiny village, and I heard the name Terry from an American radio show. I wanted to live up to her, so I copied her name. But it's not my real name. And to be honest, I've seen very little in this world. I'm not qualified to give advice to others. There are many nights when I am lost and confused and don't know what to do. I feel a lot of pressure. I feel tired. I wish there was someone who could tell me what to do. But when I look at the adults around me, they seem just as uncertain as I am. All of us are flailing around, trying to figure out how to find that vague thing, happiness.

"And so to all the desperate, lonely girls out there, and to everyone else who might be feeling a little alone tonight, I just want to say one thing. Take care of yourselves. Take it easy. Let's not put too much pressure on ourselves. And just know that there are others listening right now who are also uncertain and lost, and listening to the same song tonight."

And then she brought in the track "Lose You."

The sound mixer stopped Jinyi as she started walking toward the bus. "Did you eat? There's a noodle restaurant I like a few blocks away, wanna go?"

"Oh, sure." She was still brooding while she followed the sound mixer. She'd been so earnest. And naïve. It was ridiculous. It was humiliating. What were people going to think of her? "Idiot," she muttered, not realizing she'd spoken aloud.

The sound mixer gave her a look. "Hey, Jinyi," he said. "You know, you're doing fine."

"What?"

"You're twenty-four and hosting your own radio show!" he said. "Not many people can say that. And you're just trying to figure things out. Like everyone else. Just like you said."

His serious attention made Jinyi embarrassed. She turned her face away. "As long as this show doesn't tank," she said, but a little warm bubble of gratification swelled inside her.

The noodle restaurant was on an empty street next to a karaoke studio and a yogurt shop. There was only a single black SUV with tinted windows idling against the sidewalk. Jinyi walked past it to peer at the menu plastered on the noodle shop window. The sound mixer thumbed through WeChat. Briefly, Jinyi wondered how the fangirls with the bloody posterboards were doing. Were they feeling ashamed, embarrassed? Would one of them ever hear her broadcast? Maybe, just maybe, Jinyi thought, it might make her feel a little better.

"Hey, where did you get that file today?" the sound mixer asked. "For the 'Lose You' track."

"It's not the one we always use?"

"No, it didn't have the usual backing track. It sounded different. Wing's voice was so much louder than usual."

Jinyi thought back. She had been in such a trance in the sound booth, she had hardly paid attention. "I don't know," she said. "I'll have to listen to it again."

Just a few steps behind them, the black car's engine rumbled to a start. A moment later, it pulled down the road and turned at the light.

Over the empty street, the night was warm and still.

THE GIRL WITH THE

DOUBLE EYELIDS

PROLOGUE: AFTERNOON

LiLi's head was in my lap. Her hair, falling away from her face, was spread over my thighs, leaving exposed her right ear. LiLi was self-conscious about the size of her ears, saying they were too small for her head.

Her head pressed against my legs, a warm, heavy globe whose heat radiated from below the center of my body, hotter than everything around it. I imagined the blood circulating just under her skin. The parts of her hair caught in the sunlight glimmered, a paler black than the rest, and were warm to the touch. I leaned down—my shirt fell to touch the back of her head—and peered into her ear canal. The skin inside was so pink and soft-looking, like a baby's. The wax, I was sure, would also be soft and clean. "I'm going in," I said, keeping my voice very neutral, "don't move." I took the wooden pick and angled it carefully. My fingers trembled slightly.

"Ah, it's so hot today, I can't stand touching another human body," LiLi groaned. She squirmed and the weight of her shoulder lifted, the gap between her body and mine introducing a tiny interval of coolness.

Yes, she was right, it was hot, it was an afternoon at the end of summer. It was the time of day and the time of year for suspension, for longing—for a person, a song, a walk, a tree leaf, a fall of hair—the time of year for standing in front of electric fans while the cicadas whined, waiting for something to happen.

LiLi's head in my lap was heavy, it was hot, I was so hot, I was burning. Her eyes were closed, the curves of her lids like the keel of a boat. The afternoon sun through the window was glaringly bright.

"Stay still," I coaxed her. I looked deep into her ear canal and searched for the deepest pieces of wax.

1

I was born with small eyes. My aunt, when she saw me, exclaimed, "She looks like her mother!"—divining in my wrinkled newborn features my future square-jawed face, delicate ears, long eyebrows, and well-shaped neck. I weighed eight pounds; my mother had eaten four, sometimes five meals a day during her pregnancy. "The only shame," my aunt continued, "is that she didn't get her mother's eyes," for while my mother had brilliant, bright, wide double-lidded eyes, mine—alas!—were small and hooded, like my father's, a thick strip of flesh and no visible crease at the top.

When I was thirteen, my mother took me to a photo studio where a makeup assistant cut out slivers of tape in the shape of fingernail clippings and pasted my eyelids up. While powdering my face, she asked my mother, "Ma'am, you have very big eyes. Have you considered getting your daughter's eyelids done? If you do it while she's young, people will think it's more natural when she's older. Some people get double eyelids naturally through puberty, you know."

"Did you get yours done?" my mother asked. The makeup assistant had a soft, doll-like face, her hair piled in an updo, her big, round eyes framed by luxurious lashes.

"I was born with mine," she said matter-of-factly. "But that girl over there did," and she nodded at the makeup assistant at the next counter, who looked edgy and bold with thick wings of eyeliner swept right above her creases, making her eyes look long and elegantly tilted.

"She's pretty," my mother said.

When the photos were developed my mother came into my bedroom with the album in hand. Impossible images of me flicked by on thick matte pages, a skinny teenager with fake Sailor Moon–style buns engulfed in tulle dresses, wearing fluffy shorts and holding a large stuffed rabbit, or buttoned into traditional high-collared two-pieces that looked like they were from the Tang dynasty, hair in long artificial braids.

"Xiao Yun, look how pretty you look," my mother said. "Everyone said you look like a model." Her hand, with the red bracelet she always wore around her wrist, trailed along the lower corner of the book.

It wasn't even the heavy makeup or Photoshop retouching that had made the biggest difference. It was my eyes, so bright and so wide. The makeup assistant had glued on false eyelashes that flew to the ceiling and dusted the inner corners of my eyes with white glitter. Though I was virtually unrecognizable to myself in those photos (my smile stiff, my skin artificially pale, my expression unnatural), I startled myself with the inviting roundness in my photographed gaze.

That night, after everyone else fell asleep, I slipped out of my room to page through the album again. I lingered over the photos, over the pretty girl with the bright cheeks, the smooth hair, the big eyes. Did having double eyelids make such a difference? In the photos, I had the expression of a kind person, of someone at peace with the world. What, I wondered, did that girl in the photographs see?

*

The chemistry teacher was a family friend who came to our mahjong nights every Friday. He had gotten his PhD in the UK and spoke good

English; despite this, he had chosen to return to China. He always wore long, tailored pants made of a thick, expensive material, even in the summer. He was not old, but sometimes he used a polished wooden cane, which only made him seem more British. He had a clear forehead, thick hair, severe glasses, and a quick, intelligent voice. He was always reading foreign novels, he wore cologne, and whenever he smiled, it was with his mouth closed, so it felt like he was hiding a secret, that he was laughing at something behind you that only he could see.

He and my uncle had once worked together at the paper factory where my uncle had been a foreman and the chemistry teacher was a laboratory researcher. After the factory closed down, the chemistry teacher got his job teaching chemistry and my uncle didn't get another job at all.

When I was young, before I entered high school, the chemistry teacher used to take me out for ice cream. Whenever we walked home through the park, he would lean down and whisper to me: *See that woman, pinched around the nose because she is stingy with money. And that tall woman, long-necked and slender—she sleeps on her stomach, has bad dreams and insomnia. And that young boy scampering around the playground—has no stamina, he will certainly burn out by thirty.*

As humbly as I could, I would ask the chemistry teacher how he knew these things. He would shrug. "I can just see it," he said, "just by looking." And I never quite managed to ask him what he saw when he looked at me.

When I was sixteen, in my second year of high school, I finally took his class. On days we were scheduled for chemistry I tried to look my best, brushing my hair, straightening my bangs, hoping the smell of my scented body soap would linger, putting on a little bit of the sheerest lip gloss and eye makeup that you could get away with—a bit of mascara, a little tape. I rolled up the hem of my uniform skirt and put a tiny pin inside my jersey to emphasize my waist.

I was one of the best students in his class. "If a strip of magnesium metal is added to a solution of silver nitrate"—he'd tap his chalk against the board—"what is the balanced equation for the reaction?"

Often, I would be the last one he called. "Xia Dengyun," he'd say, and there was something in his voice when he said my name that made my spine straighten. *Well, everyone,* his tone implied, *now that you've all tried and failed, here is Xia Dengyun to show you the way.* And up I would go.

$$Mg + Ag^+ \rightarrow Mg^{2+} + Ag$$

At school the chemistry teacher and I spoke formally, as though we did not know each other. We spoke of personal things only once. The spring I took his class, he called me to the teachers' lounge. He looked through the papers on his desk. "Xiao Yun," he said, calling me by my family's nickname for me, "you'll be taking the entrance exam next year."

"Yes, Tang Laoshi." I was never talkative in the best of circumstances, but around the chemistry teacher I grew even more tongue-tied and shy, always looking down at the ground, never knowing what to say. Now I looked at the ground again, at his pointed-toe oxford shoes. There had been a rumor going around in PE. An older girl told us that she had seen Tang Laoshi's pants leg lift up once and there had been a gleam of metal, she said that in his shoe he had a metal foot. We were all awed into silence. *It makes sense,* LiLi had said. *This is why he carries a cane.* Another girl said softly, her voice filled with wonder and pity, *I wonder what happened. He's so handsome.*

"You're a diligent student." His voice came down on me. "Have you thought about where you might want to go for university?"

"Nanjing University," I said, only because it was the most well-known university in the area.

"That's a very good choice. Though perhaps you could also study abroad. Your English scores are high. What do you think? That would be good for a young woman like you."

"Really?" I asked politely. "I never thought about it." And it was true, I hadn't thought much about my life beyond the next day, the next week, thinking about the future was like looking through a telescope the wrong way—everything so small I couldn't make anything out.

"Your parents told me they might be interested in sending you abroad."

"I didn't know that."

"You're a curious girl. Would you like to see more of the world?" His voice was commanding, and I looked up. I liked his straight eyebrows, and his forehead, so noble and clear.

"I don't know, Tang Laoshi." Though my classmates all seemed to have dreams and interests, to go abroad, own a coffee shop, start a fashion line, earn a large salary, I was not in such tune with my own desires, or even aware if they existed. I had lived in the same neighborhood in Nanjing all my life. I was comfortable living with my talkative mother, my old-fashioned grandmother, and my stoic and hardworking father. I knew which bookshops and convenience stores to go to for the latest magazines, which dessert shops gave the largest portions, which cosmetics stores had free samples, and I knew how to study. I read magazines, watched TV dramas with my mother, and on the weekends, talked on the phone with LiLi, my first friend after entering high school. And aside from all of that, when I had extra time, I memorized chemistry. What kind of life did I want after this life? Why should I want any other kind of life?

2

Though the education at my high school was mostly academic, I was, along with the other girls, also undergoing an alternate education— how to become a woman. We knew the best dieting tricks, how to eat noodles made from a root with zero calories, to drink a whole bottle of water and wait fifteen minutes when we were hungry, to avoid rice, to chew ginger root. We passed around magazine pullouts that showed stretches you could do at night to slim and lengthen the line of your legs and exercises to improve your posture. We knew how to measure the distance between the corners of our mouth to our nose to find the best side of our face to take pictures of. But for girls like me, that is, girls with monolids, the trickiest thing to learn was how to make our eyes look bigger.

I was an expert in all types of eyelid adhesives, each with its own pros and cons: single-sided, double-sided, transparent, nude-colored, eyelid glue, tape string, fiber mesh, to which you applied the glue yourself, from a bottle like that of nail polish. There were different sizes and different shapes, long and narrow, short and wide. There was eyelid tape printed black on the front side so you could get your eyeliner and double eyelid in one go. There were tips for how to cut the tape, where to place it, high or low, near the inner corner of your eye or at the outside. There were tutorials on how to shape your eyes like Jolin Tsai's, Scarlett Johansson's, Maggie Cheung's. I had my preferences and go-to brands, and each morning I could put on my eyelid tape, using the double-sided type, which I cut myself, in three seconds flat.

Finally, the summer after my year of chemistry, the summer before my last year of high school, I went under the knife. My mother saw my grades were good and convinced my father for me, as a reward. She asked around to find the best surgeon who would give the most natural results. We went to Shanghai for the most modern doctors, and found one who had studied in Seoul.

At the consultation, the surgeon, who was not pretty, showed me different possible styles. "How about Fan Bingbing?" she asked. "Do you want a shape like hers? Or Kim Soyeon? You could get a Korean style." She cradled my face gently in her hands, touching my eyelids lightly with her gloved fingers. Ptosis, yes. Fat deposits, yes. She recommended placing the incisions low rather than high.

I told no one I was going for a consultation, not even LiLi. LiLi had bright, smooth skin, an athlete's tan, beautiful eyelids, and a gummy smile as bright as the slice of a white peach. Half the boys in our grade were in love with her. The bleached collar of her uniform shirt seemed to shine more than everyone else's. Our friendship usually consisted of her calling me on the weekends to go out for desserts and gossip about celebrity crushes and new boy idols. Meanwhile, every Friday I waited for the smell of the chemistry teacher's cigarettes to enter our apartment.

When my mother had paid the deposit with the doctor, we set a date for the appointment. Then we took the train back to Nanjing. When we got home it was Friday, a mahjong night. The chemistry teacher was in our living room, playing checkers with my uncle and smoking his sweet-smelling cigarettes. He knew all about my consultation.

I asked the chemistry teacher: "You'll keep it a secret at school?"

My aunt clicked her tongue and came over to pat my cheek. "You worry too much, everyone will think it's puberty."

I repeated to the chemistry teacher: "You won't tell anyone?"

"When school starts," he replied, "it'll be like we're meeting for the first time." He smiled with his mouth closed.

But when I got to my room, I found a fistful of white flowers sprawling from a dark green pot on my desk. The pale petals were long and ruffled, gathered in careless cascades. They looked like a flock of birds about to take flight.

"What are these?" I asked my grandmother.

Irises. The chemistry teacher had brought them for me. My grandmother sounded mildly puzzled; no one we knew ever bought flowers as gifts. But the chemistry teacher was full of strange customs.

I was tired from the train ride and lay down in the dark of my room, trying to nap, but I found it hard to fall asleep. I kept my eyes closed, and heard sounds from outside, muffled by my pillow. The front door opened when my father came home and, sometime later, there was the clatter of the mahjong tiles, my uncle's guttural laugh. When my mother came in to check on me, the faint smell of cigarette smoke floated through the crack in my door. I could distinguish two types of cigarettes: one, the typical sour odor from the Baishas my uncle smoked; weaker than that was the faintly cooler, minty-sweet smell of the chemistry teacher's cigarettes. I didn't know which brand they were, but I had never smelled them anywhere else.

Whenever I cracked open my eyes I'd see the irises, waxy and astonishing against the shrouded window. The green glass of the vase glinted. I wondered how my life would change now that I was going to be beautiful.

*

For two weeks after my surgery I stayed at home. LiLi called me to say a boy she was dating wanted to introduce me to a friend, but I told her I had allergies, I was sick. With the oppressive summer heat, my parents turned our air conditioner on full blast, while the humidity outside turned all the trees a brilliant yellow-green.

Even after my stitches were taken out, the healing incisions looked red and raw. In the mirror my face was bruised and swollen, my eyes inflamed and weeping—a nightmare face, the face of a demon. My grandmother brought me congee with pickled vegetables and soup with carrots and goji berries. I watered the chemistry teacher's irises and kept them turned to the window in the kitchen, the sunniest part of our apartment. Each day, I looked at myself in all the reflective surfaces I could: the iron of the water kettle, dark windows before dawn, the distorted metal of the showerhead.

Fifteen days after the surgery, my mother declared me recovered.

"They look so natural," she said admiringly, brushing my bangs back in front of the mirror. "Look, your eyes look so much brighter and more awake."

"We should go to a photographer," my grandmother said, "and order some professional shots."

We decided to go to a restaurant, and invited my aunt and uncle and the chemistry teacher as well. For the first time in two weeks I put on nice clothes, a short dress with a tiny floral print and white sandals with a heel. I went through my makeup bag and threw away all the substitutes: the eyelid tape, the eyelid glue, the fiber mesh, the adhesive string. I drew dark lines across my new creases and stepped back to judge the effect. I added mascara and pink lip gloss, and patted shimmer powder onto my cheekbones and the inner corners of my eyes.

Under the fluorescent lights at the restaurant, everyone else looked tired. My grandmother's pink blush was too strong, and her lips were brittle and thin. My father wiped his hair away from his face, showing the shining forehead, the receding hairline. I lifted the tablecloth to peek underneath. The chemistry teacher's feet were directly across from mine. His shoes were polished, shining and clean, and I could see his socks, a rich navy color with brown stripes, probably expensive. He always had been a well-dressed man. I looked back up. The chemistry teacher licked his dry lips and got up to go to the bathroom, picking up the cane leaning against his chair.

When he turned away, I saw the *thing* on the back of his neck: an enormous white-coated pink tongue. I knocked over my soup bowl with a clang. Heads swiveled around to us.

As I fumbled with the napkins, my mother took over, blotting the tablecloth with her napkin. I blinked again and again.

"Xiao Yun, do your eyes still hurt?" she asked me.

"They're fine," I said breathlessly.

When the chemistry teacher sat down again, I excused myself to the bathroom. On the way back to the table, I deliberately walked behind him. I hadn't been wrong. The tongue was really there on the back of his neck. It looked almost like a tattoo. It was big, bigger than a normal tongue, and underneath his hairline I could see the mouth it came from, a red stamped line. It looked greedy, I could imagine it licking me up, from toe to scalp, taking a little more of me with each lick until I was gone.

But even as I looked, I could tell there was something extradimensional about it, something that indicated it was not really part of his skin. I blinked again and again. I knew the chemistry teacher would not have gotten such an ugly tattoo.

And it was ugly—it looked like a sick tongue.

During dinner, everyone laughed and ate as usual. From the front, the chemistry teacher looked clean, handsome, and kind. He spun the lazy Susan, leaned over to place morsels of fish on my mother's and aunt's plates. No one else seemed to notice anything wrong with his neck.

When we got back to our apartment I watered the irises. The dark window reflection showed the top of my head, the overhead lamp, the steel cabinet handles. I looked down from the window and back at the counter. Along the stems of the irises a hundred eyes blinked open.

I dropped the watering pot and covered my eyes. Spilled water dribbled over the floor, wetting my socks.

Then I removed my hand and looked again. The eyes on the flower stems blinked occasionally, some of them looking at me, others looking away. There were so many tiny eyes, it should have been disgusting, but my body didn't react with fear, I didn't tremble or feel nausea.

I closed my eyes and gingerly reached out to touch the flowers. I didn't feel anything out of the ordinary. The smoothness of the stem, the velvety texture of the petal, they all felt the same as any unremarkable fresh flower. My thumb and index finger found one petal, and I crushed it between them.

When I opened my eyes, there was a soft white smear on my fingertips. But the eyes on the stems of the living flowers still blinked slowly, unchanged, some looking at me and some not looking at me. They had the same tattoo-like quality as the tongue on the chemistry teacher's neck.

I threw the crumpled petal away, went into the bathroom, and washed the makeup off. What was happening? What was going on? My face floated up before me—bright-eyed and pretty, prettier than before. My eyes were definitely bigger, and I knew instinctively that I, too, was now someone who could see things without being told.

3

That was the beginning of the end of my ignorant child's life. The following week I looked at my aunt and saw red markings covering her face. They felt menacing, and inspired in me a feeling of great unease, so I stopped looking her in the face. "What's wrong with this girl?" she asked exasperatedly. I fidgeted in my seat around her, answering monosyllabically when she talked to me.

"Xiao Yun," my mother would snap at me, "don't be rude," but I had no explanation for her.

I saw the image of a snail peeking out from my mother's T-shirt sleeve, or a string of dark alphabet letters on my father's wrist. Another time, my grandmother called me in to bring her a towel after her shower, and through the steam I saw a chain with a medal hanging down her chest. The tattoo went over her wrinkled breasts with the enormous areolas and stopped at her belly button. If the medallion were real, it would have been so heavy it would have bent her whole back. It looked so familiar I kept staring at it after I handed over the towel, until my grandmother shooed me out.

In the evenings, instead of doing my homework I surfed the Internet looking for answers. I came across fearsome terms: *psychosis, schizophrenia, optical hallucinations.* I read about religious visions like the kind the Christian God gave to believers. I read stories about paranormal sightings and poltergeists, about alien abductions. I read about drug-induced breakdowns.

I went to a temple and gave my pocket money to the gods. I brought oranges as an offering, burned incense, and pulled a slip of paper. There were other students there, probably praying for luck in school or exams. My slip of paper said, *Small bad luck. Be prudent. Wait for clarity.* In the temple I watched people come and go, catching sight of a tattoo-like image here and there, on the back of someone's hand, on a thigh peeking out from underneath a short summer skirt.

I knew I would not tell anyone what I could see. I would not go to a doctor. From deep within me, intuition—bestowed by whom?—told me I should wait and see what else I'd see.

After the summer recess, I came back to the classroom and found my classmates had grown up. This was the year we were all busy cramming for the college entrance exams, but in the meantime, they had switched from flip phones to smartphones, from QQ to WeChat. They'd started dating. An underclassman asked Song FanFan out. Jiang Yutian and Huang Geyan started holding hands. Some classmates studied my face, seeming to notice a change, but I had been wearing eyelid tape for so long they couldn't say for sure what it was.

One girl insinuated, "Xiao Yun, you look prettier now. Is it that change they say, that girls transform when they're eighteen?"

"I'm not eighteen yet," I said.

LiLi winked at me and defended me. "Maybe it's love? Love makes a girl prettier."

"I'm not in love, either," I said, trying to smile mysteriously.

LiLi had cut her bangs. We hadn't seen each other much over the vacation. After the first day back at school, she invited me to her house to study. Her mother brought us cubed watermelon. LiLi told me she'd gotten her first kiss that summer, then she'd broken up with the one who'd given it, Liu Peiwu. "He's not mature enough," she said. "I couldn't talk to him about anything intelligent."

LiLi was wearing sweat shorts and a loose tank top, and her hair was up in a ponytail that showed her graceful neck and small ears. So much of her skin was visible, from her thin feet to her long arms, but I didn't see any tattoo-like symbols on her. She told me more about Liu Peiwu, how they had walked in the park together and he had put a hand around her waist, how his breath hadn't smelled like anything when he kissed her. "I was expecting to feel something different," she said. "I still don't feel like anything happened to me." In the middle of our conversation, she put out a hand and brushed an eyelash from my nose. Her face startled me, so close to mine. Her skin was so smooth and healthy. I looked in her eyes and saw guilelessness, an innocence that even I knew was dangerous.

"Your eyes look great, by the way," she said. Her voice was so sweet.

*

One day, LiLi texted me that Meng Weishi said he wanted to meet me in private, in the park by the convenience store. But when I went there after class and found him waiting, I saw an ugly tattoo-like image peeking out from under the sleeve of his uniform shirt, the head of which looked like a crow or other unfriendly bird. I could not stop looking at it. We walked under the dried-out trees. He told me he wanted me to be his girlfriend, but I thought I knew better.

When I turned him down, he said, "Why?"

I didn't say anything and the silence stretched out longer and longer, as long as our two shadows lengthening with the late afternoon.

"Why do you take so long to reply?" Meng Weishi finally said. "Your brain is fucking broken." On his way out of the park he kicked a tree so hard its branches rattled.

The symbols I saw on the bodies of people around me crowded my field of vision. I couldn't unsee them, I couldn't focus on anything else. I stopped taking care of my appearance; I forewent makeup, dressed indifferently. I began to spend more time among safe, inanimate things, books, magazines, television. When I spoke to people my dialogue grew very slow and distracted. I looked down at the ground often, or up at the sky, and hardly met anyone in the eye. "Look at this girl," my mother sighed in exasperation. "Can you believe she's almost an adult?"

Sometimes I simply closed my eyes and hoped the world would be solid and ordinary again when I opened them.

4

One Friday, I came back from studying in the library, expecting the weekly mahjong night. Instead, when I walked in, the house was quiet. No one was cooking, no food had been set out. My uncle and father were gone. On the couch my mother had wrapped her arms around my aunt, who was huddled next to her, making soft, whimpering noises.

As soon as I entered, my mother looked up at me and mouthed for me to go into my room. But as I tiptoed past them, I caught sight of half of my aunt's face—behind a tangle of hair, covering her entire eye, there was a vicious purple bruise. I almost stopped breathing.

The bruise was the size of a palm and shades of dark purple, blue, and orange. This was no hallucination, no second sight; I could immediately tell it was real.

Instead of going into my room, I went to my grandmother's. She was sitting at the old wooden desk with her glasses on, looking through a photo album. On the desk next to her was a familiar-looking medal. It was half the size of my palm, gold with dark red lettering, hung on a thin chain.

I recognized it—this medal had been awarded to my great-grandfather, her father, who had died in the civil war. She had shown me this medal before. She kept it in the drawer.

And it was the real-life version of the enormous tattoo I'd seen on her in the shower.

For a moment I was stunned, my body cold and clammy.

"Xiao Yun," my grandmother said, as I quietly absorbed this new information, the correlation between my new sight and the real world. "What's wrong?"

"What's happening with aunt?" I asked.

She sighed deeply and took off her glasses. She patted the bed for me to sit down. I looked at her neckline, and yes, the tattoo-like image of the chain was there, I could see the edge of its outline under her collar.

"This isn't something we want to worry you with. This is an adult thing." My grandmother looked at me carefully. "You saw her face?"

I nodded.

My grandmother whispered that last night, my uncle had thrown a bottle at his wife.

We all knew how my uncle was. I saw the way he would drink down glass after glass of whatever alcohol was on hand through dinner, how when he walked through our door, he'd immediately pour himself a glass from the *baijiu* bottle he always had ready. He and my aunt had been high school sweethearts. I heard she had never wanted any other man, that she was completely devoted to her husband, whom no one could compare to, even though ever since the paper factory closed down, he'd been hard-pressed to keep a job, even though he lay around the house drinking, while my aunt did all the cooking and cleaning, and worked part-time on the side, too. My uncle had a red face, I had seen how he could get frustrated, irritable when something didn't go his way. I had seen the way he sometimes snapped at my aunt when she did something small that irritated him, like clinking a spoon too loudly against her bowl.

"Is this the first time he's hurt her?" I asked.

My grandmother didn't reply.

"What did they argue about?"

"Their family is missing a child, it's incomplete," she said, and I couldn't tell if this was why they had fought or if this was meant as an explanation. My aunt and my grandmother were not related by blood. How would she have felt if it was her own daughter?

"You should know," my grandmother said heavily, "we all carry different ghosts on our back."

That night, my aunt stayed with us, taking my bed while I slept on the couch. I lay awake in the living room long after the apartment had gone quiet, staring at the ceiling and piecing together what I had learned. There had been so many nights when my aunt came to see us by herself, to cook for our family, watch TV with my mother, and when it got too late, spent the night in our living room. Why did she come to our home, if not to escape her own?

And I thought about the symbols I saw, on my family, on the people I loved. The medal on my grandmother's neck: it had a connection to her father, the soldier, whom I knew she had loved, whom perhaps she still grieved. And the red squares on my aunt's face like a veil revealing, instead of hiding, real pain.

These images I was given access to meant something, but they were like a language I had no access to, an alphabet I couldn't read. And not only could I not read the language, the language itself was also inconsistent. What was the use? What was I supposed to do with all this? Why was I tormented with secrets I didn't ask for, knowledge I didn't know how to apply, data that wouldn't cohere to conclusions? I thought crying might bring me relief, but though I blinked again and again, tears didn't come. Would my world never go back to how it was, would I never get my innocence back?

Why me?

Eventually I got up and went to the kitchen to pour myself a glass of water. The hundreds of eyes on the stems of the irises blinked slowly. No other plants had taken on the life that they had; I wondered what was special about them, knowing I'd probably never figure it out. I only knew that they had been a gift from the chemistry teacher.

I stood next to the flowers. The eyes gazed at the world without intelligence, but also without judgment. They wouldn't share my secret with me, but perhaps they were the only ones who could see the things I saw.

*

Because I was no longer taking his class, I saw the chemistry teacher less and less. When I started my final year of high school, he had stopped coming to our family's mahjong nights, though I didn't know why. At school, he always wore high-collared shirts and his hair had grown out to cover part of his neck, so I almost never saw the tongue, and almost forgot about it. Our family circle grew distant. There were more and more Friday evenings when, if I wasn't studying, my parents and I would watch a movie together or walk around the mall instead of having anyone over. In physics, I no longer felt the need to study so hard, and my rank slipped. Besides, I wasn't sleeping well, and was often tired, and my parents were worried, thinking it was the stress of school. I occasionally passed the chemistry teacher in the halls, and he would smile distantly at me, but we never stopped to talk.

At school, I was spending more and more time with LiLi; one could justifiably say I was clingy. After class, I always asked if she was free to study, if she wanted to go for ice cream. She was loving and sweet and often said yes, but the times when she was busy, or if I saw she had plans with someone else, anxiety twisted in my rib cage and I had to work harder to keep my composure.

Though I looked earnestly, even searchingly, at LiLi's face, her arms, the skin above her socks and below the hem of her skirt, and had glimpsed her creamy belly when she stretched and her shirt lifted, I never saw any strange symbols. I thought she must be the only person in my life who had no secrets.

One day LiLi told me the chemistry teacher was starting a supplementary group for English learners. It was to be a small group, only for the most dedicated students. We were walking back from the convenience store with a plastic bag of chocolate and milky drinks, and she'd slung an arm around my shoulders in her usual friendly way. The night before, I had had a series of nightmares and jerked awake with a gasp, short on air. LiLi's touch made me want to lean into her, a yearning so intense and fleeting I was dizzy, and momentarily closed my eyes.

"Why him?" I asked when I reopened them. "Why not Wei Laoshi?"—who was our official English teacher.

"The chemistry teacher studied in England, and he likes books. His English is really good." She chewed a green apple candy and swallowed. I thought her breath would smell like apples, later. "It makes sense. And we're going to read novels. It's like free tutoring. I want to go. How about it?"

I wondered why the chemistry teacher had told LiLi and not me. Previously, I would have been jealous that he had another favorite student, but instead I was startled to feel jealous that LiLi was sharing an intimacy with someone other than me.

When I was home, I told my mother about the new class. "Tang Laoshi probably speaks the best English in the school," she said approvingly. "He's so smart and generous. You should go. It will be good if you want to study abroad."

Whenever she mentioned the future, I mumbled and found a way to sidestep the conversation.

From the beginning, LiLi took charge of the new English group, which met in an empty classroom once a week after school. On the first day, she passed out blank forms on which we could fill in what books we wanted to read. I couldn't think of any in particular. At the bottom of the form was the question "Why did you join this reading group?" My potential answers all seemed inadequate: LiLi had asked me to. I wanted to spend time with her. I had nothing better to do. Part of me missed seeing the chemistry teacher. I needed to fill my time with something. Reading was better than seeing. Real life hurt too much to look at.

The first few meetings were boring. We didn't talk much. The chemistry teacher gave us worksheets with vocabulary words and paragraphs taken from random books, with blanks where we should fill in the appropriate words. But sometimes the chemistry teacher would read out loud to us, which I enjoyed the most. He was good at reading, with a clear, strong voice and even pacing:

The real evils, indeed, of Emma's situation were the power of having rather too much her own way, and a disposition to think a little too well of herself; these were the disadvantages which threatened alloy to her many enjoyments. The danger, however, was at present so unperceived, that they did not by any means rank as misfortunes with her . . .

Of course, we didn't understand everything he was saying—how could we possibly? English remained as remote to us as a receding wave on an opposite shore. But it was the rhythm of his voice, the soft slur of vowels and syllables that flickered and caught, provoking occasional understanding, that I enjoyed when I closed my eyes and listened. I could imagine a different world through the cadence of this other language, of the images that sometimes caught in my imagination. What kind of world? A world in which all the people around me looked different, felt different, were concerned with wholly different issues I had no conception of. A world so different I could not even conceive a picture of it. A world in which I was a baby, ignorant and useless, understanding absolutely nothing.

*

One day, when we were jogging in PE, LiLi told me she had a crush. No, more than a crush; it was love.

I immediately felt a pang of jealousy. "Is it someone in our class?" I felt that I would have to guess. In the world of girlhood, one could not outright ask for secrets.

"I can't tell you yet." Her breathing was even and easy as we circled around the field; I glanced at her, and her cheeks were flushed a rosy pink. "It's a little bit sensitive." She picked up the pace; I jogged harder to keep up.

"I wrote him a poem," she confided. "I was so nervous. And recently, he wrote one back."

"Did he give it to you in person?"

"We exchanged books. I lent him *The Little Prince*. My favorite book." She was quiet for several moments.

"This is the first time I've been in love," she said at last.

I hadn't read *The Little Prince*. With her flushed cheeks, LiLi seemed more excited than I'd ever seen her. My mind raced. Who was the boy? How could they have met? Was it someone top-ranked? Someone with glasses? Someone who liked books, a quiet student who had square, neat handwriting? Was it someone in our English study group?

"He'll definitely like you," I said, to be encouraging. The words slipped out unwillingly. But it was my job to be encouraging, after all, and it was also true; LiLi was pretty, sweet, and popular with everyone. I didn't totally understand why she spent her time with me. I thought sadly about how sometimes, when I went to LiLi's house to watch TV, she would get sleepy and her head would droop onto my shoulder or arm. Her hair was always clean and fresh. That time late in the summer when we were at her house, and she had put her head on my lap and asked me to clean her ears, I went home afterward daydreaming about the pink nap of her ears. I had secretly wanted her to do the same for me, I had been working up the courage to ask.

If LiLi fell in love, I would be all alone.

"Are you going on a date?" I asked. We had slowed to a walk, but I sounded out of breath.

"Soon." She dimpled. "He said he'll arrange something. We have to meet privately."

From the end of the track the teacher called our names sharply, and we started jogging again. A few minutes later, she asked: "Xiao Yun, what about you? You never talk about boys."

Boys? I thought about the boys in our class. Meng Weishi, of the crow's head on his arm, was still avoiding me. Even the boys who were nice, who I felt were trustworthy, had symbols and marks I avoided looking at. Their voices were scratchy, and when they were hot, they wiped the sweat off their faces with their shirts, which bothered me because it seemed dirty. And when the girls giggled over boy idols on magazine covers, I could only think how far away and flat their photographs seemed.

Then I thought about the chemistry teacher, the walks we'd once gone on when he would tell me what he saw, his immaculately pressed clothing, the minty smell of the cigarettes he smoked in our living room. How I had brimmed over when he gave me attention, how I would roll my skirt up and put lip gloss on for his class. I had never been able to say more than a few sentences to him. My feelings had been so strong last year, before my eyes changed; now they seemed to belong to a completely different person. Had that one-sided love been love?

"I'm too immature for love," I said instead.

"That's not true," LiLi said. "It's just that you're so practical and down-to-earth. You're not a daydreamer."

We crossed the end of the track and slowed to a walk. My cheeks and lungs were hot in the cool autumn air.

I snuck a glance at my best friend. Even the slight sweat on her forehead was clear and bright. LiLi, LiLi, she was leaving me behind, and for whom?

"You're standing firmly in the real world," LiLi said, easily hooking her arm through mine and patting my hand. "It's a good thing."

5

Near the end of November, my uncle returned to our mahjong table. He'd finally gotten a new job—at a real estate company, showing properties. He arrived alone, in the middle of the afternoon, jovial and in a grandiose mood. He said our aunt was coming after getting her nails done.

My parents switched on smiles. I wasn't sure how much of it was pretend. We hadn't hosted him since the night my aunt had showed up with the bruise.

"And listen," my uncle said, draining his glass of wine—I saw how my father tensed as he reached to refill it—"he's going to be late, but our old friend Tang is coming tonight."

"Oh my goodness, it's been so long since we've seen him," my mother said. "Where has he been hiding?"

So the chemistry teacher was finally coming back to see us. Out of habit, I went to the bathroom to check my appearance. I re-brushed my hair and swept my bangs out of my face. My eyes looked pretty. I had on a new blue skirt. My appearance would do.

My aunt showed up with a bag of oranges. When I opened the door for her, I saw that the tattoo-like red squares on her face had completely disappeared.

Her face was just her face.

"What are you looking at?" she laughed at me. I was staring. I dropped my eyes quickly. It was the first time a sign had vanished. What did it mean?

My aunt looked happier, and I was glad. She smelled good, too, fresh, there was a subtle smell like mint. It was nice to see her face—I had almost forgotten what it looked like without those red squares. When she sat down, I kept looking at her, making sure they were really gone. Were they really gone?

She moved loosely, with a freedom that felt new. She and my uncle didn't sit very close together, but when they poured out the mahjong tiles, she shuffled them with gusto.

When the chemistry teacher arrived, he brought kebabs from the barbecue restaurant down the street. He had cut his hair and looked clean-shaven. He was also in a cheery mood, gripping my father's hand, greeting my grandmother, tousling the hair I had just brushed. His palm was warm and heavy on the top of my head. "Xiao Yun," he said, "it's so lonely without you in my class now!"

"Her grades are slipping," my mother sighed at him, "it's a shame you're not her teacher anymore!"

"Tsk," he clicked his tongue. "You can't slack now, Xia Dengyun. Not if you want Nanjing University!" I remembered the tug of his charisma, the pleasure of making him laugh, the old draw of wanting him to share his knowledge with me, of wanting to impress him. But when he sat down at the mahjong table, I could still see the tongue tattoo on the back of his now-bare neck. It looked redder than I remembered, swollen, larger. I stepped away from the table.

"Go get some kebabs for your grandmother," my mother ordered.

In the kitchen, I heated the kebabs on the stove and brought tea water to a boil. "Peng!" I heard my father call out, and the chemistry teacher groaned.

But when I brought the teacups out and passed one to my aunt, I saw something on the back of her hand. There was a new symbol. White, long-lashed, with a blue iris—an eye. It was blue where the whites should have been, and the pupil was white, but it was undeniably an eye. A new symbol? What did it mean?

No. I forced myself to ignore it. These images were nothing, nothing. They were like bracelets or rings, random accessories, nothing more. I walked back to the couch. I passed my grandmother her tea. The apartment was full of the sounds of laughter and company, food and warmth. It had been a long time since our apartment was so full of life. Everything was back to how it used to be. I inhaled deeply. I felt almost relaxed for once, for the first time since my operation.

When I sank into the couch, I saw the chemistry teacher's satchel carelessly tossed on the ground by my feet. The top was undone and some papers and the spine of a book peeked out. It was thin, white and blue. I glanced at it. An English book. On the spine: *The Little Prince*.

"Xiao Yun," my aunt called, "how about I take you shopping this weekend?" Her voice came out girlishly high-pitched.

"She needs to study," my mother protested.

I stared at the satchel. Was this LiLi's book? The one she'd given her crush? Why would the chemistry teacher have it? Was it pure chance? We weren't reading *The Little Prince* in our English group. We were reading an abridged version of *Great Expectations*.

I thought about how LiLi had giggled while we were out running, how infatuated and distant she had seemed talking about her crush. Was this why she couldn't tell me who it was? Was this why it was sensitive? Could I . . .

My mother and grandmother were transfixed by the TV. Stealthily, with a duplicity I didn't know I had, I slipped a hand over the front of the couch and pulled the book out.

"Why, Tang Laoshi," my aunt said coyly from the mahjong table, "it seems I just beat you," and there was laughter. I quickly slipped the book under my shirt.

"Ai," my grandmother said, disgruntled at something happening in the TV drama she was watching. "Look, she's lying to him again. I knew it."

"I'm going to do some homework," I said, holding my hands over my stomach, and fled into my room just as I heard the tiles being shuffled.

*

In my room, I turned on the desk lamp and examined the book. The cover had a curly blue typeface and an illustration.

It could just be a coincidence, I thought. The chemistry teacher read a lot of foreign novels. And this was a famous book.

I opened the book. The cover page. I turned the page. Words, just words, some of which I recognized: *heart, children, rose, fox, the.* I quickly thumbed through, and then found it—a slip of white paper. Folded and sealed shut with a sticker.

The skin around my skull tightened. Reality dripped and expanded. I still wanted to preserve my understandings of the people in my life, to continue to believe that the chemistry teacher was polished, kind, and smart, that my aunt and uncle were a happy couple, that my family life was happy. I was still just a girl. Some secrets, most secrets, I didn't want to know.

I was aware of the insistent thudding of my heart. The folded paper I held between my index finger and thumb was physical evidence. It wasn't something no one else could see.

And the neighborhood I had grown up in, the wide street with the white apartment buildings, the cherry trees, the little shop with the walls painted red where my mother liked to get noodles, the graveyard behind the park—all of it, the whole environment, suddenly seemed inscrutable, unsafe, full of hidden truths that might erupt at any moment.

With my palm pressed against the smooth pages of *The Little Prince*, I recalled LiLi's pink and hopeful face. She had sounded feverish, excited, when she said her crush wrote her a note back. I peeled the sticker off the paper—it came off easily, it had already been taken off before—and unfolded the note. The first line was in LiLi's handwriting. *I'm so shy, I can't believe I'm writing this*, it began.

I didn't want to read more. I sealed the note again, feeling sick.

"Xiao Yun." Someone tapped at my door. It was my father's voice. "Why are you working so hard? Come out! We haven't gotten together like this in a while. Do you want ice cream?"

"One second," I called. I shut the note back in the book and hastily put *Great Expectations* on top of it. I opened the door and forced myself to yawn. I told my father I was going to sleep.

"Is everything all right?" he asked, his face kindly, and I wondered what things he might know that I didn't.

After he left, after I had changed into my pajamas and brushed my teeth, I returned to my room. I felt nauseated, still, and my breath came short, like when I had been running alongside LiLi.

On my desk, I uncovered *The Little Prince*. I was too exhausted to return the book to the chemistry teacher's satchel, to do the work of sneaking out, slipping it back in. *An ugly tongue*, I thought, thinking of the back of the chemistry teacher's neck.

And anyway, what does he know, I thought, petulant, frustrated; *he has no idea what I know. Let him wonder.* I took some books out of the bottom shelf of my bookcase and hid *The Little Prince* flat against the back. I reshelved the books so that they stuck out only a little more than before.

Then I lay down in the dark and breathed slowly, in and out. It was a long time later that I heard chairs scraping back, the chatter fading, and smelled the mint smoke of a freshly-lit cigarette.

"She's asleep?" I heard the chemistry teacher say.

"High school students have it hard," my aunt sympathized. "Let's not bother her."

Then the shuffle at the door, the sound of farewells, the squeak as the hinges closed. My parents continued to speak in a huddled whisper, discussing something fervently between themselves. I put my pillow over my head so I didn't have to hear the sound of more secrets. I drifted, not into sleep, but a calm of deep logic. There were emotions in me, suspicion, fear, doubt, hurt—if I had to articulate them, I would articulate them as images, a heavy umbrella, a lichened boulder sunk into a sea hole.

I pinched myself on my inner wrist, hard. The sensation cleared away the thoughts for a moment. Maybe what I had done was enough. And maybe if I didn't think about anything, then everything would solve itself.

6

I began skipping the English reading group. I said I had to study, put my attention on other subjects. LiLi was disappointed, but she only said, "You're being practical. I bet you'll get into a top university."

It grew colder. My uncle worked late at his new job. My grand-mother started knitting me a new scarf. My father was promoted. One Friday, my aunt came over alone, said she was staying the night, and took me out to hotpot.

She was wearing a long-sleeved dress. She ordered herself beer. Over the steam of the broth, I looked at her arms, wondered if she had ever covered up bruises.

She asked me, "So, Xiao Yun, have any boys in your class been interested in you?"

"No," I said, dropping a piece of taro into the broth.

"It's good to focus on your schoolwork," my aunt said confidingly, "but you're a young girl, you should enjoy life a little, too. You should date around while you can, figure out what you like. What about get-ting your ears pierced? I can take you!"

We dipped pieces of pork, cabbage, and baby corn into the broth.

Finally I asked her directly. "How are things with uncle now?" I didn't look her in the face. When she replied, I could feel her gaze on me, her voice gentle.

"Were you worried about that? But Xiao Yun, your aunt knows how to take care of herself."

"Has he done it before?" I still didn't name the deed.

"Anyone who stays together will have their differences over the years. How can two people stay the same forever?" She put her chop-sticks down and leaned across the table so I had to look at her. Her face was damp from the steam. "Let me tell you something. You're almost an adult, you can understand."

Her voice was bright and conspiratorial, with a hard, self-preserving edge. "A woman has to protect herself. You have to have other options."

Then she giggled and raised a hand to her mouth. It was the hand with the tattoo of the vivid blue eye. The uneasy thought came to me that her new tattoo looked a bit like the chemistry teacher's tongue. "That's why I'm telling you, you should look around when you can."

*

Perhaps it was what my aunt said, or perhaps it was that my grand-mother finished my scarf. Perhaps it was that it was almost the end of the year, and almost my birthday. Or perhaps it was that LiLi finally confessed to me that her crush was on the chemistry teacher.

We were out together drinking hot milk teas. The closeness between us I had felt for those months during the summer and early fall, when she had put her head in my lap and asked me to clean her ears, when we walked together arm in arm from the convenience store, had diminished. I still slid behind her like a puppy, hoping for affection, but since the English classes had started she was more distracted, sometimes melancholy, returning my messages more slowly and often hard to reach.

That afternoon, she gave me an early birthday present: a makeup kit with glittery lip gloss. She wrote me a card with a bunch of stick-ers inside it. I looked searchingly through the short message and felt disappointed: *Happy birthday, Xiao Yun! Let's both get into great col-leges and fall in love!* she'd written. I had hoped for something more intimate than that.

"How is it going with your crush?" I asked, sliding the card back into the envelope.

LiLi sighed and looked mature. "He's distant. It's hard to meet up."

I sipped my milk tea and tried to look curious instead of dismissive.

LiLi leaned closer. "It's Tang Laoshi," she whispered. "That's who I like. That's why it's hard. I know he likes me, but he doesn't want there to be any trouble."

When I didn't say anything, she asked me, "Aren't you surprised?"

Even with my suspicions confirmed, I was surprised at the hurt I felt. "Oh," I said faintly, trying to playact a normal reaction. "I mean, he's an adult . . ."

These few words were invitation enough. "Yes, he is!" LiLi burst out, eyes shining. "He's so smart, he knows so much, he's completely unlike anyone else at the school!" Her voice turned yearning. She had clearly been desperate to talk about him. "He knows your family, right? Do you know what he's like outside of school?"

"My uncle knows him," I said slowly, not wanting to divulge how close we actually were, how many hours he had spent in my family's home. And since the time I had stolen his copy of *The Little Prince*, the chemistry teacher had not come to our mahjong nights again.

LiLi's expression turned dreamy. "I wish I knew more about him. He said we have to wait until I graduate to date. I can't wait, I wish I was older badly. But look, he gave me this." She pulled something from her backpack: a tube of lipstick with a flower on the case. "I only wear it to the English group."

I should have stayed in that class, I thought.

"My mother says he's very smart," I said, not knowing what else to say.

"Oh, he obviously is," LiLi said, lost in a fantasy. "Sometimes I go to the English group a little early and he'll tell me about his life overseas, and all the things he can show me . . ."

Perhaps the moment I really grew up was when I looked at LiLi's pure, blissful face, suffused with a young girl's love, and felt inside the red-hot blistering of rage. And even then, there were none of those tattoo-like symbols on her—my eyes told me nothing, nothing.

＊

"Dad," I asked the following Friday, "where does Tang Laoshi live?"

My father was reading the newspaper and crunching sunflower seeds. "Tang Laoshi? Near the university . . . why?"

The lie came easily. "He said he was going to give me some English prep books, but didn't want to bring them to school or the other students would say it was favoritism. I wanted to go pick them up."

"Oh really? That's nice of him." My father's voice sounded a little uncertain. "Do you want me to go with you?"

"No, I'm meeting LiLi afterward," I said. My parents trusted me implicitly; it was so easy.

My father gave me the address. I didn't have a plan, not really. I only knew what I had seen, which was the red tongue on the back of the chemistry teacher's neck.

I put on a hat and covered my face with a mask, like I had allergies. On the kitchen windowsill, the irises blinked dumbly. I left the house and got on the bus, and went to the address my father had given me.

The first day I staked out his apartment, I didn't see anything. He lived in a clean, pale-yellow building on a pleasant street with stationery stores and used bookshops. His building had a pretty little wrought-iron gate. His unit was on the ground floor. I walked by a few times, pretended to browse a shop stall, and bought a cold drink at the café down the street. I waited for an hour. His apartment seemed empty, he didn't come out.

The second time I went on Saturday morning. I went to the same café, wearing a different hat. I didn't see him come out of his apartment then, either. There were college students all around, and for a brief moment I remembered this was Nanjing University, which I'd said I was aiming for. This street might be my future.

The third time was Sunday. I woke up early to get to the café right as it opened, thinking if he had plans today, he might leave in the morning. I had almost dozed off watching his building when a man came out of the gate. He had a cane. It was the chemistry teacher. The anger that had been growing hotter and hotter in me suddenly froze. I had half planned on confronting him, on asking exactly what he was doing with LiLi. I even half stood up. But then I hesitated. He was our family friend, an adult I had respected my whole childhood. I remembered him buying me ice creams in the park. Yet how many words had we really exchanged between us, all my life? What was his whole life that I didn't know? The chemistry teacher turned and walked up the street.

It was easy enough to follow him. It was easy enough to see that he went to a bus stop, that he was waiting for a bus there, and while

I debated with myself, hiding behind two tall girls in thick jackets, wondering if I should get on the bus, too, it was easy enough to see something else that would make the whole story change. I saw the bus appear at the end of the road. Before it arrived, a girl came up to him at the bus stop, put her arm around his waist, even tiptoed up to kiss him. What a display of affection out here on the street! The quickest of kisses, but I had never seen a real-life kiss before.

The girl wore a white baseball cap and a gray sweater set with a long skirt. Under the baseball cap she had a round face and pink lips. She didn't look much older than me, her face even looked a little bit familiar, like I had seen it on TV or something. My first, instinctive thought was that she wasn't prettier than LiLi.

But I couldn't ignore the look on her face. It radiated with love.

The bus arrived. I took out my cell phone and snapped a picture of the two of them. She was holding his hand as he followed her onto the bus. I wondered what I would do with the picture. Would I show LiLi?

The two girls I was standing behind moved. I took one more picture of the chemistry teacher and the girl as they went up the steps. On the back of his neck, I saw the chemistry teacher's tongue again. It looked just how I remembered, red and greedy.

7

We celebrated Spring Festival with my father's family, away from Nanjing. And when I came back to school after the break, the chemistry teacher was gone.

The truth came out only drop by drop, like a delicate titration of poison, in hushed sentences and whispered rumors among the students. I heard it not from LiLi but from Song FanFan, who had heard it from someone else.

The chemistry teacher had been dating a graduate from our high school. She was a first-year college student at Nanjing University. Someone had mailed the high school principal a picture of her holding hands with the chemistry teacher at a bus stop. Then her parents discovered cigarettes in her purse; she wasn't a smoker, but had a pack of Esse menthols.

The girl was only one year older than us. Their relationship had started when she was still in high school. The rumor was that she had even once been pregnant, but had gotten rid of it.

The day the school announced that the chemistry teacher was not going to be coming back to teach, I texted LiLi between classes, *Are you doing okay?* But when she didn't reply, I was not surprised.

When classes were over, I saw her hiding by the track field, her face in her hands, shoulders trembling. I wanted to go up to her, but I didn't know what to say. And the way she was standing, the way she was crying, so still, like she had stopped breathing—looked so private, so secret, that I didn't want to break in on it. Even seeing her felt like a violation.

Before the holiday, I'd met up with LiLi and showed her the photos. We were in her room. She pressed her lips together and started trembling so hard I had reached out to steady her. "Stop," she'd said, shrinking in on herself.

"I'm sorry," I'd apologized, even though I didn't know if I was the one in the wrong.

"Send me those photos," LiLi had said. "I know who that is."

I dutifully texted them to her. She hadn't spoken to me since.

My own feelings were confused. I hated seeing LiLi so hurt, but knowing that she knew the truth about the chemistry teacher made me happy. She was avoiding me, and that wasn't what I wanted, but the chemistry teacher wouldn't have her, either. I thought if I looked at myself, I might find an ugly tattoo, too, like Meng Wei-shi's crow.

That day, when I got home, my mother came to my room and closed the door. "Xiao Yun," she said in a low voice, "you had classes with him last year. You visited him to get textbooks, right? Your father and I are worried. Did he ever . . . Did he seem strange? Did he ever tell you to . . . do anything?"

"No," I said slowly. "He treated me just like any other student."

My mother twisted her fingers together. *My parents, they don't know anything either,* I thought, and this realization made me incredibly sad.

"You think you know someone," she sighed. "And with a young girl like that . . . He'd been our family friend for so many years . . ."

"Where did he go?"

"I don't know what his plans are." She shook her head. Then, probably because she was so shocked, she told me, "Your aunt even told me, a while ago, that she thought he would be a better husband than your uncle. They were a little flirty. Some nights, when your uncle was drinking, she didn't come stay with us. And I did wonder if she ever went to him."

I examined my feelings. Another surprise? Something I hadn't seen, or known?

Coming to her senses, my mother looked at me quickly. "That was just your aunt talking, of course." She patted me on the shoulder. "Forget about Tang Laoshi. He won't be part of our lives anymore."

When she left my room, I took the books from my lowest shelf. For two months, I had left *The Little Prince* hidden behind the other books.

I rifled the pages looking for LiLi's folded note with the sticker. A piece of paper I hadn't seen before fell to the ground.

It was a torn and crumbled strip, hastily ripped from some notebook. There were two sentences on it, in two different handwritings.

The first line:

So we're leaving together?

The second:

You know I hate this place.

I looked at the two sentences carefully for a long time. It was the chemistry teacher who had written the second line—that handwriting was unmistakable. How often had I seen his writing on the blackboard? But the first line, I couldn't say. It wasn't LiLi's handwriting.

So he had hated this place. Another thing I hadn't known. And why did this conversation have to be documented on paper?

Long ago, it seemed, he'd asked me if I wanted to study abroad, what I wanted to do in the future. Looking around my room, I came to the calm realization that the safe, familiar neighborhood I'd lived in all my life would change with or without me. The people would change, the houses, the stores. My classmates would go to college. People would get older, get married, get jobs, struggle, leave.

I wouldn't stay here forever, either.

I leaned down to reshelve *The Little Prince*. Then I caught sight of the old photo album, the one my mother had gotten done when I was thirteen. I pulled it out. The pictures flipped by—me in puffy skirts, wearing elaborate hairpieces of dynasties past. My face was small and young, round-eyed and friendly.

I closed the photo album in which I looked so naked and naïve.

In the kitchen, I shredded LiLi's note and the second piece of paper into tiny slivers and dropped them into the garbage. I took out the watering pot and sprinkled water over the irises the chemistry teacher had given me. Through the kitchen window, past the winking, sleepy eyes of the flowers, I saw a single winter butterfly winding its way around the bare-branched trees, its white wings flapping gently, as though just for me.

THE VIRTUOSO

It was cool inside the auditorium, dim and tall-ceilinged, baroque wooden ornaments gracing the walls beside hieroglyphs of gold leaf. There was no sense here of the world outside, of the wind, the blue sky, the green-yellow trees, the baked smell of afternoon pavement. The fluorescent lights above the stage cast the emerald velvet chairs and their seated figures in shadow. The keys in front of her were white and cool as bone, the sheet music the aged yellow of a skeleton's teeth.

The announcer spoke: "Continuing with the upper division advanced roster, we will now have Nora Ren, eleventh grade, playing selections from Robert Schumann's *Carnaval*."

Nora waited, taking a moment to re-scan the first bars, mentally rehearsing what they should sound like. The auditorium was stagnant. The softest rustle of adjusting clothes, a creak of chair springs.

And then in the second just before the silence would become too much, Nora took a deep breath and began at the pickup, her fingers nimble through the triumphant beginning of the "Préambule" as she kept the time precisely with her breaths, *one-and-two-and-three-and-one-and-two-and-three-and*. She leaned fearlessly into the quick fingerwork, the crescendos and diminuendos, careful not to play too quickly, not to feel anxious. The page turner behind her flipped the sheets just as she reached the last bar and she was on to the next page, smoothly, without a hitch, she could play this piece blind, her fingers were faster than thought, her muscles knew exactly where, when, and how to press, not too soft, not too hard, don't go too fast, keep breathing, count.

After the applause, she stood up, the folded folio under her arm, and bowed to the audience, making sure to meet the eyes of the judges, who sat scribbling in the front row—this was a mind game, to make sure they saw how confident she was. Her head was hot with triumph, but she kept her expression unsmiling. She walked off the stage slowly. She had played perfectly. She knew.

Her scuffed heels clacked down the steps. She settled into her seat three rows behind the judges, ignoring the other contestants. The next competitor came on stage and Nora barely listened, through this girl, the next boy, the next girl. Familiar faces, faces she had seen time and time again over the competition circuit through the years.

The Southern California Association of Music's annual piano competition was a hotbed of seething envy, neuroses, backstabbing, and tears. Only the best and most bloodthirsty advanced from the local competitions to the county level, and from there only the most vicious and technically precise would be awarded the crown at the final state competition in Los Angeles in June. Her mind drifted to the future: today she'd win first in county, and then all that was left was the advanced upper division state-level competition. Last year she'd gotten second in the final round, losing to a high school senior from Arcadia, but with that senior off in college, she was sure to be first this time, and so end her years on the competition circuit triumphantly before college applications in the fall.

She had fallen into half a trance, listening to the babble of piano music, slow and fast, Grieg and Kabalevsky, but then—she didn't know how many songs later—something pricked her awake. On stage was a boy she knew, a competition regular, tall and spindly, with long arms, a straight nose, and rectangular glasses. Derek Ma. He was playing a piece she recognized, something ponderous, even lugubrious, except for the quick trills and flutters of energy that accelerated the heartbeat of the harmony. She tried to keep time in her head: the rhythm was maddeningly difficult. His fingers were light as butterflies. She opened the program and read, "SELECTION FROM LISZT'S HUNGARIAN RHAPSODY NO. 2."

Nora sat up straight through the end of the piece. An hour later, she emerged from the Jacobs Music Center onto the warm green lawns outside, one of the last from the flood of escaping music teachers, parents, and black-jacketed youths, many of the latter dazedly clutching folios and possessed of the lost, listless look of soldiers in a fugue state.

Nearby, a mother hugged her daughter, a twelve- or thirteen-year-old blonde in a perfectly fitted green dress, her hair falling in pretty waves. "Congratulations, sweetie! Fourth place!" Nora cast them a contemptuous glance. If the girl got only fourth place *now*, she'd be out of the circuit in two years. She would probably never make it to state.

Nora's mental calculus was automatic. She turned away from the blonde girl and immediately forgot her.

Her piano teacher appeared to congratulate her: "Nora, you played well."

"Thanks," Nora said mechanically. In her right hand she held the silver trophy for second place.

"We'll start preparing for June."

They exchanged no more words. Mrs. Lisowski had been a master of Chopin in her native country of Poland; she had met many students through her career, but Nora, moody, intense, self-driven Nora, whose habitual tight ponytail pulled her sharp-featured face and taut cheekbones into a shark's grimace, and who sat at the piano as though it were an enemy to be wrestled down, sometimes chilled her.

*

Derek Ma. How had he beaten her? At this same competition last year, Nora had gotten first easily, and Bradley Philips—surprising everyone—second. Bradley was a brunette and languid-limbed boy a year older than her who, against her will, attracted her gaze to his long lashes, the sprinkling of freckles on his cheeks, the shoulders stretching his suit jacket. He played show tune accompaniments at their high school's theater productions, which Nora collected the brochures for but never attended. But when he came up to her after the awards ceremony with his second-place trophy and smiled, offering a hand to say "Congratulations," Nora, stalky and twiggy in the same boxy black dress she'd worn this year, hadn't known how to say anything but the shortest of "Thanks."

She had even thought of Bradley with a mix of pity and preemptive regret, for though he was handsome and gentle, she would have to leave him behind. Bradley was good enough at piano, but he never took the certification tests, was only in one or two AP classes, and was certainly not serious enough in his life to be going somewhere like Stanford, or Berkeley, or Columbia, the places for which Nora knew she was destined.

And Derek Ma had gotten third.

Third, and this year he was first.

She'd met his parents at some piano examination or other, and they'd said he wanted to study engineering. He was on the robotics team at his high school, one district over, renowned for their award-winning, nationally ranked team.

He didn't even practice that much! she thought, though she didn't know if this was true. But how could he do everything? School, tech competitions, *and* piano? It was unfair. The only thing Nora did—the *only* thing—was piano. Two and a half hours a day, every day, weekends included. And theory classes on Friday evenings.

Piano was her golden ticket. Like every other Asian kid at her high school, she had good grades, took advanced classes, had high test scores, volunteered at a senior home some Sundays. Other kids played the piano, too, or the violin, or were in band or orchestra, but none of them—Nora thought—were as serious as she was. If she proved herself at the state recitals this June, if she got first place, she'd show she had talent. Discipline. She'd stand out.

And without the distinction of first place, what did she have? Nothing.

How had she lost? *What had she done wrong?*

She turned into her cul-de-sac. Her SUV was a dirty, dented, unloved old thing, which she usually drove in abject silence, bought secondhand eight years ago and passed, thirdhand, to Nora when she got her license.

She pulled up the parking brake and was about to turn the engine off, but her hand stopped. No one would be expecting her just yet. In the car, she had a few minutes of privacy before she had to go through the front door, eat dinner with her family, help Maya with her homework, and start her own. A few minutes before she would have to tell them how she'd done.

She decided to drive to the neighborhood exit and back again.

She pressed the power button for the sound system, and whatever CD had been left inside started to play. A delicate instrumental accompaniment, piano and the murmur of violins, spun out of the speakers. It was some syrupy sentimental song, with a soprano's breathy warble. Sidewalks and oak trees slid past the window. She listened, trying to place the song. A girl crooning for someone to think of her . . . think of her . . .

Andrew Lloyd fucking Webber. It was *The Phantom of the Opera*. This must be Maya's CD. She'd been obsessed a few months ago, Nora had gone to Blockbuster to get the DVD for her. The cover with the pretty curly-haired girl. Pretty *and* talented. When you were both, you didn't have to give anything up. Nora was seventeen and had never been kissed.

This song was so cheesy. So easy. So romantic. This was why she didn't listen to this stuff. It was undemanding, unrigorous, cheap, commercial—

And yet—

She turned around only as the next song, even worse than the first, was starting. As she straightened out in front of her house, the wheels scraped the curb loudly. She turned the engine off and "Angel of Music" cut out mid-warble.

She went in. "I'm home," she called, and immediately headed up the stairs.

"Is that Nora?" her mother's voice floated out from the kitchen.

"How was the competition?" Maya poked her head out.

"I'm going to change," Nora said loudly.

Maya followed. "Nice dress."

This dress is not nice, she thought contemptuously.

"So did you win?" her sister persisted.

"I got second," Nora said, entering the bathroom and closing the door behind her.

*

She'd started the piano when she was six. Her mother had played Beethoven and Mozart, the only composers she knew, to her in the womb. She'd wanted Nora to be a prodigy.

Nora half remembered, in the way that memories might be constructed rather than formed, walking through the music store the day they bought the piano, the soft lighting glinting off the polished surfaces of the wooden cellos and violas and violins, the mysterious, feminine swells of the black instrument cases, the soft carpeting, the glass windows and high ceilings—and in the center of the showroom, taking center stage, the grand pianos. Their covers were lifted to show the endless stacks of ebony and ivory teeth, regular, uniform, begging to be pressed. Nora put her finger down on one key as she passed and heard the note chime out into the room, lovely and sonorous and bright.

They got a cabinet piano. Not a grand piano, but still, a cabinet piano all her own, walnut-colored, KAWAI printed in gold lettering on the wood. When it had been installed in their living room Nora was allowed to insert the little brass key, unlock the lid, and lift it to reveal the velvety red dust cover. Everything about the piano was, to her, sumptuous and sensual, replete with mystery and richness.

"We'll get a big one later," her mother promised her. "When you get better, we'll definitely get a big one."

Her first teacher was soft and motherly, and praised Nora for learning to read sheet music so quickly. By now she had forgotten that teacher's name. She remembered only the amiable aura, the gentle way she had corrected her posture. She'd hummed occasionally. At the end of their lessons the teacher always gave her a warm hug good-bye, though Nora never lifted her arms back.

Just as she had finished learning to read her bass and treble clefs and how to play the C major scale, Maya was born. During this pregnancy her mother had spent a lot of time looking at old master paintings. When Maya was brought home, Nora peeked in the crib at this new pink, sleeping baby-sister-*thing*, and Maya coughed and let out a cry. "Well, Nora, you'll have to be a good big sister," her mother whispered to her, clasping a heavy hand on Nora's shoulder, near her neck. Since then her mother had not said much about Nora's piano at all.

*

Tuesdays were Nora's lessons with Mrs. Lisowski. In the Polish teacher's brocaded living room, Mrs. Lisowski showed her the video she'd filmed of Nora's weekend performance. Nora watched herself ascend the stage, her expression on the computer screen stony and still. She viscerally *relived* the sensation of sitting at the grand piano, the lights beaming bright from the ceiling, the hard, cold floor she could feel through her heels.

But she also remembered that sensation of triumph. She remembered how she had been sure, so sure, she had played everything right.

Now she knew she had been wrong. Second place. Just barely eligible for the state finals.

She let herself dwell on her appearance in the video. In the poorly fitting dress, square around the waist and short along the thighs, she looked sullen and plain. But what did it matter? She was not there to be beautiful. She had always known she'd prove her value another way.

But as she listened to her own performance, she could hear none of that triumph she'd been so sure of. Why? The piece—it still sounded *good*. It sounded just as it was written. She hit the notes, she kept the pace, she was faithful to each command on the sheet.

There must be errors somewhere. She returned her attention to the sheet music in front of her. The copy of the Schumann was scribbled and dog-eared, Mrs. Lisowski's handwriting scrawled all over the margins: underlines where Nora needed to add emphasis, *softer here* written over the bass clef. *Yes*, Nora thought, finding her place in the sheet music. There, she had sped up just a bit too much, and there, the volume of her crescendo was too loud, and there, a little skip where she transitioned badly between difficult chords. She knew that spot well, where her fingers were too short to make the jump easily.

She and Mrs. Lisowski went exhaustively over the bars they had marked, practicing each section again and again. Finally, she asked Mrs. Lisowski to put the digital camera on the edge of the piano, angled so only her hands and wrists were visible. Nora imagined herself ascending the stage again, ready to dominate, succeed, bend the piano to the force of her will.

When she reviewed the second video on the Sony's built-in display, it did not sound so very different from the first video. Nora knew she should listen carefully, focus on all the minute details that did make a difference. Instead, she could not stop looking at her hands on the tiny camera screen. They were like scurrying little rats, frantic and ungraceful. Against the beautiful row of white keys, the contrast was shameful. How had she never noticed it before?

She crossed her hands in her lap. Her nails were plain, uncolored, clipped short and hastily. A cooking scar was under one knuckle. She wriggled her fingers. They moved so lissomely, dexterous from her years of unforgiving practice. She controlled every joint, every tendon. But she could not do anything about the fact that her hands were small. They were dark, squat, and ugly. Chords stacked in notes of four or five were a challenge. When she jumped octaves she always had to use the pedal.

She recalled Derek Ma as he'd stood on stage—his uncomfortably tall frame slightly stooped; his pale, computer-nerd skin; the wrists poking out of his too-short suit jacket. And his hands. They were milky white, with prominent knuckles, but his fingers were long and loose and that was all that mattered. Rachmaninoff was famous for his enormous, octave-eating hands. Derek Ma had the hands of a true virtuoso. That was what she had to compete with.

*

Friday lunchtime, which Nora spent in the media center reviewing physics, sneaking bites of cold cafeteria pizza while the librarian pretended not to notice. "Hey," someone said behind her.

Nora spun around, eyebrows knitted together in alarm. It was Bradley Philips. She put her hand over her mouth and swallowed. "What?"

He was wearing a bomber jacket over a white T-shirt and frayed jeans. He had a stack of pink papers in his hand. "Just passing around flyers for this," he said, and handed her one of the papers. *Chicago!* the flyer announced. *Murder, Jail, and Jazz! Presented by the RB Players!* Followed by a string of student names Nora knew but did not associate with—Emily Stepman, Dylan Harris, Melinda Ghosh.

"Opening night's tonight at seven." Bradley grinned. "I'm on piano. You should come, it's going to be fun."

The pizza seemed stuck in Nora's throat. "Sorry," she said, casting her eyes down at Bradley's knees. "I have to be home." She handed the flyer back to him and forced herself to look up and make eye contact.

"Well," he said, with a half smile that made her stomach burn, "sorry to miss you." She watched him leave and head to the kids at the next table over, openly passing a bag of onion-flavored corn rings back and forth and clearly not paying attention to the textbooks stacked carelessly next to them. She heard his easygoing voice again: "Hey, you guys busy tonight? You should come to *Chicago* . . ."

They were all empty words. He wasn't going to miss her.

In the afternoon, after seeing Maya settled with snacks and homework in the kitchen, she flipped open the piano lid and started running through her scales. Her fingers stumbled a little; her rhythm wasn't steady. She opened the Schumann. Played the first bars. She thought of Derek Ma playing the Liszt so confidently. Her fingers faltered. She started over and after a page and a half of determined, ruthless playing, banged her left hand down in a sharp, atonal jumble of keys and broke off abruptly.

Her mother came home at dinner. Nora had already prepared the rice and reheated the previous night's soup. Her mother tied on an apron and got out the meat.

"How did everything go today?"

"Fine."

"Everyone got their homework done?"

"Yup."

"Did you finish the laundry?"

"Maya did."

Her mother frowned, as though trying to place something. She had been, still was, a beautiful woman, with fine cheekbones, expressive eyes, an elegant tapered jaw. She watched Nora beat a bowl of eggs, then said, "Why aren't you at theory class?"

Nora stopped. "Crap."

"You *forgot*?" Her mother looked at her with bewilderment.

She looked at the clock—8:00 p.m. The class would finish in half an hour. Maya popped out of the den. "What's going on?"

"She missed her theory class," her mother said. "Nora, that's not like you."

"Mom!" Her pulse accelerated and shame flushed her neck. "I—"

I was busy, she wanted to say. *I was thinking about the competition . . . I have been so tired . . . I . . .* She couldn't swallow. There was a brick in her throat. The walls were pressing in around her, the faces of her mother, her sister, their heads cocked in the same way, their identical curious eyes.

Late. She'd missed it. Then she was grabbing her key-chain wallet and jamming her feet into her battered sneakers. Maya followed her to the door. "Where are you going?!"

"It's too late!" her mother called.

But she was out the door, she was in her car. The rumble of the engine startled her. She sped past still trees and silent buildings, the dark road and the moonlit night pooled around her. Perhaps she could still—

She moved onto the I-5 south. An exit later she met a huddle of traffic and slowed.

She was slightly calmer now, her body cooled, her brain clearer. She felt foolish. She had left her phone behind. Her car idled. Again she did not want the car to be silent. She turned on the radio and sound flickered on. Worship music. The singing that filled the car was dreamy, rapturous, wholly unfamiliar. She imagined church choirs with their high angelic voices. A part of her wished she could believe in this, a force greater than herself, so she would not feel so alone.

She should turn back, but she did not want to face home yet, face the explanations and questions.

Off the side of the freeway there was a big white billboard with a smiling woman's face. Her skin was smooth and unblemished, her eyes almost alien in their blueness, her blonde hair pulled back into the perfect ponytail. She held up a hand encased in a clinging white doctor's glove—*Don't let nature do the work! Radical cosmetic surgery to change your life. Free consultation.* Followed by a phone number. Nora's eyes lingered on the billboard until a honk behind her startled her into pressing the gas.

She ended up at the high school. At the far end of the lot, underneath a shivering pine tree with a spindly bench, she found an empty space. She parked and contemplated getting out. She was here, after all. She was right across from the theater. Bradley's show. The lights were all on; she could see them from here. She killed the engine and the headlights flickered off. The radio, which she had forgotten about, played on. It was some classical music now.

She imagined the state competition in two months' time. In those two months, her days would be filled with exhaustive practice, two and a half hours, or three, including weekends, the arpeggios, the technical exercises, the recordings she'd listen to, the Schumann she'd play over, and over, and over again. She felt tired all the way down her arms.

And in a fearful whisper she hadn't dared voice to herself, she wondered, What if she didn't get better? If after all that she still wasn't good enough for first?

What if someone else still beat her?

After all, what could you do when you hit your limit? When you'd done everything you could to improve and there was nothing else you could change?

She remembered the billboard: *Don't let nature do the work!* The perfect woman with the gloved hand.

It wasn't fair that she had practiced so hard to be defeated. She had put everything in, and it still wasn't enough. If, Nora thought half dreamily, she were to change something about herself . . . If she could replace her hands with someone else's . . .

Because then she would be perfect, she would play perfectly. She imagined the procedure. The surgeon's blade. The swapping, the stitching. There'd be physical therapy, obviously. She wouldn't be able to use the hands as her own right away. But over time, she'd be able to start from the beginning again, relearn it all better, the scales, the notes, C-D-E-F-G. She even felt happy at the thought of taking the doctor's directions day after day, with nothing to think about except move this finger, stretch that muscle, don't move that IV drip, as the daylight passed through the hospital ward and dropped into night.

Whose hands would she take? Derek's. Her thin arms, the burnished skin of her wrists, suddenly bifurcated, his huge, heavy, ghost-colored hands hanging off her bony wrists. She pictured what she could do with those hands, stretching the thumb on the keyboard from middle C to the next C, C to D, C to E.

She imagined ascending to the stage of the Jacobs Music Center and bowing to the audience with those alien, better hands. The horror of the audience, their sudden alertness, their helpless morbid fascination. She'd look like Frankenstein's monster. The judges' faces!

They could not help but pay attention to her then.

But. Nora touched her face. If she were honest. If she were really honest with herself. If she could change herself, she'd soften her features. Round out her chin, raise up her nose. She imagined walking through sliding glass hospital doors, her hair down, not in a black dress, but in something nice, maybe green. Or low-slung Levi's, new from the mall, with little suede flats like she saw other girls wearing.

But she couldn't *see* it. She couldn't imagine what she, in this fantasy, looked like. There was no use, she thought against herself, repeating her old mantra, in wanting something you could not have. No use, for instance, in imagining Bradley Philips picking her up in his car, a nice silver sedan. No use in imagining spending her time differently, sunny afternoons when she did not have to pick up Maya, go home, open her test prep guides, then her practice books, think of ways to do more, be better . . .

"Danny Wright playing Pachelbel's Canon in D, arranged for piano," the smooth radio announcer's voice said.

Nora was jolted. She almost turned the radio off, with half a mind to go outside after all, get some air, listen to the tail end of the show. But the music stopped her.

A child's song. The tempo slow and easy, the main melody and chord progressions easy to remember, easy to play.

And of course, the tune. She could hum along, if she wanted. Every child knew this tune even if they didn't know its name. Simple, joyous, subtly nostalgic. One of the classic songs, popular, beautiful. Too popular. Too familiar. There was nothing interesting about the song, and yet, now, Nora was lost.

The left hand played the same harmony over and over. Her ear training kicking in, she isolated the same eight notes: D, A, B, F# . . . F# for D major, of course, this was why it was the Canon in D, she thought inanely, automatically, like she was answering a question on a test.

In fact, she recalled, she had only ever played one version of the song. It was when she was eight. Or nine. Just before she had left that first teacher, the soft one whose name she couldn't remember. She had had one of those beginner piano primers, CLASSIC MASTER-WORKS ARRANGEMENTS VOL. 1. It had a yellow cover. And she remembered the teacher now, putting on the CD of a more complex, fuller version of the canon and saying, "One day you'll play this one!"

She dug her nails into her palms. Back then, when she had had no expectations of herself, it had been an immediate joy to open the piano and touch the keys. More than joy, it had been magic. Press a key, make a song. Press two keys, three keys, four keys, all at once, and they could sound jangled and ugly, which was pleasing in itself, or they could resolve, sound perfect, like a key clicking in a lock.

She had loved the little arrangement she'd played. She had played it over and over. She could remember the giddiness with which she swung her elbows as she ran her fingers up the arpeggios, and the self-importance with which she turned the page.

Her father (before the divorce, before the once-yearly calls on New Year's) had joked, "Don't you know how to play anything else?"

And her mother had defended her. "This is a famous song!"

But the canon on the radio was winding down now. The notes were coming further and further apart, softer and softer, and it was going to fade soon, complete. Nora could feel the end of the performance coming. She felt sad, there was a whole emotion coursing through her body that she would have to examine later, after this experience was over. Inside her chest there was a loosening, as though a stitch had been undone, something had given way.

The feeling she had was something like mourning, also like forgiveness. And the sadness had an ecstatic side to it, too, because of the way the melody lifted at the end of each repetition of the theme; one could not help but be uplifted, was this not the reason people continued to listen, to make these sounds, to stitch them together into feeling like this? She never felt the way she was feeling listening to this song now when she played the piano.

All those years she had spent practicing (eleven! eleven years!). What had they all been for?

She groped for some understanding of what it was she wanted to change. There was a thought out there she could almost catch, drifting on the currents of the night like a fallen leaf, slipping around the pine tree, over the bench, over the side mirror just next to her. *I wish . . .*

Then she heard a different noise and looked through the window. A shadow moved across the sidewalk in front of her. Nora ducked and flattened herself against the seat. After a few moments she heard a car starting and cautiously raised her head. Across from her, the lights in the theater were dark. Bodies were trailing out. The show was over.

LET'S GO

LET'S GO

LET'S GO

DIRECTOR'S NOTE: THERE WILL BE NO MUSIC THROUGHOUT.

They are scuffing through the trees, swinging their flashlights back and forth. The smell is of damp earth, running water, ancient green things breathing in the night. The sound of their sneakers as they push through the forest reminds Emi of when they first arrived at the center, how brightly the sun had shone, how hot and blue the sky had been, how quickly the temperature dropped at night.

"Lily!" A man's voice, Reiya's, calls from the left.

"Lily!" Another male voice, Goto's, calls. Through the bushes Emi can see the glow of his white pants.

"Lily!" she calls, eyes darting around the shrubbery, imagining the scene as it would look through a camera: the shakiness of the frame, the wobbliness of the lighting. She wonders again whether they are not all participating in some larger scheme. At what point does the line between art and reality blur, at what point does the performance become the life?

*

The first scene was this: Lily had turned her camera on Emi as they hiked up the long flight of steps to the Play Center. It was one of those bright, windless days in late July that make it seem as though summer will go on forever, the sun, the stillness, the cicada cries as constant as youth. Warmth and light fell through the canopy formed by the cypresses.

Emi was tired of the heat. She did not like summer. Sweat dampened her hatband, her feet were stuffy in their New Balance sneakers. She scowled under Lily's lens and heard the click of the shutter. "What's this for?"

Lily always looked fresh; she was annoying in that way. Even when she was sweaty, she emitted a clean, energizing glow. She had clear, lightly tanned skin, big, Western eyes, straight shoulders, and a tall, long-legged frame. At the beginning of summer she had cut her hair into a modern bob. She looked like she was from California, like she was made for the sun.

"Emiko," Lily sing-songed. Emi slightly relaxed. Lily had been saying her name like that, in that childlike, wheedling tenor, since middle school, when they'd first met; when she had heard it again, half a year ago, she had immediately been pulled into the rush of familiar, easy intimacy.

"Are you grumpy already? Are you worried about the next two weeks?" Lily prodded. Her voice was half film director, probing and warming her subject up; the other half was the genuinely concerned and interested friend. Emi wondered if it was going to be hard to distinguish between the two.

"Why would I be worried?" She shrugged her backpack into a different position; the strap hurt her shoulder.

"Need help?" Reiya called.

The two boys were far ahead of them, leaning in the shade against a tree. Reiya was tall and sporty, with long, carefully gelled hair and stylish sunglasses, trekking uphill in blindingly clean Nike Air Jordan sneakers. He had the easy air of someone who came from money and had been handsome and well-liked from a young age.

And next to him was Goto, his profile was so familiar to Emi she didn't even have to look to know what he looked like, white socks up to his ankles and wiry, spiky hair, his Adam's apple moving under his stubborn jaw as he swallowed from his bottle of water.

"If you don't hurry up we won't get there till, like, midnight," Goto complained.

"Not midnight." Lily pushed forward easily. "We'll be there in half an hour."

"Are you sure we're not lost?"

"How can we be lost? The stairs only go in one direction. Besides, I've been here before, remember?"

Emi knew the other three weren't tired. It was her, Emi, keeping their pace back. And she *was* tired; her shoulders chafed from the backpack and her lower back was starting to hurt. Out of embarrassment, she muttered, "They sure make getting there a big deal. Like we couldn't just take a bus? Or drive?"

Once she and Lily drew under the tree, Goto reached out a hand for her backpack.

"You can't carry it," Emi said, swatting him away. "You've got your own."

"I'll carry it with one hand. Come on, just give it to me."

Intensely aware of Lily's camera and Reiya's eyes, Emi shook her head and frowned. Goto rolled his eyes.

"Emi, let's switch," Lily said. "I don't have a lot of stuff in mine." And this, for some reason, was easier to stomach. She shrugged off her backpack with relief and took on Lily's, which was much lighter. What about the two weeks' worth of clothes and makeup, the shampoo, the paintbrushes and papers weighing her own pack down so the zippers barely closed? Emi felt a stab of shame. Lily's backpack was so light it seemed like there was nothing in it. Lily was so free and airy, untied to the world, and Emi was so solidly trapped on the earth.

*

On the evening Lily had come back into her life, Emi had been waiting at the green frog train carriage outside of Shibuya station. Her phone was out; she was texting. She'd been back in Japan for just two months.

"Excuse me. Emiko . . . ? Emiko Miri?"

She looked up to see a tall girl standing in front of her, one hand laden with Tokyu Department Store shopping bags. She was pretty but basic, with her dewy makeup, creamy white sweater, and tall black boots.

"You're Emiko, right?"

"Um—who—" Then it hit her. "Lily?! Lily Bae?"

Lily broke into a wide smile and started speaking in English. "Oh my god! It's been so long!" She reached her free arm out and Emi automatically stepped forward for a hug. Instead, Lily dropped her hand and they ended up half holding, half shaking hands. Her skin was warm, and she squeezed Emi's fingers tightly, in what felt like real welcome.

"I'm waiting for a friend—Ken Goto," Emi said. "You remember him, right?"

"Oh wow, I haven't heard that name in years!"

They stood outside the green frog carriage talking. Lily was effusive—but then, she always had been. Emi could not get over the feeling of shock. How to react when you meet one of those figures from your past whom you had once known intimately, but was now a stranger, with years of distance in between?

Emi had spent her elementary school years in Maryland and moved to Japan with her parents for middle school. She went to M International, which was filled with the children of diplomats and expats and returnees from abroad. That is to say, they were students on the fringes; the school was populated by transplants, transients, and outsiders.

Lily had been president of the art and design club at M International. She had an older-sister vibe, which Emi, an only child, newly arrived to a different country, at first tried to resist but felt inexpressibly comforted by. Though Emi didn't stay in the club long, even after she left, Lily reached out often, checking in on her, advising on teachers, classes, homework, tests, or coming to eat lunch with her and catching her up on gossip. On weekends, Lily sometimes came to Emi's house and watched TV with her or helped her sew. There were certainly times when Emi wondered what Lily, the pretty, popular, older girl, saw in her, but then again, Lily seemed to be friends with everyone, so perhaps the attention she showered on Emi was no different from what she gave others.

"So, you and Goto went to the same college?" Lily asked.

"No, I went to a college in the States. Have you heard of the New School?"

"Not sure . . . Where is it?"

"New York."

"Oh, wow! That's so cool! What did you study?"

"Um, fashion design."

"Oh my god, that sounds so glamorous."

"It wasn't, seriously. But what about you? I can't remember where you . . ."

"Oh, I went to school in Kyoto. But what are you doing, are you back in Tokyo for good?"

Emi explained briefly that she had just moved back after interning for a year in New York and that she had landed a new job at a design firm. "Goto and I are going out to drink, do you want to come? He found this old-fashioned standing-only sake bar in one of those back alleys."

"No, I have to deliver these." Lily indicated the shopping bags. "I'm kind of a personal assistant to this weird lady, I'll have to tell you about it next time. We've got to catch up now you're back!"

"Sure," Emi said, pretty sure this, their first meeting, would also be their last.

But instead Lily actually dropped her shopping bags and pulled out her phone. "What's your number now?"

When Goto found Emi, several minutes after Lily had disappeared into the crush of people entering the subway, Emi told him, "You'll never guess who I just saw."

"Who?"

"Lily Bae!"

"*Really?* That's crazy. Was it just like, a total coincidence?" He pulled a face. "Did she explain why she dropped off the face of the earth?"

And this was the real reason Emi didn't think she was really going to see the other girl again: at the start of Lily's final year of high school, she'd ghosted.

Lily had been out of town for the summer recess, visiting family in Korea, and when she got back, she and Emi were supposed to meet at a café. In fact, Emi had wanted to confide in Lily, lean on her; her parents had been fighting, and Emi was afraid of a divorce. But when she showed up at the café, Lily wasn't there. She never arrived, and when Emi called and texted, she didn't pick up her phone or answer any of her messages.

The next day Emi came to school angry and ready to hear an explanation. But Lily was absent—and none of her friends knew where she was.

Lily didn't show up to school that day, or the next day, or the day after that, and when Emi eventually asked her homeroom teacher, and Lily's friends in the grade above her, she heard Lily had suddenly withdrawn from school.

The abandonment was like a shock of cold water. Emi wandered the school halls half-dazed, feeling like she couldn't be sure of what was real. Eventually she learned that Lily had moved to Seoul, but this didn't explain the emails, texts, and voicemails Lily had failed to return, or the fact that she had just up and left without any warning. Emi was devastated that she had had to hear the news through a rumor and not from Lily herself. How could she have left without saying anything? No warning, no closure, no last hug goodbye.

*

It was with a sense of déjà vu that she took the train to a café in Nakameguro to meet Lily for lunch after their run-in. The walkway by the river was shiny in the aftermath of a rainstorm. Emi wove between the weekend shoppers, pulling her hat lower over her eyes.

Lily really *was* in the café. It was surreal to see her sitting there, in the flesh, chatty and friendly, with her hair long and loose, asking cheerful questions so Emi didn't have a second to feel awkward: what she'd done at school, how she'd gotten her job, what it was like being a designer at an advertising firm.

"Are you happy there?" Lily asked intently.

Emi shrugged and sipped her milkshake through her straw. "It's fine." She was a contract employee, and the work was boring, but it was a job.

"What are you working on in your free time? You were so creative at M International." Lily laughed.

"I'm not really working on anything . . ." And in front of Lily, she felt small. In high school, Lily's energy and praise had rubbed off on her; Emi had picked up on the enthusiasm, threw herself into activity after activity. With Lily's encouragement, she had believed in her own boundless potential and creativity.

But after Lily left, she stopped her hobbies. She lost all her inspiration. Had she ever been creative, or had it all been Lily, had Emi only been leeching off Lily's zest for life? Emi had never felt that same sense of possibility again. After Lily, her days felt so thin and wispy, like scraps of tissue all pressed together, combined into an opaque curtain that she couldn't see through. It didn't matter where she was, New York, Tokyo, the moon—nothing in her life ever moved.

Though Emi desperately wanted to, she didn't ask Lily about her disappearance in high school. Lily acted so naturally, as though they had been apart for only a few months, not years. What would she even say? *Hey, remember when you just stopped talking to me without any explanation? Remember when you disappeared from my life for seven years? Remember when I left you a thousand voicemails, emails, and messages asking what was going on, and you totally ignored them?*

Lily wore her hair in the same long style she had as a teenager. Her style of speech was the same. It was like time had not moved at all since high school. Emi suddenly wondered: The life she had lived in the years since she'd known Lily—had it been real? The places she'd been, people she'd met, the little she had accomplished; suddenly she doubted whether it had all even happened.

For her part, Lily said she had gone to Kyoto Arts and Crafts University and was working as an executive assistant and an occasional model. This was, Emi reflected, the kind of job pretty girls like her would have.

"I'm just temping at different places, mostly." Lily waved her hand. "I have to have room for my other projects."

"You mean your modeling?"

"No, no, I've been getting involved with this arts collective. Well, it's an arts collective, but they do a lot of other stuff, like meditation, classes, workshops . . ."

"That's super cool," Emi said, envisioning the artsy, creative people Lily must have surrounded herself with. "What is it? What are you working on?"

Lily leaned in. She had a way of cupping her chin in her palm and looking at you when she was explaining something, a behavior that was maddeningly familiar, and Emi tried to sit back, but already she felt herself invested again, wanting to stay in the warm glow of

Lily's company, her attention, her obscure plans. Lily looked at her consideringly.

"What?" Emi asked.

"Have you heard of the Anti-Civilization Committee?" Lily asked.

*

Which was how they had ended up, the four of them, walking up the side of Mount Haruna that hot summer day in July.

Finally, the staircase flattened out and they came to a one-story house, with sliding doors and light wood. Emi instinctively softened her footsteps. The quiet surroundings, the austerity of the building, their long walk; all these combined gave the place an air of sanctity. At the entrance, they slipped their shoes off and went inside. A woman sat behind a desk with a glass of water.

"Hi," Lily said, going up to her. "We're the group from Dr. Matsusaka . . ."

"Welcome to the Play Center." The woman stood up. She looked to be near Emi's mother's age, with a determinedly placid expression and eyebrows drawn on sharply. She introduced herself as the house-keeper, but Emi missed her name. The woman consulted a paper list.

"Lily Bae . . . Reiya D'Aramitz . . . Ken Goto . . . Emiko Miri." Even when she got to Reiya's last name, she pronounced it smoothly, no stumbling. Then she held out a clear plastic box. "Please place your phones here. They'll be returned at the end of your stay."

Lily already had her device out. The other three were slower, reluctantly pulling their phones from their pockets, checking for one last text. But Emi had already tried outside, and the signal on the mountain had been bad.

Goto hesitated. "What if we have an emergency?"

The woman said, "There's a landline you can use."

Goto scowled and handed the phone over, and the woman closed the lid to the box with a final-sounding click.

"Let me show you to your rooms," she said.

"Are the cameras on already?" Lily asked.

"Yes, they're on right now," the woman said.

*

After their café date, the first event Lily brought Emi to was called "A Performance of Nothingness." It was held on the first floor of a plain office building on a quiet street. The sliding door had paper flyers taped up that said, "ANTI-CIVILIZATION COMMITTEE ☺." The smiley face threw Emi off.

Despite the out-of-the-way location, the event was crowded. As they walked into the auditorium, Lily exchanged smiles and greetings with the people she knew, which were many. In fact, it seemed to be everyone.

"Is this your first time?" one of those passersby asked, stopping Lily and homing in on Emi.

"Oh, yes," Emi said.

The stranger beamed. "How exciting! You'll love it. You've got the absolute *best* guide." He patted Lily on the shoulder with fatherly familiarity and left before Emi could ask what he meant.

Inside the auditorium, the stage had what looked like a glass shower, a mirror, and a stool. Digital display screens on either side of the stage showed a close-up of the stool and mirror.

Before the audience had even completely quieted, an older man walked onto the stage. There was no fanfare or announcement: he just appeared. He was dressed in loose black robes and had a close-cropped head of gray hair. Without looking at anyone, he began untying his robes. They fell in a puddle at his feet. Emi wrinkled her nose—what, had she come to see a perverted public display of nudity?—and glanced at Lily and the audience. They were all observing the stage with expressions that could only be described as rapt.

The man had an aging body, once taut but now sagging, with skinny calves and loose skin on arms that had once held more muscle. He looked totally naked, until Emi realized he was wearing flesh-colored underwear.

He sat on the stool. He picked up a calligraphy brush dipped in ink and, facing himself in the mirror, began writing on himself. The characters were bold and powerful. Emi looked to the digital displays to see them close-up. They were random words, concepts: *eat, prey, dream, home, equinox*. When he had written over his arms and legs and belly, everywhere he could reach, he got up, opened the door to the shower, and got in. The water turned on. Emi watched as all the beautiful words he had so carefully written washed away.

In the second act of the performance, the man—Dr. Matsusaka, Emi figured—sat on the stool again and the audience called out words. He wrote them down, some serious: *death, birth, memory, transcendence, obscenity*, others seemingly frivolous: *Hermès, radio, McDonald's*. The calligraphy brush moved over his still-damp skin and the characters came out blurred, weaker. When he had covered his body in words again, he got back in the shower and washed them all off until he was once again clean. He bowed and left the stage to loud applause. The shower shut off, the glass walls were streaked with water.

That was it.

There were supposed to be speakers after the main event, but Lily suggested they leave. They walked to a Mister Donut nearby. Emi didn't know what to make of what she had seen, and wasn't sure what Lily thought of it. Sure, it could be deemed art, of the conceptual performance type that her peers in art school following in the footsteps of Marina Abramović might produce. This field—idea-based, gestural, unrooted in a tangible product—wasn't her specialty. She also wasn't sure what the "point" of it was. If it was conceptual, what was the fundamental concept? What was the whole performance *about*?

In the coffee shop, Lily ate two crullers and explained. She'd met Dr. Matsusaka when she was studying in Kyoto. He had gotten a doctorate in conceptual art after leaving a career in the steel industry in his late thirties. He was the founder of the Anti-Civilization Committee, a collective that believed in the "cheerful nihilism" of the world based on his philosophy.

"So what is it, like a death cult?"

"No, not at all," Lily said, eyebrows raising. "It's about anti-materialism. The rule is: Everything we make has to disappear."

She leaned forward, her hair falling over her elbow. Emi remembered how winning she was, how bewitching she could make her ideas sound, whether it was something as mundane as trying a new ice-cream parlor or something like shoplifting from the most expensive department stores in Ginza.

Lily continued: "Fundamentally, it's about acknowledging there is nothing behind everything we live for and assign meaning to. Everything will vanish, but it doesn't have to be depressing. We just know that none of this is going to last. But this makes life easier. We can just play and do what we want."

Emi didn't miss that "we." "So what does that mean, what do you guys do, exactly?"

"We just go to workshops, make art, and do performances. It's fun. It's like a club. People come and go all the time."

Lily didn't say anything specifically to recruit Emi that day, but the next time she went to an Anti-Civilization Committee event, Emi tagged along. At first she told herself it was just out of curiosity, or to prove to herself that Lily was a whacko and she could be done with her erstwhile friend once and for all. They went to a pottery class, and after they'd fired their bowls and cups and covered them in glaze, they smashed their pieces against the wall. When she was riding the train home alone, Emi was surprised to find herself feeling very . . . clean.

Another time, Lily made a film of Emi pinning strips of fabric onto canvas and lighting them on fire. One night, they joined a group working under the cover of dark, guerilla-style, to fill an abandoned parking lot with giddy armfuls of cut flowers. It was there that they met Reiya, an actor and singer, half-French, born in Switzerland to a wealthy, pedigreed family. Reiya kept showing up to other events after that; he was a solid, unimaginative kind of person, who didn't seem the type to be into woo-woo things, and Emi suspected he had a crush on Lily. But she understood: by then she was already spending most of her spare time with Lily and, by extension, Lily's activities for the Anti-Civilization Committee.

Privately, when Goto asked Emi what appealed to her about the whole group—though he used the word "cult"—she waved him off. He was an engineer, not an artist, and his comfort was with circuits, wires, straight lines, and measurements on a computer screen. As far as she could tell, the Anti-Civilization Committee was innocent. They didn't ask for anything of her, besides an occasional fee for classes or a request for small donations. The events were fun, and, above all, she liked the feeling of being creative—actually creative— again. The stagnant, listless feeling she had been filled with before Lily came back into her life, before she'd found the intrigue of the Anti-Civilization Committee, dissipated.

But she failed to grow close to any members of the group besides Lily. It was something in the flow of their conversation, the way their eyes wandered, or fixed *too* intensely on her face. Sometimes she felt like she was talking *to* a conversation, rather than having one. Most of all she felt a carelessness—a lack of rootedness about place, about action. Whether the members of the Anti-Civilization Commit- tee were sitting in a quiet room or eating in a crowded restaurant, whether they were playing futsal or whittling wood, it was all one and the same to them; it didn't matter. Everyone she talked to was vaguely detached, impenetrable.

Rather than being put off by this, Emi caught herself wondering how she could emulate it. She cared too much about life. Her choices, actions, regrets, lack of daring, and losses weighed so heavily on her that she was afraid to act, and it would be easier if they didn't. This was why she had never forgotten Lily, why she rarely made new friends and barely dated, why she was unhappy in a boring job and didn't have any idea what she wanted to be doing in a year, two years, three years. She couldn't shake the fear that she had failed herself. Meeting Lily's friends, she wondered: What was it like, to wear life so loosely? Was it freer?

She watched a few of Dr. Matsusaka's videos. "That which humans make will eventually perish, humans will eventually perish," Dr. Matsusaka said. "Contemporary civilization is nothing but a mistake. But this landscape of nothingness is nothing to grieve. Sooner or later we will comprehend that matter is futile . . ."

It wasn't like that wasn't true.

*

The Play Center really belonged to Dr. Matsusaka. Originally, it was his family's summer home, until he renovated it and made it available for his collective, and Lily had been there once before, on a separate retreat with five other members. His only rule at the retreat was to cut connection with the outside world—no Internet, no cell phones.

Emi unpacked in the room she and Lily were sharing. The single window looked out onto a beech tree, and into the glow of early evening. It felt like being on vacation. Until Emi finished her shower, toweled her hair dry in the bedroom, looked up, and saw the white camera blinking from the top corner of the room. She felt the impulse to turn toward it, open her towel, and flash her body at the lens.

The housekeeper gave them a tour of the house: the kitchen, dining room, two studio rooms with exercise mats and art supplies. CCTV cameras, one in each room, which no one remarked on.

Then she took them to the back of the building and held up an electric lantern. "This is what we set up for you." In the clearing behind the house, there was a giant wooden sandbox, like the kind children might play in. It was filled with tiny dunes and valleys of a pale, glittering powder. "Just as you requested."

"And here . . ." She led them to the side of the sandbox, where a large branching tree stood away from the edge of the building. Her lantern illuminated a small wooden door fixed facedown into the dirt.

Goto asked: "What's that?"

"This is the Hole." The woman leaned down and dragged open the heavy door. A crude ladder hung over the side into a deep, dark space. In the dim light, against the mountain's night sky, Emi couldn't see how big or deep it was.

"There's a soundproofed room down there, with no light," the woman said. "People go in and sit. It's from a monastic practice."

"What's the point?" Reiya asked, his face perturbed in the stripe of orange from the lantern.

"The idea is that you are experiencing hell. Going in is completely voluntary, of course. Not many people use it." Abruptly, the woman swung her lantern back and walked ahead of them, leading them back into the house.

The four of them were left alone with a refrigerator of supplies. Dinner was quiet. Reiya asked Lily, "Was the Hole thing always part of the house?"

"Yeah. Dr. Matsusaka put it in when he did the renovations."

"Did you ever go down there?" Goto asked. He was resting his head on his forearms, and looked up at her with what Emi thought was an unusually intimate glance.

"I did, the time we came here on retreat," Lily said placidly.

"What was it like?"

Lily tilted her head back thoughtfully. "It was scary, and kind of cold. I couldn't hear anything at first. And it seemed like I was down there for a really long time. I think I might have cried a little. But when I came back outside I appreciated the night more. Compared to

being in the Hole, the night wasn't dark at all. When I came back out
I realized there was all this light in the night sky I'd taken for granted.
And I felt that life was very precious."

*

The first night, the branches of the beech tree scraped the glass by Emi's
window, and the last thing she heard before falling asleep was Lily sighing, curled in a fetal position on the futon across the room from her.

She woke up far earlier than she normally would have. She sat up
and stretched, then looked out the window. She realized, with a jolt,
that the trapdoor to the Hole was right there. Last night, she hadn't
understood the layout of the house and garden.

She looked to the other side of the room, but Lily was already gone.

Emi felt the sting of the camera's eye on her. She had not forgotten
it, and she could feel herself shrugging into her performance persona,
a spark of self-consciousness, excitement. Perhaps she had felt this
while she was sleeping, too, perhaps this was why she had woken
up so easily. In the bathroom, she pinned up her hair and put on a
hot-pink wig, powdered her face, and changed her pajama pants for
perforated black leather shorts she had punctured with silver grommets. It was an outfit she had not put on in a long time.

She found Goto downstairs, making breakfast—boiling water for
instant coffee and grilling small, bony mackerel.

"The coffee is going to taste weird with this stuff," Emi said.

Goto looked at her and didn't say anything about her outfit. "You
don't have to drink it." He dissolved the granules into a mug and
stirred with a chopstick.

"Do we have any bread?"

"Yeah, that lady left some."

"Maybe we should just eat the bread."

If it had been just the two of them, unwatched, somewhere else,
Emi might have teased Goto more, he might have said something

sarcastic in reply, or elbowed her. She found herself searching for something to say, but couldn't fill the pause.

She had known Goto for ten years. At M International, they had been polite classmates, then Lily disappeared and they became friends. Even when Emi had been in New York, whenever she sent him a message, he answered. His presence had been so reliable, so constant, she knew she sometimes took it for granted. He was part of the reason she'd moved back to Tokyo.

They talked and texted every day. More than once, she'd felt sure he loved her. Sometimes, she thought she loved him, too. But Goto was honest, his personality was fundamentally straightforward and wholesome; he believed that people's intentions matched their words, like his. And Emi thought his worldview was naïve. She knew that people could be twisted, with strange and conflicting motivations obtuse even to themselves. This, she felt, was something Lily not only understood but also celebrated: the inconsistency of human beings.

Reiya wandered sleepily in. "Nice hair," he said to Emi. He saw the camera in the kitchen, went up and waved to it, and pulled a silly face. When neither Goto nor Emi laughed, the three of them sat down and ate in silence.

Reiya washed the dishes. Opening the fridge, he said, "Hey, we even have watermelon."

"We should eat it soon."

"Maybe we can smash it outside."

It was mercifully cloudy after the heat from the day before. Outside, Lily was squatting barefoot in the sandbox. She had a bottle of black ink and a tiny brush, and was painting a small patch of sand the size of a tennis ball black. The patch was growing steadily darker with each layer she added.

She smiled at Emi and wiped her forehead. "You look cool." Her palm was smeared with ink.

The piece was called the "Vanishing Sandbox." Lily had designed the concept, a mix of reality TV and performance art. Each day, they would take their bottles of dye and tiny brushes and paint the sand, an exercise in futility. In the evening, they would rake anything they'd painted in the sandbox over, starting each day with a fresh slate. The CCTV cameras mounted around the center broadcast a livestream of their daily lives in each room to a website Lily had set up, which, without their phones, none of them would be able to watch.

When Lily had first floated the idea, Reiya dismissed it as boring. No one would want to watch four people doing nothing—playing in a sandbox, reading, cooking food—in some secluded rooms in the mountains, he claimed. Besides, the video quality would be poor, they wouldn't get a close-up of the sandbox, there would be no audio; it wasn't good production value.

But Emi knew better. She knew a little about performance, about life as content. When she was a student in New York, she'd first donned the pink wig and elaborate harlequin outfits of "Emilia." She cammed on Chaturbate at first, then moved to Twitch. Sometimes she played video games, sometimes she just left her webcam on while she was dressed up and clicked around on the Internet, online shopping, watching cooking videos, doing her homework.

She didn't let it get sexual, at least not explicitly. It was her secret, unreal life. Sometimes, a man would pay her to play a game with him, or to say something directly to him on cam, or read something out loud. Sometimes she might fulfill a different request: sleep on camera, try to follow a ballet routine, eat a strawberry cake. The people she performed for could be terrifying, creepy, explicit, demanding. They were mostly men, mostly angry, all of them lonely. But Emi understood. She even had empathy for them: she was angry, too. On camera, her alter ego, Emilia, could do things Emi would never do—dip her finger in whipped cream and lick it off; drip wax from a candle held two feet above her arm onto her skin; dance to slow music, swaying her waist, hips, arms. Emilia could act in ways Emi would never; Emilia could cater to vague, unspoken desires.

People thought they wanted stimulation and excitement, but what they really wanted was the bleed of authenticity. This was why there was such outrage when people found out reality shows were actually scripted, or the incredible memoir they'd loved turned out to be fake. Emi, Lily, Reiya, and Goto didn't have to do anything to make their videos more interesting. The boringness made their livestream interesting. The access they provided to truth without artifice. For their audience, it was the very ordinariness they consumed that anchored them to reality in an increasingly unreal world.

*

The next day they did smash the watermelon, finding a thick fallen tree branch and making a blindfold out of a clean sock. Reiya, who had borrowed Emi's paints and spent all afternoon in the room he shared with Goto, emerged outside with a mask made from several pieces of paper glued together and cut into a fox-like profile. It covered his face down to his mouth. His mouth looked ferocious, his eyes, peeping through slits in the mask, were mere pupils.

"I *love* it," Lily said approvingly. "Are you going to wear it all the time?"

"Even when I'm sleeping," he said, flashing his teeth. His easygoing voice sounded strange coming from behind the mask. Lily laughed, and as Reiya tied the blindfold over his mask and swung at the watermelon with the tree branch, she snapped photos.

They ate the broken watermelon sitting in the shade, holding the pieces to their faces. There were birdcalls, faint rustling in the bushes. A bead of sweat traveled from Emi's eyebrow to her chin.

"It's peaceful here," Goto said, tilting his face up at the sun.

Lily was sitting next to him, again. She handed him another piece of watermelon. "You don't even miss having your phone, right? The world back there is too full of *stuff*, it's overwhelming."

They watched a spotted bird take off from the trees beyond the house, arcing high above the cypresses.

Lily waved a hand at the house, the woods. "Coming up here makes you realize how bullshit everything is in the real world. Don't you just wish you could stay here forever?"

"I get it," Reiya agreed. He sat with his back against the house, arms sprawled over his knees. With his expression hidden, the colors of his mask—white, red, black, and orange—formed an uneasy pattern.

*

Over the next few days, they made sandcastles and wrote long poems with calligraphy brushes in the sandbox. Goto vanished for hours, taking long walks in the woods. He came back with flowers, which he pressed into hot water for fragrant teas.

When he wasn't hanging out with Lily, Reiya strummed chords on the ukulele he'd brought and wrote lyrics on scraps of paper, which he later buried in the sand. Similarly to Emi and her wig, Reiya never took his mask off, except when he showered. He even slept with it on.

Emi had taken to staging performances around the house in the afternoon, making costumes by gluing leaves and broken branches to her clothes. She choreographed fluid, repetitive motions, like dangling her right forearm from her elbow in front of a camera for twenty minutes. In the hour or two after lunch, she sometimes joined Lily in meditative painting, the two of them working in silence, the time passing like a dream.

In every room she stood in, she was aware of where the camera was and the angle she was showing to it. She took her wig and makeup off only to sleep. With each outfit change, Emi felt she was slipping deeper into the skin of a person who was a little harder, sharper, more irreverent, crueler. If she was in a room alone, she might wave at the camera, and once, she flipped her shirt up and flashed her bra.

Another time she did a handstand, letting her skirt flop over her torso and reveal her underwear. But privately, when she walked though doorways, she gripped the wooden frame, the hardness digging into her palm a reminder of a sensation that could not be seen by others.

As the days passed, she felt something expectant, heavy, like pressure gathering in the atmosphere before a summer rainstorm. She had come up the mountain expecting mostly banality, essentially four friends on a quiet vacation. But this was something else. Were they being changed while they were here? What were they being changed into, what different things would happen to them?

One afternoon, bored of the house, tired of painting in the sandbox, she went out looking for Goto—he had gone on a long walk—but wandered through thickets of crisp, green leaves and snarled roots without finding him. When she came back to the house, the sun was setting, and Emi saw Lily sitting by herself in the sandbox. She had made an enormous intricate pattern, almost like a mandala. While Emi walked up quietly, she saw Lily cup a palmful of sand and drop it into her mouth, swallowing it.

*

Eleven days into their retreat, the very atmosphere had seemed to absorb the pressure Emi felt building. The air was wet and electric and the afternoon had dripped by slowly, sweatily, painfully. She lay on the floor fanning herself with a magazine, waiting for rain, or a breath of wind.

The housekeeper had come by with new groceries. They made a light cucumber salad, started mixing together ground meat to make dumplings. They had cold beers. Their conversation was superficial. For each individual, the other three had faded into the background, become like wallpaper. Then, pleating a dumpling shut, Goto began to tell them about the time he had carried a ghost down a mountain on his back.

One summer in college, he said, apropos of nothing, he had gone hiking. On the way back, his shoulders started to hurt, as though from a heavy backpack, but he'd barely carried anything with him.

"*Here*?" Reiya said.

"No," Goto said. "It was Mount Takao." He seemed like he was in a bad mood. Emi looked at him and wondered why. She had never heard this story before, either.

He was living with his parents, he continued, and when he got home from his trip, he began having sleep paralysis, immobile in his bed, feeling an invisible pressure sitting on his chest, making him short of breath. He had trouble waking in the mornings—he was always groggy, disoriented, woke up with neck and shoulder pain.

He ascribed it all to stress. Then one night, he went out drinking with friends, missed the last train, and ended up staying over at someone else's apartment. Goto wasn't drunk enough that he forgot to go into the bathroom to brush his teeth, using his finger as a toothbrush.

In the bathroom, he noticed a cut on his lip. Then his shoulders started hurting again. A thin line of blood trickled over his lips, which were cracked and dry.

He splashed his face with water and wiped the blood off, then went to sleep on the couch. Only a few hours later, his friend was shaking him awake.

"Hey, hey dude," his friend said—breath sour, hair uncombed. "Wake up."

Goto's head was so heavy he couldn't lift it. "What?"

"There was this *girl* just like—sitting on you!"

His mouth was parched, he could barely move his tongue. "What are you talking about?"

In the middle of the night, the friend woke up because the light in the bedroom was on. He thought they'd forgotten to turn it off. When he stood up to flip the switch, he saw Goto lying with his eyes wide open.

"What's wrong?" he'd said, thinking Goto was awake, but Goto didn't answer. It was creepy, but okay. He shrugged it off. Some people slept with their eyes open. Then he flipped the light switch, and just as the room went dark, he saw the figure of a girl squatting on Goto's chest. She was young, a teenager, like fifteen or sixteen. She had bobbed hair and a round, moonlike face.

The friend immediately turned the light on again and the girl disappeared. Then he saw Goto's eyes were closed, and his mouth was bleeding. That was when he shook him awake.

Goto sat up and realized the cut on his lip had opened up again.

So the next day he went to a temple and talked to a priest, who asked him where he'd gone the last few weeks. Finally, the priest traced Goto's story back to Mount Takao. He said he had probably picked up a spirit on the mountain, most likely a girl who had died up there.

The priest burned a candle and gave Goto a charm. And then Goto went home.

"And everything stopped after that? The sleep paralysis and lip bleeding?" Emi asked.

"Yep."

"And nothing else ever happened? In the mirror, or when you were sleeping?"

"No. Nothing did."

"So what was it? Was it a real ghost?" Reiya's voice sounded skeptical. He carefully wet the lip of a dumpling skin.

Goto shrugged. "If you don't believe me, you can ask the friend I stayed with. He moved apartments, he lost his deposit and everything. He was freaked out."

Reiya shook his head. "I'm not saying I don't believe you."

"I've heard the spirits of teenage girls are the most powerful," Lily, who hadn't said a word through the entire story, offhandedly cut in. "I heard they have the most attachment to the world because of all their unfulfilled desires."

There was a moment of silence after that.

"Creepy." Emi smiled, raising Lily's camera to take a picture. She imagined what was showing on the livestream: the four of them around the clean room with the big bowl of dumpling filling in the center of the table; Lily like an advertisement for bottled water with her straight teeth and glowing skin; Goto, serious in his white shirt and stubborn expression; Reiya in his strange mask; Emi herself, with her pink wig and the whirls of silver acrylic paint she had put on her face and fingernails that morning. What kind of scene was this?

Again she had the feeling she was not in her own body. How odd it all was, that she should be up on a secluded mountaintop with these people. Lily, who had waltzed back into her life like they had never been apart, and yet about whom much remained unanswered. Like, why had she moved back to Tokyo? Why had she disappeared from high school?

And as for Reiya, what did she know about him, really? Emi felt a flash of unease, even danger; in fact, how could she know anything about anyone? How could she be sure of what these people, fundamentally strangers, would do? The only person she *really* knew here was Goto. And yet even he had whole stories she'd never heard before.

You're being paranoid, she told herself. "Say cheese," she said, and aimed the camera at Goto, the most familiar, for comfort. Through the lens, he looked at her distantly, and for the first time since she could remember, she couldn't decipher his expression.

*

After dinner, Reiya caught Emi while she was heading to her room. Under the mask, his mouth was lifted in a smile.

"Crazy story, right?"

"I guess," she said. "But I believe it."

She imagined him looking at her appraisingly. But the only part of his face she could see—his mouth—didn't move. His mask had become crinkled and stained through the past week and a half.

"Hey, you've been friends with Goto for a while, right?"

"Yes," she said.

"Why is he here anyway? He's not into this stuff. He barely talks to any of us, even you. He just disappears all the time. Where does he go?"

Emi shrank back and shrugged. "It's a free country."

Reiya's teeth were straight, white, bright. "Your American influence."

Emi didn't say anything.

"So how long have you guys known each other? What's the story there?"

"We're high school friends."

"Sure about that?" Reiya drew closer, pinning Emi to the wall. In a friendly way, he put an arm in front of her, his hand against the wall, blocking her from walking forward. "He's got incel vibes to me. You don't think he's got the hots for you?"

She met his eyes, brown, friendly, like a dog's. She was aware of the camera in the corner of the hall, and even as she felt partly wary of Reiya, part of her also felt her performative switch turn on.

"Don't talk about Goto like that," she said sternly.

With his other hand, Reiya pulled at her pink wig. "Why do you dress like that, by the way?" the smiling mouth said. There it was again: the streak of aggression in his voice.

"Like what?"

"Looks like you're wanting attention."

She shrugged, and said again, "It's a free country."

Reiya nodded at the camera. "So why don't we give a little show? You like that kind of stuff, right?" His tongue wagged. "For all our viewers out there."

She lurched against the slyness in his voice; she wanted to break it down.

"We're not all exhibitionists like you," she said sarcastically.

His laugh was hard and sardonic. "Maybe not all of us, but *you* are, right?"

"You're being weird." Her voice was as cold as she could make it. She imagined shoving him away. She imagined kissing him, biting his hand, ripping his shirt off, the two of them having sex on the floor.

His mouth stopped smiling. His fingers twitched. For a second, it seemed like he was going to put his hand around Emi's throat. Her breath stopped.

Reiya released his arm. His voice came out harshly: "Isn't it time something happened around here?"

When Emi got back to her bedroom, Lily wasn't there. It was hot; she felt flushed. Wasn't the room too stuffy? She opened the window and stepped into the bathroom to wash her face. She took off her wig, took a shower.

She rolled out her futon and lay there, with her hands palm up toward the ceiling. She didn't know what to do with them. She waited for Lily to come back so she could tell her about Reiya, but time stretched on and Lily didn't enter the room. What was she doing?

She stared out the window at the beech tree. The forest beyond was a fumbled outline of leaves. She looked for the stars, the moon. She imagined there being so many stars she couldn't see, crowding the sky, as many stars as there were grains of sand in the sandbox.

At some point her eyes half closed and she began dreaming.

In her dream, she and Goto were walking through an empty Tokyo at night. The subway stops, clothing stores, bars, neon lights of Kabuki-chō, and lantern-lit eateries of Asakusa had half-clean plates and open doors. It looked like everyone had just stepped out momentarily. But the streets had the vacated, blue-lit dust of a city that had been abandoned for a long time, remaining perfectly preserved. She felt very cold.

They walked and they walked. Then, when the city stopped and turned into a deserted road, Goto took her face in his hands and lifted it up to his. He kissed her on the forehead. Tenderly, he traced the rest of her face with the tip of his nose—her forehead, the left cheek, the right cheek, the jaw. His nose, which was cold and clammy, exerted a gentle pressure along the perimeter of her chin, and then, softly, he kissed the tip of her nose and released her.

Emi woke with a gasp. The room was cold. It was still dark. And Lily's nose was inches from her face.

She turned her face and jumped, clutching, ridiculously, her blanket to her chest. Lily was crouched by her side, looking at her like someone studying a microbe on a glass slide. She was so close Emi could feel her breath on her cheek.

"What are you *doing*?"

"You were talking in your sleep, Emi*ko*," Lily said in that sing-song way.

"What . . ." Emi shifted her body so she was farther away from Lily. "What was I saying?" Her mind was scrambled, from the intensity of the dream, the touch she thought she had felt, the shock of waking up and finding Lily *there*. Had Lily been the one touching her? Had that been the touch in her dreams?

"Hmm." Lily sat back and rocked on her heels. "Something like, 'Let's go'? What were you dreaming about?" She was wearing a T-shirt and jeans.

"Where were you?" Emi asked. "Were you out until now?"

Lily smiled, a little bit mysteriously. "Nowhere, really."

Emi scrubbed her hands over her face and shivered. "It's cold."

"Close the window, then. Do you want some hot water?" Lily reached over her to pull the glass panel down. Underneath the T-shirt, the curve of her breast: she wasn't wearing a bra.

When she leaned back, her shoulder brushed Emi's nose. The moment of contact was so fleeting, so warm. Reiya's mouth, mocking her, flashed in Emi's memory.

"Lily—" she said, then an uncontrollable yawn escaped her.

"I'm going to get you that hot water," Lily said comfortingly, before she got up, went out of the room, and closed the door.

Then Emi must have drifted back to sleep. Her doze this time was punctuated by fits of cold, and dream-memories. Reiya's mask, the dumplings at the dinner table, Goto's white T-shirt, the mark the ghost of a teenage girl had left on his lip, the first day she'd seen him after landing at Narita. The staircase up the mountain. Lily in the sandbox, Lily's hand dropping sand into her mouth, a clink and the feeling of heat near her face, "Emi, the water," a silken touch that could've been a hand, on her cheek.

"I'm sleepy," she sighed, or tried to sigh, and there was a shifting movement next to her, or was it just a dream? She put out her hand, like a child, her fingers crawled up a forearm, she remembered in high school, on a warm afternoon, sitting on the bus, putting her head in the crook of Lily's shoulder. "Where are we getting off?" she mumbled. The bus view was full of spring greenery.

"I'll let you know," Lily said. Emi said, "Okay, make sure to wake me up." Emi said, "It's so nice being here with you." Then it was raining inside the bus, and Emi was sitting near the docks at Yokohama watching the boats, but she had forgotten her umbrella. She felt cold again. Then she woke up for real.

For a moment she thought she was just waking up in a normal house on a normal day. She saw the cup of hot water, now cold, had been knocked over, soaking the blanket and futon. And Lily was not there; Lily was gone.

*

In the kitchen there were no bread crumbs, no dirty dishes. The house felt empty. How late *was* it? Emi sneezed, wondered if there was medicine, or if they would have to go somewhere else to get it.

"Lily?" she called out. "Lily?"

No reply. She drank a cup of coffee, and looked at the sandbox through the window. She wished she had a photo of what it looked like when they had started. Had it changed at all? Here and there, there must be black spots, blue dots, surely the sandbox was a little muddier than the pristine white it had been when they arrived a week ago.

No one was in the sandbox, but she saw there was something inside.

Emi went outside. There were brushes abandoned at the edge of the box, a turned-over bottle of dye. Inside, black letters, each half a meter long. They were long and thin, written in frail, wobbly ink, but against the white sand, the words were clear:

LET'S GO!

"Lily?" she called again.

She walked around the back of the house, her heartbeat getting faster, then she started running.

"Lily?"

There wasn't *that* much space to hide. If Lily wasn't in the house, she had to be outside. Maybe she had just gone into the forest. She couldn't even be sure Lily had written the words; it could have been Reiya or, less likely, Goto. She remembered Lily had been wearing jeans last night.

Emi walked through the kitchen, the workshop, the bathroom, her bedroom. They were all empty.

With a sudden suspicion, she ran back into their room. Lily's futon was rolled up, or it had never been laid out. Her backpack and toothbrush were still there. Then Emi found Lily's camera in the backpack. She opened up the back. There was no film cartridge. The compartment was empty.

She caught sight of the omnipresent white camera in the corner. She realized, suddenly, she didn't have her wig on. She hadn't put on her makeup. She was in her natural clothes, natural hair, natural self.

The only place for privacy was the Hole.

Emi went back outside. It was starting to drizzle, a very fine, light rain. The door under the beech tree was closed. She squatted down and dragged it open. The door was heavy, and she grunted with strain.

"What?" a voice yelled-called. This voice, she knew.

"Goto?" Emi yelped. "What are you doing down there?"

At the bottom of the ladder was a tiny space. Goto was sitting on a thin cushion with his knees hugged to his chest.

"What do you want?" he said.

Emi hesitated. She put a hand on the ladder and prepared to climb down. "I was . . . I was looking for Lily. What's going on? Why are you down there?" A horrible thought came to Emi. "Have you been here *every day*? Do you just sit here all the time, when I thought you were out walking?"

He snorted. "We've been here for how long, and this is the first time you've thought about asking me what I'm doing?"

His voice was low, aggressive. Emi swallowed. "I don't—are you mad at me? I'm just—"

"Off in your little Emi world," Goto said bitterly. "Because whenever you need someone to cry to or whine to, you know you've got me to listen."

"I just . . . I'm sorry," Emi said. She didn't know what else to say. Her throat tickled, and she let out an enormous sneeze.

"Little Emilia," he spat. "Or Emi*ko*. Lily's little pet name. Always have to be the center of attention, don't you? As long as you've got at least one person looking at you, you don't have to think about any others."

Emi's head was hot; she couldn't process his words. Last night's dream Goto had been so tender and silent. "I . . . All of a sudden, this . . ."

Goto shouted: "Did you think my life was smaller than yours?!"

Who was this angry stranger, yelling from the bottom of the Hole?

"I just . . . Look, I'll leave you alone," she said. "Have you seen Lily?" Her throat burned, she suddenly let out a coughing fit. She couldn't tell whether it was the coughing or real tears that made her eyes wet. "I'm just worried," she said. "Lily left a message in the sandbox. And last, night, she was dressed like she was going out. I don't know. I'm sorry. I'll leave you alone."

But Goto came alert. "What did she write?"

*

They stood at the edge of the sandbox together. The drizzle coming down had darkened the sand around the letters.

"Her mom has schizophrenia, you know," he said quietly. "She used to think Lily was an evil replacement of her actual daughter."

"How did you find out?"

"I asked her."

An umbrella opened over them. It was Reiya. Instinctively, recalling the previous night, Emi flinched away, then let out another hacking cough.

"What's going on? I heard arguing outside." He looked at the words Lily had left behind. "What's that?"

Goto was the one who explained. "Lily's gone. Did you see her today?"

"What? Did you check everywhere? What about her stuff?"

"There's not that many places to check," Emi said. "And she took her film. Or else there wasn't ever any film in her camera."

Reiya pulled his mask up and looked them face-on. "Don't worry. I'm sure she'll be back."

Seeing his real face for the first time in what felt like forever, Emi was startled by how serious he looked.

"I think we should look for her." Goto crossed his arms, his voice decisive, authoritative.

Once they had gotten their ponchos and sneakers, they walked into the wilderness behind the Play Center. Emi's sneakers squished in the soft dirt. Her throat itched and burned. Her wet hands were cold. She sneezed as the sound of water hit the leaves above her. Under the cloud cover, it was dark between the trees.

"Lily!" Reiya called, somewhere from her left.

"Lily!" Goto called, somewhere on her right.

"Lily!" she called, too, but her voice was weak. She almost didn't recognize it as belonging to her. The three of them were finally beyond the reach of the cameras. The screens would be showing nothing: empty rooms, discarded mugs. Like they had just stepped out and were going to come back. Where had Lily gone? Had she been planning this escape, to dematerialize, from the very beginning? When Emi had first seen Lily after their seven years apart, it had been like seeing a ghost. She had been almost afraid to touch her, lest she vanish again.

"Lily," she called again, but the sound didn't carry. It seemed to Emi that her voice had dislocated itself from her body, that the name she was calling had expelled itself into the forest, two faltering syllables floating detached in the wilderness, fading unseen into the tangles in front of her.

POWER AND CONTROL

Keychain was Brian's friend first. Greta saw her for the first time in July, on the screen of Brian's phone, when she was helping him pack up his place for his move to Pittsburgh.

"It's not *that* far," he said over the packing tape.

"Who's going to look after me when you're gone?" she teased.

"Maybe you should try taking care of someone else for a change. I know someone who just moved to Brooklyn, she doesn't have a lot of friends."

Brian and Greta had met four months previously, right after Greta and her last girlfriend broke up. Brian ran a film Meetup and Greta, who didn't like being lonely, joined them to see Teshigahara's *The Face of Another*. She could tell he was a normal, trusting guy who liked to be helpful. From there it was easy enough to charm him, to say she needed a friend for hotpot and take him to Flushing to get all-you-can-eat, to appeal to his kindness by playing up her sadness, her sense of being adrift. Brian laughed when she cracked jokes about coworkers and patients. He brought her as a guest to his two-hundred-dollar-a-month gym, and he shared the vegetables he got from friends who ran an Amish farm in Pennsylvania.

The woman in the photo had short black hair and a close-lipped smile. Her skin looked pale and easily bruised. She didn't look that friendly. Brian said she was shy. They had volunteered together at a community garden when he lived in New Orleans.

"Not a lot of Asians in New Orleans," Greta observed.

He smiled. "So you can show her what's good in New York."

"Why did she move here?"

"A new job. She's going to be doing conservation research at the botanical gardens. But I think she was feeling pretty stuck before she moved. You know how it is. After the lockdown, two years stuck at home, people just gotta do something different." Brian himself had spent the lockdown years learning UX design so he could get out of project management. It was because of his new skill set he was moving to Pittsburgh, where he had been hired by a language-teaching app. His example inspired Greta to look into returning to her first love, which was theater. She'd given it up after performing in some student roles in college.

Now what she did was work at a dentist's office, cleaning: teeth, gums, tartar, plaque. Trapped behind her face shield, she sprayed down tongues and scraped mashed pork and white scum from yellow crevices, shined a light in the dark corners to look for signs of decay at the edges of white and silver fillings. She aligned image receptors and placed bite blocks in mouths for the X-ray machine. Her days were spent spelunking in the foul-smelling tunnels of people's appetites.

"She'll be at my going-away party." Brian smiled. "Isn't she cute?"

Greta hadn't told him much about her last breakup. All he knew was that it had been sudden, her ex had taken all her things, and Greta had stopped going to the lesbian bar in Park Slope where she might run into people they knew in common.

She looked at the picture one more time. The woman's face was very haunted. It was the hollows under her eyes—it wasn't right for someone their age to have such hollows.

"Not my type," she said, turning away.

*

Early on, Greta gave her the nickname Keychain, for the rattling keys she was always fishing out of her pocket. Keychain kept her keys attached to a slim card case in which she kept her ID, metro card, credit card, and a few folded dollar bills. Later she added a keychain with pepper spray and a safety alarm that sounded when you pulled out the pin.

Keychain was a careful person by nature. If she was not new in town, and if Brian had not introduced them, Greta knew the two of them might not have had a chance. In those honeymoon, scrabbling summer days, she showed the girl around New York. She looked for small openings to get Keychain to trust her: a moment to brush her arm, opening the door for her if she had bags, grabbing her elbow when a car sped across the street. Greta could read how these little gestures touched her all over her face.

She trawled Keychain's Instagram to see what photos she posted (plants, dogs on the street, an occasional selfie) and which accounts she followed (indie musicians, designers from LA). She spent hours researching places to take her, intuiting what she might like:

the Japanese flower shop and café with the riotous interior near Murray Hill,

the SoHo cupcake shop with the frosting decorated to look like tiny succulents,

Joe's Pub, where they listened to an experimental jazz-R&B-electronic duo while sipping on highballs two yards from stage.

And when she nailed it, when she found the perfect spot to take her, Keychain's face would brighten, the hollows under her eyes seemed to lighten, and Greta would bask in the gratitude. And wasn't Keychain so adorable, with her tiny smile, her careful expression, the earnest way she knit together her eyebrows?

Keychain liked to draw, and after one of these summer outings, she gave Greta a pastel doodle on a small white card. "GRETA spells GREAT," the little cartoon lovebird she'd drawn cooed into a speech bubble. "I'm so glad I met you!" Oh, the very proof of love. Greta kept the card in her wallet, carefully protected by two credit cards.

Then the day came when Keychain was at the botanical gardens, dropping something off at the gift shop. A guy came in from the street, looked at some ZZ plants, turned around, and flashed her. She screamed and he ran out of the store, pulling his pants up.

She called Greta, who Ubered from the dentist's office to the gift shop immediately. There were other patrons, other garden staff, it was a raw and disorienting mess. In Keychain's upper-floor room an hour later, Greta hugged her, stroked her hair, and made her mint tea.

"I can't believe this happened to me, I can't," Keychain said, sobbing on her bed. "I literally just moved here. I'm so unlucky."

"But it's lucky that you moved here and met me, right?" Greta said, cradling her cheek. Keychain's eyelashes were wet. She'd been crying for almost forty-five minutes. This was the moment, the chance, Greta thought, when she would make herself indispensable. "I'll take care of you, you don't have to worry," she said. The girl snuffled; Greta kissed her eyelid. Keychain's shoulder stiffened. "Hmm?" she said, a little confused. Oh, here was a girl, soft, sweet, trusting, looking for safety. *It's all going to be better now*, Greta thought. All the difficult relationships, the arguments, the fighting, the loneliness, her smallness, her rage, it was all over. Greta would be all right now. She brought Keychain's haunted little face closer and Keychain didn't resist. That was their first kiss.

*

At the time, Greta was living with a roommate named Aileen. She'd gotten the room through a series of coincidences. After her ex left, she couldn't afford their lease alone, and Aileen's last tenant had given only two weeks' notice. Greta heard about the opening from a botanist acquaintance who had briefly sublet Aileen's extra room. Aileen's father was ill; she was looking for someone to move in quickly. She said Greta could do month-to-month. The first time Greta went to see the place, she noticed the deep green color of the front door. Back then, every morning, Greta drank a green juice. The knocker was a brass mermaid.

The three of them—Aileen, Greta, and the botanist—were all in the network. They were all scientists, or more accurately, alchemists. Alchemy was a slow process, involving experimentation and communion with a set of half-known principles. The knowledge was minor, but it couldn't be found on the Internet. People learned informally, half through experiment, using stranger processes, subtler compounds, alien chemical formations that were not commonly known. When she first got her start, Greta transformed a broken watch into a clear, glass monocle lens. When she raised it to her eye, everything looked younger: cats turned into kittens, Leonardo DiCaprio looked like young Romeo, radiators lost some rust. The lens lasted a little over an hour, just long enough to liven up an evening.

Now, Greta mostly specialized in metalworking and tinctures. On her first visit to Aileen's house, she peeked into the other woman's room and saw her tools: tiny brass scales with gold dust and crystals, trails of snail slime in a glass tank, grams of crushed blue thistle on a silver plate. She didn't ask, but she suspected Aileen was doing mirror work. Why else would mirrors be hung everywhere in the house? There were triptychs in the halls, irregular circles on the walls, rectangles stacked like Tetris blocks over doorframes.

There were more than a few alchemists in New York, though they didn't congregate; practitioners of the science tended to be solitary. Perhaps they saw themselves too clearly in one another, one line of thought went—recognizing in each other their own anxiety, single-mindedness, desire for control. But around the time Greta moved in with Aileen, one practitioner sent out a rare call to the whole group. She was Chinese. In her message, she named Asian people who had been hurt—the woman with the acid thrown on her face, the man stabbed in Chinatown, the woman stomped in the head at the revolving door in Midtown, the subway attacks, the slurs. *We can't do nothing,* she said. *We have power, we should use it to protect those who are being hurt.* She was making charmed safety pins—a tiny decoration one could stick onto a bag or a jacket that, if it sensed something awry, would influence the wearer to take a different route, to turn a few steps away. She wanted to donate them to Asian families.

Please volunteer if you have time, the girl said.

Greta ignored the message; she suspected so did Aileen. Aileen was white, it didn't matter to her; as for Greta, she had things of her own to worry about. She could protect herself, why should she protect others? The Chinese girl was being naïve, Greta felt. The teachers had emphasized from the beginning how futile all their experiments were, how temporary. *None of it lasts,* everyone said. Really, in the end, alchemy could only pull off a few party tricks, a few minor manipulations. You can't save the world, you can't change the weather. You won't have power over life, or love, but—oh—you can try.

From Aileen, she heard about darkrooms one could rent in Gowanus. Not long after she met Keychain, Greta went to check them out. The rooms were in the basement of a metalworking shop, cheap and open for access at all hours. There was a chocolatier next door.

The first thing she took to the darkroom was Keychain's mother's necklace, a silver piece with a jade pendant. Keychain always wore it around her neck. One day, not long after their first kiss, in that ambiguous stage between infatuation and commitment, Greta had been kissing Keychain in bed and tangled her fingers in the necklace. The chain was delicate. The clasp tore off.

"Oh, I'm so sorry!" Greta stopped what she was doing, while Keychain struggled—Greta could see it—to not be too upset. Greta felt cold: What if this made Keychain like her less?

"It's okay, it's okay," Keychain said, a little grimly, sitting back on her naked haunches and holding the chain in her hand. The pendant gleamed green between her fingers. It was clearly not okay.

"I can fix it," Greta said. "No, really. I can. Give me a few days?"

She bought a new chain, pure silver. The metal was pliable and easy to bend. Eagerly, she went down to the basement in the building in Gowanus. She heated together a few ingredients, cadmium and ylang-ylang oil and wax from a certain honeycomb, and a little bit of gold dust. She went carefully, for the chain was expensive, and each ingredient was expensive; she had gone to all corners of the city to look for them. Then she heated up the new chain and hammered it down with a new coating. When she gave the necklace back to Keychain, she put it over her neck and carefully closed the clasp herself.

Greta had hunted hard for this recipe, which was supposed to be reliable. Metal was difficult to work with, but the results were longer-lasting. Into the chain, while she had been hammering down its new coating, she had worked: an openness to love.

They were falling in love anyway; she was just speeding up the process.

*

August ended, then September. Time, so gray and unhappy since Greta had been alone, came alive again. There was something to look forward to in the days. The dentist's office was awful, but Keychain was waiting after work, Keychain was texting her where did she want to go to dinner, Keychain was curling her small hand into Greta's shyly, Keychain was eating a mint and pressing her insistent lips against Greta's.

"Greta, I thought you said she wasn't your type?" Brian asked, teasing, on the phone, the one time he called from Pittsburgh. "I vouched for you, don't let me down now."

"I don't think you heard right. I said she's exactly my type," Greta said flippantly. What was he talking about? They were perfect for each other. They were everything the other could ever need.

*

In October, Greta finally signed up for the acting classes she told herself she wanted to do. It wasn't too late, Keychain encouraged her; lots of actors got their start when they were thirty. The class met at a rented studio space in Times Square. Ten chairs were arranged in a circle in the airless, fluorescent-lit room. The other students were all in their early twenties, nervous, arrogant, limp, and sweaty, and Greta regretted coming, as if by sitting with them, she was making herself as pathetic as they were. But then the teacher came in. She was a fashionable, slim woman, with sexy, curly dirty blonde hair and purple lipstick. She smiled at Greta, welcomed the class, and Greta told herself she might as well stay.

*

Once in a while, Greta would feel curious about her ex. After their split, her former girlfriend had become so extreme, had gone private on everything, and when Greta checked, she couldn't find any details. There were no profile picture updates; the number of posts on her locked Twitter account seemed to be exactly the same. Sometimes Greta got the funny feeling that her ex might not even exist in this world anymore at all.

It was one night while she was running through Facebook, Instagram, LinkedIn, Twitter, and even Venmo, trying to find details—proof—about her ex, that she heard the choir singing. At first she identified it only as some kind of music practice—there were practice studios in a building behind Aileen's house, and sometimes, they would hear bad metal music, or trap or house, emanating from those aggrieved spaces.

But this time, it was a high, ethereal singing, like what she had heard when she went to church when she was younger, coming from rows of mouths all held in Os. But that was impossible; there was no church nearby, and when she looked out the window, she didn't see any crowd or anything that could have been a congregation. The sound was eerie, low, and startlingly resonant, as though the singers were in a huge and high-ceilinged nave. The words, whatever they were, were indistinct.

It must have been coming from the music practice rooms—but how? The music felt ominous, and hearing it, Greta felt a little nervous, without knowing why.

*

News of the subway attacks had dwindled by the day she and Keychain were walking in Madison Square Park, and someone—a man—stopped them on the sidewalk. He was slightly hunched, with a wind-chapped face. "Can I just say," he said, his voice unctuous and slippery, and Keychain's hand in Greta's tightened, "y'all are *so, cute*," and a tension Greta hadn't realized they both had been holding slightly relaxed.

"Thanks," Greta said guardedly, edging her body in front of Keychain's. The man had a smile like an oil slick. He leered at Keychain, who smiled nervously, and seemed about to say more, but Greta started walking, pulling Keychain. Greta imagined him watching from behind as they left—his eyes lingering on Keychain.

"That went a different direction than I was worried it would," Keychain said afterward when they were back in her room. She sounded terribly relieved. "I thought he might say a slur or something."

Greta imagined how he must have seen Keychain walking away from him: a pretty girl, on the short side, with a delicate, kissable mouth, thin skin with the blood near the surface. She imagined the man looking at Keychain's butt in her jeans, her shoulder blades outlined against her black top, her monolidded eyes, symbol of that contradictory cocktail of fetish and hate.

"It's so scary going out these days," Keychain sighed, "but that makes it so hard to meet people."

Meet people? Who did she need to meet?

"You didn't like his attention?" Greta said.

"What? Of course not, why would you even say that?" Keychain looked shocked.

The words slipped out so easily: "I'm not the one wearing thigh-high black boots, am I?"

"Are you *fucking* serious? Are you actually—"

She'd gone too far. Greta backpedaled. "I'm sorry," she said, softening her voice, putting out a hand to hold Keychain's wrist.

"What the actual fuck?" Keychain flinched back and shook off Greta's hand.

"Oh my god. I don't know why I said that. I'm sorry. I was so rattled, I was just so scared, you know? I'm sorry, I really don't know why I said that. I'm sorry!" A spurt of cold fear: What if Keychain got angry at her, what if she left? Keychain had latched on to her when she was new to the city and didn't know anyone else, what if she met someone who was a better match?

Her anger suddenly deflated, Keychain looked confused. "Yes, that guy was scary," she said in an uncertain tone of voice. "But still, you shouldn't have—"

Greta spoke fast. "I wasn't thinking straight. I was afraid he was going to hurt you. I just lost it, I know, I shouldn't have." She warmed her tone. "But I mean, he's right about one thing, we *are* cute together." She pinched Keychain's cheek and looked in the mirror. They were a study in contrasts: Keychain's short hair, milky skin, Greta's warmer-toned hue, her larger build, long hair.

"That was a weird thing to say," Keychain said, but still with uncertainty. Without answering, Greta started to kiss her. Their bodies lowered in the mirror, their reflections slipped out of sight.

*

Dentist's office, acting classes, the Gowanus darkroom. It was a busy life. Keychain's birthday was in late November, Sagittarius season.

The day of Keychain's birthday dinner, Greta's acting teacher took her aside after class and said, "You're doing great. And you have such a striking look, great for stage," a compliment on which Greta preened. She also put a hand on Greta's wrist—but that was her business, nothing Greta had to feel guilty about.

Keychain texted while Greta was getting ready. *My friend Janey wants to come to the birthday dinner and meet you! See you soon.* Heart emoji.

Who the heck is Janey? In the living room in Aileen's house, Greta heard the weird choral singing again. It was the third or fourth time; she hadn't been able to determine which building it was coming from, and each time, the singing made her feel unsettled and restless. She wandered into her bedroom, the bathroom, and the living room again; the sound was inescapable.

"Do you hear that?" she asked Aileen, who was in the kitchen.

"What, exactly?" Aileen asked absently, but she was always distracted, anyway, this time banging around making some witchy wellness broth in an enormous tureen boiling with sachets of herbs and ginger-like roots. The steam had flattened her already-flat blonde hair to her forehead.

By the time Keychain and Janey showed up at the restaurant, Greta had the uncomfortable feeling of her skin being too tight for her body. Irritation bristled inside her, an internal inflammation. Keychain was walking with a woman Greta had never met before, and when had she started making new friends, anyway? Seeing Greta at the threshold to the restaurant, Keychain bounded up eagerly and said, "Oh, sorry we're late—look, this is—"

"Took you long enough! It's raining! Let's go in, they've held the reservation for ten minutes already." She pushed open the door and didn't acknowledge the girl behind Keychain, who was dressed in a sleek trench coat and had immaculate makeup and blown-out hair. Something about her face felt recognizable, but in the way a stranger can remind you of someone annoying you once knew. Greta immediately didn't like her.

It turned out Janey was a new hire at the botanical gardens working in the fundraising department. Previously she'd worked in public health handling vaccine distribution, and had burned out. "She does so much good work," Keychain said earnestly, "she's been organizing these community self-defense classes in Chinatown, for Asian people."

"The food here is taking so long to arrive," Greta complained. Janey raised an eyebrow. Greta could tell she didn't like her, that she was looking down on her, why? Because being a dental hygienist wasn't as great as working at a charity asking for money?

After dinner, Greta and Keychain went back to Greta's room, and there was a fight:

KEYCHAIN: "Why were you so rude? That was so embarrassing, and I was trying to introduce Janey to you, I don't know *what* she's going to think."

GRETA: "Rude? She was the one who was rude to me, she kept talking down to me."

KEYCHAIN: "What are you talking about? She was just asking you what you do for work! It's a normal question!"

GRETA: "And what were you two doing before, why were you late! I was waiting in the rain!"

KEYCHAIN: "I told you, there was this whole thing at the gardens, we were running late! It wasn't our fault."

GRETA (*sarcastically*): "*Our*? Oh, so you two are a unit now?"

KEYCHAIN (*voice choking*): "No, we were at *work*—we *work* together!"

GRETA: "Oh, come on, now you're going to *cry*? That's not fair! I should be able to express my feelings!"

KEYCHAIN (*inhales sharply*): "You—you—"

GRETA (*taking a gift box from her bag and hanging it to Keychain, turning her voice sweet*): "All right, you're right, you're right. As usual. I'm wrong. I'm sorry. I was just mad because I wasn't expecting someone else. I thought it was just going to be the two of us. I wanted it to be a special night. And I wanted to give this to you, but I was too embarrassed in front of her."

KEYCHAIN (*softening, staring at the anklet in the box*): "Did you make this? It's so pretty."

GRETA: "I've been working on it the last month. Every time I go to Gowanus. Do you like it?"

KEYCHAIN: "Thank you, I love it. I'm sorry we were late. I'm sorry we didn't get to have a private dinner. I should have told you earlier."

GRETA: "It's okay. I love you."

KEYCHAIN: "I love you, too. I'm sorry."

Keychain kissed her. Fight won, Greta took the anklet and bent low to fasten it above Keychain's foot. It was heavier than it looked. The beads were not all the same size, and undulated like the crests and troughs of waves, connected to one another by a thin copper wire. The anklet had taken her weeks to make and much trial and error, but when Keychain wore this anklet, she'd feel encouraged to stay home. She'd be more unwilling to go outside, feel more afraid to go anywhere new.

It was safer this way. The streets were dangerous. Greta thought of the man who'd said *cute* in Madison Square Park, of how even Janey had looked at Keychain with a certain glimmer of desire. Greta knew. She would be able to relax, worry a little bit less, and not have to always be guessing what Keychain was up to when she wasn't around.

*

Two weeks later, on the subway, she watched a little boy, maybe five years old, scoot over to smack his older brother on the seat. The older brother squeezed the younger boy's wrist until he cried. Their mother tried to pull them apart half-heartedly while the younger boy wailed. Everyone in the car ignored them.

People do terrible things to one another, Greta reflected, standing holding the strap from the steel railing. It was only an ignorant minority of repressed people who were surprised by the selfishness, brutality, and disregard most humans had for one another. Morality was a fairy tale told as a bedtime story to brainwash children. One Christmas, when she was visiting her parents, she'd seen her uncle throw a clock across the room at her aunt. As for her aunt, she used to sit in the dark, drunk, chanting curses when her husband came home—mumbling insults at him, at her good-for-shit parents, at all the teachers, institutions, and agencies that had failed her, and above all, God, who had failed her most by not existing. Oh, her aunt and uncle were horrible, miserable people. But then, most people were.

When she burst into fresh air she had a few new text messages.

Are you busy tonight? from Keychain. *Not feeling like going out, wanna come over and watch a movie?*

Greta gloated.

And surprisingly, there was a message from her acting teacher.

Hey, you work near West 4 right? I'll be there tomorrow for an audition if you want to get a drink after?

*

Christmas. Greta gave Keychain a little bottle of perfume she had concocted (a floral, sweet-smelling mix treated with extract of gingko and wasp venom and a keratin treatment from hedgehog spikes) that, when sprayed, would make Keychain feel a little bit uglier, so prevent her from getting any ideas about other people liking her. Keychain gave her a small photo album with pictures of the two of them from the last half year.

For the holidays, Keychain went home. She wasn't out to her parents. She asked Greta if she wanted to come with her under the guise of a platonic friend, but Greta, both because she was feeling tired and for another reason she didn't completely understand herself, said no. She and Aileen spent New Year's Eve alone, passing a joint back and forth on the snowy fire escape and looking at the muddled sky.

Greta inhaled the sativa. She regretted not leaving the city. She missed Keychain and wished her girlfriend was with her, and sulked that she hadn't gotten a text back to the message she'd sent earlier. What was Keychain doing? Meeting up with high school friends, a high school ex? She shouldn't have let her go alone.

"Did you hear about the botanist?" Aileen asked. The botanist they both knew from the network, who had told Greta about the vacant room.

"No, what happened?"

"He was growing a replica of his dead wife," Aileen said. His wife had died of pancreatic cancer two years prior. Aileen stubbed the remains of the joint out and gave a few details. The botanist had used the cross cuttings of a bamboo shoot and a spring mandrake. It had taken a year to grow. Apparently, the plant wife was very pretty, her entire body was an amazing shade of pale green. She needed a lot of water and the botanist kept his entire apartment filled with misters and humidifiers. It was all very high-maintenance.

"I was just on Facebook Marketplace," Aileen said, "and saw the planter was for sale."

She gestured at the living room, in which there was a new fiddle-leaf fig in a large terra-cotta pot.

It clicked for Greta. "Wait—is that—"

"No," Aileen said. "It's just the pot he used. That's a new plant I bought."

"What did he do with the plant wife?"

179

"I don't know," Aileen shrugged. "He should have known better. When you start out, they all say, don't mess with the fundamentals."

Was that a warning Greta heard in Aileen's voice, or was she imagining things?

A few moments passed, during which Aileen, inscrutable, dusted a light coating of powder off her jacket. She stood up.

"Hey," Greta finally asked, "what *are* you trying to do with all these mirrors, anyway?"

The older woman shrugged. "To see myself clearly," she said, like it was obvious. "It's so hard for anyone to see themselves clearly."

When she clambered back into the kitchen through the fire escape window, Greta heard her mutter, "Some say it takes a lifetime."

*

Another fight scene:

KEYCHAIN (*setting a plate of pasta in front of Greta*): "Janey and I are going to see that musical next Friday—"
GRETA (*not looking up from her phone*): "What musical? Why didn't you tell me?"
KEYCHAIN: "*Hadestown.* I told you about it!"
GRETA (*who had started sleeping with the acting teacher over New Year's*): "You know how I feel about Janey. And I thought we were going out to dinner that day. You know I've been wanting to go to that new restaurant."
KEYCHAIN (*hesitantly*): "You didn't tell me we were going to dinner. And I asked you if you wanted to come two weeks ago and you never answered."
GRETA: "Did you ask me? I don't remember you asking me. Besides, I made a reservation. I told you."
KEYCHAIN: "Really? I don't remember that."

GRETA (*who had not made a reservation*): "I did. But I guess now I have to cancel it because you got these tickets without me."

KEYCHAIN: "I texted you about the tickets again yesterday and you didn't reply. And we couldn't keep waiting and booked the tickets."

GRETA: "I never said I didn't want to go. But whatever. I'll do something else on Friday. It's fine. It's not like you have to get my permission."

KEYCHAIN: "Are you going to be mad at me if I go?"

GRETA: "Why would I? You're just ditching our date to go see a musical with your friend who doesn't like me and doesn't want me there."

GRETA (*looking up from her phone and suddenly noticing*): "Hey, where's that necklace? The one your mom gave you. The one I fixed the chain for."

KEYCHAIN (*surprised*): "I took it off. Are you sure the chain was pure silver? I was getting a rash."

＊

The acting teacher was hot, but a little bit boring to talk to outside of class. Still, she had a tongue like cream and was so intense in bed it made Greta dizzy. After the second time they hooked up, Greta took the C and the W from the tiny Bed-Stuy apartment the teacher shared with three others (actors, all of them), got off in Gowanus, and entered the darkroom.

She got together her things. She had tried making this device before, in different, failed iterations, but had gotten the idea of trying it as a mirror from watching Aileen. She had a framed photo of Keychain, dressed in her black coat and red muffler, standing in the botanical garden. She had a pocket mirror she'd stolen from one of

Aileen's drawers. The pocket mirror had a brass cover that clipped shut. When she cleaned the smudges off the glass, she saw a tiny little chip.

In the darkroom, she measured out silver nitrate, barium chloride, mercury, lithium, and a few drops of an inky blue acid she had gone to great and illegal lengths to obtain. She heated the mixture over a Bunsen burner. It was hot and stuffy inside the darkroom, the radiator clanging and the heat too strong. She put the framed photo into a basin with the silvery liquid.

The photo and the frame would slowly dissolve into the acid. She would come back regularly to coat and recoat the mirror with the substance. If everything worked, once the mirror was complete, Greta would be able to look into it and get a glimpse of where Keychain was, what she was doing. She'd see anything Keychain was keeping her out of. There would be no hiding.

＊

There was that weird choir singing again. Sometimes it sounded ominous, sometimes ecstatic, revelatory, and angelic. Each time, it gave her the creeps.

＊

The end of February. Practically a blizzard outside, but the darkroom was sweltering. The heat felt like a punishment, the way some punishment felt like purification. Greta laid another coat of silver over the compact mirror and watched it slowly harden. Keychain's photo had almost completely dissolved; the mirror was almost done. In the silver reflection, she could see an indistinct shadow forming, moving around—Keychain's shape?

On her way out of the darkroom, in a surge of generosity, she stopped by the chocolate shop to buy a box of truffles for Keychain.

Taking out her credit card, her fingers brushed against the little drawing Keychain had made for her in the summer (so long ago it seemed like another century). Keychain had been so sweet. For a moment, she imagined what it would be like to not make the mirror, not make the anklet, not charm the necklace chain, to not lie, not worry, not obsess. For a moment, Greta felt sorry.

"How's the photography going?" the man boxing up the truffles behind the counter asked.

"Going great," Greta said automatically. "I'm working on some exciting projects, really looking forward to seeing how they turn out."

Don't be a fool, she reminded herself. She remembered Janey's look of contempt, and the way the acting teacher had, before anything happened between them, started things off by putting a hand on Greta's wrist. There were traps all around that could take Keychain away, and then where would she be?

Free tonight? the acting teacher texted.

Greta looked at the notification and decided to reply later. She wanted, all of a sudden, to see Keychain tonight, to kiss her, rub her feet, nuzzle her sweet-smelling neck. She paid for the chocolates and left.

*

It was a bad day at work. A patient complained that Greta had scrubbed her gums too hard, and the DDS had given Greta a stern talking-to. She seethed, humiliated. She was late coming out of the dentist's office, and sleet was coming down as she slogged to the darkroom. Maybe it was time to talk to Keychain about moving in soon; that would take some of the pressure off, she thought, the going back and forth.

After leaving Gowanus, she dawdled on the way home. At the basketball court by her station, she watched three young men in sweatpants play, one of them in short sleeves despite the slush and winter. She tried to imagine spring coming, and couldn't.

It was a surprise to see Keychain's boots at the doorway when she went in. Keychain and Aileen were sitting around the kitchen table nursing mugs with Tazo tags sticking over the side. Aileen had a bunch of items spread out in front of her, a bundle of dried lilac, a cluster of beads, an old handheld bronze mirror. Keychain was still wearing her coat. She was explaining something, pointing at the fiddle-leaf fig Aileen was growing in the botanist's old planter. When had they gotten friendly? Usually the two of them only exchanged hellos.

"Hey," Greta said, putting down her bag, suspicious. "When did you get here?"

She immediately felt that Keychain's mood was off. She seemed a little distant, not meeting Greta's eyes, not standing up to hug her.

"Like twenty minutes?" Keychain said. "Not that long."

Aileen was shuffling something around on the table in her furtive, awkward way. She was humming something. The humming annoyed Greta, who was already feeling irritated, prickling for a fight, some release of tension.

"Next time can you tell me if you're here already?" Greta said brusquely, peeling off her coat and mittens and laying them on the sofa. "I would've gotten here faster. Now you're making me feel bad."

"Something happened earlier," Keychain said slowly.

"What?" Greta snapped. Aileen's humming continued, low and insistent.

"I was walking home from Prospect Park and someone was walking beside me. I think he was following me."

"Really? How do you know he wasn't just walking?" Impatiently, Greta stalked to the kitchen to boil water for her own tea.

"When I slowed down, he slowed down. When I tried to walk past him, he walked faster. He was wearing a blue hoodie, covering his face. And his hands were in his pockets."

"So then?" Greta said, looking back over her shoulder. Keychain's demeanor seemed odd. Stiff. Cold, even.

"He was muttering something under his breath," she went on. "I didn't want to get close enough to hear, but he wanted me to hear.

"And I was scared. I tried to walk faster, to run. He started jogging next to me. He muttered something like, *hotpussywanna-fucktightpinkAsianhottiewannafuckfuck—*"

"Oh my god," Greta said, putting her hands over her ears.

"And as scary as it was," Keychain said, swallowing, her tone of voice one Greta had never heard before, wobbling, nervous, but also steely and terrifying, "I realized, after I ran out of the park and got away from him, that I felt just as scared thinking about coming here and seeing you."

"What?" White noise. Greta took Keychain in in one glance—this short, slim girl with cropped hair. She wasn't wearing the necklace. Her ankle, too, was bare.

"I was just as scared thinking, about going to see you, *Is she going to be in a good mood, is she going to be in a bad mood, is she going to say something nice to me, is she going to be mean . . .*" Keychain's eyes. They were full of dignity. Had she ever looked at Greta like that before? Greta felt naked, small, furious.

"I got all my stuff together. I'm done," Keychain said.

"You're crazy," Greta managed to say. "Some guy was being creepy to you and you're taking it out on me?"

"I kept thinking, *She used to be nicer,*" Keychain whispered, as though to herself. She sighed softly, damningly.

"How dare you," Greta spat. She had time to react now, *unfair*, she was thinking, an ambush like this, also *how close*, the mirror, it was waiting in the darkroom, it was almost complete. Rage throttled her throat; rage seeped into every cavity and orifice inside her, every wrong-shaped hole of feeling. "What have I ever done—after everything—I *love* you—I give you everything—and you're embarrassing me—in front of my roommate—" Keychain was sitting just there, within arm's distance, but Greta could see her words weren't reaching her. Her girlfriend looked closed off, armored, in a way she had never seen. *Maybe*

185

you'll never be able to convince her again? an internal intuition whispered to her. *No!* her whole soul thrashed in revolt. "If you had a problem you should've talked to me about it. This is insane. You ungrateful—"

The look Keychain cast on her was incandescent. It was pity, sorrow, contempt, and awe mixed together all at once. It was the look Greta's ex had given her, at the end, right when she had dumped Greta, taken all her things, and disappeared completely, not leaving a trace.

Aileen, goddamn her, was still humming, staring at her reflection in the little mirror on the table. The sound needled under Greta's skin, which felt too tight for her feelings again, too tight for her rage. "Stop *doing* that," she yelled at Aileen, or she yelled at Keychain, she wasn't sure which. "Stop it! Stop it! Stop it! Stop it!"

Greta strode to the table, Keychain flinched, and this made Greta even more furious, because how dare she think Greta would ever lay a hand on her? How dare she? Even on her ex she had never—she would never, never—

"Shut the fuck up!" Greta howled, and Aileen reared back, startled. Greta brought her hand down, she wasn't thinking, the motion was pure instinct, Keychain was lunging forward protectively (*protective of what!*), "Calm down, everyone needs to calm down," it was her, Greta's, voice saying those words, but then there was a scream. No, it hadn't come from her own throat. And it hadn't come from Keychain, either, who stood there with a look of horror, disgust, and a little fascination. Who was this stranger, staring at her?

The scream came from Aileen. Greta felt a stinging in her hand. When she looked down, the bronze mirror Aileen had been staring into was smashed, the silver reflective surface spiderwebbed into a million cracked pieces, and when she raised her hand, a tiny shower of broken fragments sprinkled onto the table. There was blood on her palm. Aileen's pale face was drained even paler. Everyone was dead silent. With the humming gone, Greta heard, coming from outside, that awful choir again, as though they had been singing the entire time.

WE WERE THERE

We met at a summer party. What struck me first were his ankles, visible underneath the frayed hem of his jeans, which were straight-cut and unusually short. They stopped right above his anklebone. It would have looked like they were clothes he'd outgrown, except somehow, the length of these jeans seemed intentional. He also wore plain slides, a loose T-shirt, and a pink bucket hat. I didn't think him anything special at first. But his jeans, and his bare ankles, made me think of a manga I'd read when I was in high school.

It was about a boy and a girl who started dating as students, he, popular and laid-back, she, a shy new girl in town. Then the boy moved away, and though they continued their relationship long-distance, a few months later he suddenly cut off all communication with her. His disappearance was total. No one could tell her where he was.

It ended up a sad story. The boy's mother had committed suicide. He didn't tell anyone but stopped speaking to everyone he knew and started working to support himself, falling deeper into depression each year. What I remembered most were the soft-colored cover illustrations, the boy smiling and relaxed in loose clothing and sandals, cooling himself with a paper fan. His figure always receded into the background against the hot blue sky, as though to symbolize how distant he was despite that wide smile.

The story was delicate, the author didn't rely on cliff-hangers, she didn't leave you feeling desperate and jerky and somehow frustrated, as other authors did. It was a long manga, and when I had finished all the available chapters, I would wait patiently for the next ones to be released, scanned, translated, and posted online.

I hadn't thought of the manga in years, until I came to this party and was introduced to Kane. Pronounced like *kah*-neh, not like *cane*. "Nice to meet you," he said, putting out a hand. For a moment he was fully focused on me. Then his attention turned back to his conversation with the host, which I had interrupted after I'd been led into the party by the friend of a friend I'd run into earlier that day. As I was introduced to the others, Kane and the host walked out of the kitchen to the backyard, and I saw his ankles sticking out of his jeans.

The party spilled outside. There was a charcoal grill for corn, sausages, chicken. Someone had lit a green mosquito coil, which smoked quietly on the ground. Over the fence the skyline was dotted with the burnt orange of streetlights and pollution. The air had the warm, toasty smell unique to humid summers. I'd grown up in a dry state, and this smell, the first time I encountered it and ever afterward, made me think of memory, chance, and possibility.

When I became tired of the introductions and listening and small talk, I went back inside under the pretext of getting another drink. There were a few people inside, talking quietly among themselves, absorbed in changing the playlist or stacking a house of cards. A short distance from the couch there was a plastic chair next to a window that looked out to the backyard. An electric fan hummed and rotated slowly. I sat down and leaned my head back against the wall. I wiped my forehead with the back of my hand.

Neither a very long nor a particularly short time later, Kane came inside and opened the fridge. He poured himself a pink drink from a clear pitcher.

He saw me looking. "Watermelon juice?"

I was thirsty. "Sure," I said.

When he came to hand the drink over, he also pushed the window open. Behind the pane was a fly screen.

"So the fan can blow the hot air out," he explained. And I could already feel the coolness from outside.

He perched on the edge of the sofa, not very far from me, but not very close, either. He drank from his juice. I sat up straight and drank from mine. It was chill and just sweet enough.

"Luna, right?" he confirmed. "How're you doing?"

Without really thinking about it I said, "I'm pretty comfortable."

"Good." He smiled.

The door to the backyard opened and the acquaintance I'd come with poked his head inside. "It's a little wet out there," he said. "Looks like it's gonna rain."

Kane got up and followed him out. I heard his voice through the fly screen. "We better close the grill," he was saying.

The people outside started filing in. "Where's the juice?" someone said.

"Can we mix it with vodka?" someone else asked.

I held the drink to my mouth. My fingers dampened with the beads of condensation on the outside of the cup. I thought of the manga and the illustration of the boy with the fan. I could imagine Kane with a fan, lazily waving it against himself while scuffing around.

A light sprinkle had begun outside, and when I listened carefully I could distinguish the soft *thrush thrush* of the drops hitting the fly screen.

*

I liked Kane because he was so relaxed.

"I'm a casual kind of guy," he had said at the party, and it was true, he didn't seem to have a formal bone in his body. Even when, later, I saw him in more structured clothing, a jacket with lapels, close-toed boots, he still managed to give off an incredibly indolent impression, like he was always sprawled out on a picnic blanket under the shade of a tree. The harsh things of the world probably slid off him like water from a shower curtain.

When I met him, Kane was between jobs. The company he had been at for the last four years had cut his department, and he was looking for work, with no leads. But from the unhurried way he talked about it, I thought he was still taking it better than most people would; he spent his time drinking with friends, playing video games, walking around his neighborhood, tooling around on side projects while figuring out his next steps.

I started dating someone else I met at the party, a photographer named Aaron. He was good-looking in a carefully manufactured way, the dark V-neck tees and immaculate architecture of his hair always simple, but never unplanned. He worked with a lot of high-end products, had shot for brands whose expensive window displays shimmered glassily on long, skyscrapered avenues downtown. After the party he'd DMed me and asked me to ramen. After we ate we walked around and stopped at two bars before he said, "Well, my place is up the street, do you wanna see it?"

We kissed back and forth for a while and took off our clothes before he said he didn't have condoms. He didn't seem that interested in sex, which made me pleased. Then he said that he really just wanted to keep his attention on his work, he was at an important stage where his career was taking off and he didn't want anything serious.

Curled naked on his bed, not touching him, I immediately felt a tension that had been in me relax and release. Some unspoken expectation lifted, or the fear of some such expectation. Fine with me, I said. He looked unconvinced and I added that I was applying to grad school and I didn't want anything getting in the way of that.

Aaron's whole demeanor loosened and he said that was great, great, he hated it when people asked him for a lot, like his thoughts on marriage, or long-distance phone calls at certain times every day.

"Same," I agreed, "that's too much pressure," and I believed what I said. It was better this way. While we were together that night and even later, when he said things I disagreed with, or acted in ways that I found irritating, I would suppress this instinct and remind myself we were both placeholders for each other, and in this way, not be too disappointed.

Perhaps because of this relief from expectation, Aaron was, occasionally, generous toward me. He liked to have me come over to his apartment late at night, often last minute, but he would also cook for me. Sometimes he rubbed my shoulders. With him I didn't have to talk much. He was willing to fill the silence with observations or questions that weren't too demanding. I didn't find what he had to say particularly interesting, but I also didn't mind it. Such ambivalence was new to me; I either loved someone or hated them, oscillating between extremes of loyalty and apathy, I was always anxious about one interpersonal dynamic or another. But it was tiring being such a purist. It had been a long time since I had had anything close to a romantic relationship in my life, even something as open-ended as with Aaron, and I wondered what it meant, whether something in my life had opened, or I had.

A few weeks after I met him, Aaron took me to a party. A friend of his, a potter, had moved to a new studio. At the long worktable, there were all the tools for us to make something—clay, stands, newspaper, files, glazes, picks—but most people just stood around munching on olives and grapes from the cheese board and passing around cigarettes. They were connected to one another in amorphous ways: classmates, fraternities, friends of friends of friends. They were designers, social media managers, project coordinators, tech developers, but the sexy, young kind, who worked with fashion brands and 3D art installations. A lot of the people from the first party were there. We were mostly Asian, so I felt both bored and at ease, it was a space in which I could choose to speak or not to speak and it wouldn't mean anything more than it was.

Kane arrived in a white T-shirt with strange illustrations of crea-tures I couldn't identify, worn under an expensive-looking dark jacket, and his hair, which had been as long as his chin when I last saw him, was tied back in a tiny rabbit's tail. I wasn't sure if I liked it. I was also unsure whether to catch his eye, whether he remembered me.

"Kane," Aaron said, and they exchanged greetings, patting each other on the shoulders, *Hey man, it's good to see you.* I lingered behind a little awkwardly, a lost duckling.

Aaron indicated me. "You remember Luna, from that party," he said.

"Hi," I said.

"Still doing good?" Kane asked cheerfully.

"Pretty good," I told him. "What are those drawings on your shirt?"

"Oh, they're like weird fruit."

I looked at them more closely. They were drawings of hairy, anthropomorphic fruit, such as a pear with chicken legs and covered with bristles.

"It was a concept for an advertisement that didn't get picked." He crooked his mouth. "But I still liked it."

"You drew this?"

"A long time ago."

Aaron brought over the host, who had a pixie cut and white overalls that showed off her slim arms and long body. I looked at her admiringly. The overhead lights were industrial in design and cast a yellow glow. Later the conversation turned to China. The host had just returned from a pottery workshop there; although there were many Asian people at this party, only Kane and I were Chinese. The host and Kane spoke more and more forcefully, and Aaron and I stood silent. I was unsure whether this was an argument, what emo-tions were at stake.

"People say there's all this bad shit happening there now," Kane said, "like, the government control, the censorship, the lack of privacy . . ."

"The human rights violations, the fake baby formula, the people getting arrested . . ." the host said.

"Right," he agreed. "And I get it. But I don't like hearing it. Somehow the East is always the bad guy. It never gets to tell its own story."

I nodded along. I didn't like to talk about being Chinese or Chinese American, I felt it was safer to keep my experiences to myself, unvoiced, and yet everything he said, I felt, had a point. *So he can be like this, too,* I thought.

The argument ended with a laugh, the host disappeared to get a drink. I wandered to where Kane sat at the far end of the table. He started trimming the block of clay with a wire.

I stood close to the edge of the table. "I didn't know you knew how to do pottery."

"I don't," he said. I watched him wet his fingers in a bowl of water, then shape the clay with his palms, deftly molding it into a ball. His hands were quickly covered in gray sludge. He plunged his hands into the clay and sank his fingers deep, with what looked like a very satisfying squelch. He glanced up at me and I felt the pleasurable shock of his casual attention. "Kids play with mud all the time, don't they? I'm just playing."

Something took flight in me with a wrenching sweetness. Like the feeling I got when I listened to a certain type of music when I was alone. It reverberated in a place that was hollow.

I watched him dig his fingers into the clay, feeling completely dislocated from myself.

*

At the time, I felt like I was living underwater. My surroundings, my daily life, felt unreal to me, it was as though everything traveled to me slowly, the way sound travels more slowly in the ocean. When emotions hit me, they did so with completely unexpected force and

I would be astonished, more so because I had previously thought of myself as someone very in touch with my feelings.

After college, I'd lived in China for a year and then moved back to New York. What I told Aaron—that I was applying to grad school—was a lie, but it could have been true. I had even bought a book of standardized test practice questions. I had a plethora of side projects—studying languages, French, Japanese, Spanish, or the evening classes I took in figure drawing, trapeze, guitar. I wasn't comfortable with aimless time, I always felt I had to be doing something to improve myself, though this constant reeducation was expensive and I only barely supported myself on a series of temp jobs I worked while hopping from hobby to hobby, skill to skill.

At my current job, I documented protocols and benchmarks for processes I didn't understand and products I didn't see. I spent a lot of time on calls with vendors and clients asking for status updates and whether it was *realistic that this deadline would be met*. I worked in a big, glassy building with an enormous fish tank embedded in a wall in the reception area, through which long fins of red, gold, and white flickered between undulating sea plants. I would look at the fish and imagine I was inside the tank, insulated from the reality around me through thick glass and water made a deep blue by the artificial backlight.

There was a gym on the seventh floor of the building, and very late in the evenings, when everyone had left, I would churn on the elliptical playing old albums over and over through my headphones. Afterward, if I was in a particularly solitary mood, I walked home, across a bridge chugging with car exhaust over invisible water and then into the tangle of quiet, tree-lined streets in the exquisite dark.

The most consistent endeavor in my life was the clothes I made, a whole wardrobe of patched jeans and shirts cut into strange, geometric shapes. I wasn't really a designer, more of a salvager; I salvaged everything I could from clothes people were throwing away, clothes I didn't wear anymore, thrift store finds, items covertly stolen from lost and founds. I had a mannequin I'd found on the sidewalk in Clinton Hill, and it was the host to a constant parade of changing outfits, animal-print blouses cut into bralettes, turtlenecks studded with grommets, a denim skirt with so many cutouts sewn onto it you couldn't see the denim anymore. The only bare part was the head, a blank white egg, which I had never covered with a wig or a hat.

Eventually, I thought, I would do something big, have an exhibit, costume a film—but the fact that I had come this many years from graduation and had not accomplished anything large, observable, or concrete was an uncomfortable weight. Sometimes I thought I should get a real—that is to say, adult—job. I vaguely imagined saving up and moving, out of this city, out of this country, to somewhere where I wasn't known, though I couldn't even say that I was known here. Most of my college friends had moved out of New York over the last few years, taken by new jobs, new partners, PhD programs, med school, the sunlight of the West Coast, until I was the only one left. I spent a lot of my time on the phone, my voice traveling across wires and airwaves to the ears of friends in other rooms late at night, their lamps glowing through other windows overlooking other dark streets. We were all in some ways lonely, all dissatisfied, but I felt I was the most lonely and the most dissatisfied.

Earlier in the year, I had convinced myself to go on more dates because I thought I should be more proactive, meet more people, change my life. On my way to my third first date in two weeks, Melissa, who was living with her boyfriend in Wisconsin, texted me a photo from our final year at Barnard. We'd made a double-chocolate cake with bourbon frosting and written *fuck it* in icing. In the photo I was wearing a yellow-and-blue shirt, setting candles over the cake, and smiling. Eileen, wearing glasses, was clapping her hands in the background. On the ground beside me was the blue recycling bin into which all of us had dumped the old drafts of our theses, at the time convinced they were the most important things we had done up until then.

Youthful follies, lol, Melissa texted.

I couldn't remember what I had done with that shirt. I started crying on the sidewalk a block away from the café. I wasn't sure which terrified me more: the thought that this was all there was—this limpid transience like I was being carried along from stream to stream, that it would never matter if I did something or didn't—or the thought that this was not all there was to life, but that I was missing something fundamental other people had—drive, vision, intelligence, something—which was the cause of my chronic inability to stick with anything real. Either option felt impossibly consequential.

After a minute I wiped my eyes and took a few breaths, went into the café bathroom to wash my face, and had my date. It was fine and led to nothing.

My parents still lived in a house near a canyon in Long Beach with a view dotted with agave. They never visited me. My father spent most of his time at work and my mother spent her days alone, gardening. Whenever I FaceTimed home, I thought I could see more lines on her face. In photos from her youth she was beautiful, with large, bright eyes and impossible cheekbones. Now her conversations were more fretful and she was growing more and more paranoid about the outside world. This made me sad and my calls home even more infrequent.

＊

Late in the summer, I ran into Kane at the laundromat in Prospect Lefferts Gardens. I say I ran into him, but through some sly sleuthing I already knew that he lived in my neighborhood, as well as other facts: he was a graphic designer, he had graduated from one of the best art colleges in the nation, one animated short he'd made had won a prize.

I had moved to PLG that spring. It was a coincidence that we were in the same neighborhood: as with jobs, I couldn't stay long at any one apartment, and had found a tiny sublet with a roommate who was never home. When I found out Kane lived there, too, I thought it might be a sign of some kind of cosmic fate, though really it was a popular neighborhood, one or two other acquaintances also lived here, including the one who had brought me to that first party. I began to spend more time outside of the house than I normally would have, walking in the park, lingering in the grocery store, peering into ice-cream shops and restaurants and wondering where he might be.

My laundry was spinning in the dryer and I was reading a book when he came in. He was wearing the same pink bucket hat from that first party, the same slides.

My first instinct was to turn and hide, but instead I caught his attention and said hello, forcing brightness into my voice.

He seemed to take this in stride. "Hey, cool. You live around here, too?" He sat on the chair next to me.

"How's the job hunt?" I asked him. He shrugged the topic off, started talking about an idea for a webcomic he had instead, involving aliens at church. He showed me a sketch or two on his phone. The characters were round, with flailing hands, they seemed constantly anxious; they were, frankly, adorable. The machine in front of us sudsed and tumbled. Clothes flicked by in whorls of color, white, gray, sky blue, pale pink. He shifted his weight, crossed and uncrossed his legs.

"I was thinking about what you said at that other party," I said quickly. It was true, but I also wanted him to know it. "When we were talking about China."

"Yeah? I was wondering what you thought."

While we talked I found out our fathers were both from Anhui, from the same hometown. It was a city I recalled from long childhood summers, the freeways, the blistering heat, the view of Huangshan, walking to the department stores at night with my aunts, the umbrellas they held over my head to protect me from sun. Perhaps it had worked because, even after, my skin remained very fair. It gave me an odd feeling to think that the summers I had spent lying in front of the air conditioner or feeding goldfish at the local park, he might have been somewhere in that city, too.

"And another thing," he added. He wasn't looking at me anymore but spoke intently, focused somewhere inward, beyond. "When people from the mainland say, 'Well, you grew up in America, you don't think like a Chinese.' I hate that. My memories of China are so personal, you know? It's always going to be the place that could have been for me. All those months I spent there, they add up to years, to a life I could have lived. The part of my identity, my self, that belongs there, or could have belonged there."

"Yes, exactly," I said, and in my heart I repeated it, *yes, exactly,* while a feeling of longing suffused me, while I smoothed my thumb over the cover of the book I'd closed, while the laundry machines whirred and the warm baby smell of dryer sheets thickened in the air.

*

"You're hard to get ahold of lately," Aaron said. He stood at his kitchen island, cutting open a grapefruit. Behind him eggs were frying in a pan on the stove.

"Am I?" It was a warm Saturday. I sat at his kitchen table in pajama shorts, drinking instant coffee, flipping through a fashion magazine I'd bought at the bodega before he woke up. He had a beautiful kitchen with a long, polished wooden table—perfect for working—plants in the corners, art on the walls, big windows. Signs of his maturity, his early success, even though he was my age.

"Are you busy studying?" he asked, and by the line of his neck I could tell he was annoyed. I had been saying no more often when he wanted to "hang out," which had started to mean making out and a cursory blow job from me, and last night I had almost said no when he called me at 11:00 p.m., but perhaps I was the one who was generous now, because then I felt sorry for him and said yes.

"Studying for what?" I asked. One page in the magazine announced a collaboration between a popular comics artist and a leisurewear company. They'd be printing the characters on T-shirts, leggings, workout tops. I thought of Kane's little aliens.

"When are you taking the GRE again?"

"Oh, I'm not taking it anymore." The toaster oven dinged.

"What? When did that change?" Aaron set a plate in front of me with the halved grapefruit, fried egg, two slices of toast. "Here." He twisted open a jar of orange jam.

I put the magazine away, picked up my spoon, and dug into the grapefruit. "I'm applying to schools in London. You don't need the GRE for that."

"You're going to London?" Aaron looked—as well he might—surprised. His hair was undone and he was wearing the same T-shirt from yesterday, plucked off the ground.

I felt very warm toward him, in his kitchen that morning. It had been so easy to lie. He liked me because I didn't hold him to anything, and now, I thought, I'd surprised him with my coolness.

*

"How're you doing?"

At the end of September, Kane had a party at his apartment. The invitation came through Aaron; I still didn't have Kane's number.

The last time I'd seen Kane, he was coming out of the grocery store, but he hadn't seen me and I hesitated to call out to him. Alone, his expression had been preoccupied, remote.

I wore my favorite skirt to his party, given to me by a friend who'd bought it in Vietnam. She'd described the lovely lantern-covered town, a minor stop on the old Silk Road, still full of tailors and swaths of bright colors. The skirt was dark blue and short.

"Hey, freaky," Aaron had said when he came into my room. He had never been to my apartment before. He meant the mannequin, dressed in a blue velvet dress with a vest of colored ruffles.

He sat on my bed. I pulled out a compact and swept iridescent blush onto my cheeks. While I had my back turned to him, he observed, "Nice skirt. Your roommate's out? We can come back to your place after."

Instead of responding, I walked out of the apartment ahead of him, toting a bag with the six-pack of beer and the silver packages of cream-filled wafers I'd bought. I thought Kane would like them. My grandparents had bought them for me every summer I visited them, and though I hadn't eaten them in years, when I'd seen them at the Chinese grocery store with their silver wrapping and tacky font, I recalled all the old pleasure of eating them in front of the television. At the same grocery store I had bought a box of red bean ice lollies, slightly creamy, barely sweet, which I ate in my living room, thinking again of Kane, because he made me think of my childhood, which I knew was dangerous.

It was a cool evening, and outside on the sidewalk, the air was gray and soft, only a whisper of moistness visible in the stillness of the trees.

His apartment was a one-bedroom, the living room filled with a large drafting table, a shelf of art books, and a deep-green sofa so brilliant it seemed to absorb all the other colors in the room. I walked around examining the objects with pleasure—the magazines carefully shelved in order of date, the messy kitchen with the blue-and-white kettle, a braided red good fortune hanging plastered to the back of a door. I put the beer in the fridge, carefully opened the package of wafers, and spaced them out in even piles on the counter.

I had nodded at Kane when I entered. He saw me looking at the books on his shelf. I imagined us circling around each other like the two fish I had watched in the tank at work the day before, one with a white ruffle along its upper fin and the other red and white. For the first hour, I moved through the party, speaking to acquaintances, listening in on conversations, following Kane with a sixth sense, a warm spot I intuited moving behind me like a current on a thermal map.

I wandered outside, where he was sitting with two girls on his stoop; the girls were passing a cigarette back and forth, speaking to each other in the intimate way of longtime couples. One of them was the host with the pixie cut from the pottery studio. Kane was off to the side, smoking his own cigarette, blowing little streams into the air. I asked how he was.

One of the girls smiled at me and offered a cigarette.

"You don't have to," Kane said with a quick gesture to me.

"I'll take it," I said, pleased at his protectiveness. I had not smoked in a long time. I double-checked I was putting the right end in my mouth, held it tremblingly, and inhaled as the pottery girl half cupped my hand and lit it. She and her girlfriend were watchful, like the stone dogs you see outside of shrines.

Sitting on the stoop next to Kane, I exhaled. The sky was smoggy that night, the air was full of pollen, the temperatures cool. Summer was really ending.

"How's your comic going?" I asked him.

"Oh, it's good," he said easily. "People like them online."

"I'd love to read them."

"Yeah? I'll send you the link," he said. I didn't ask how.

"I brought some cookies, you should try them."

"Really? Thank you."

"They're those coconut wafers you get at Chinese markets, you know the ones?"

"Oh—hmm? Maybe, I guess I'll see."

He wasn't looking at me. I said quickly, "I'm going to quit my job soon."

"Yeah?"

"I want to move to London and make clothes."

"That's big for you."

"Did you make your own T-shirt, that last time I saw you at the party?"

"A friend printed it for me."

He was bored, I couldn't tell how to activate his interest in me, that hot bright spark I had felt only a few times before, when we shared the watermelon juice, when he'd spoken to me in the pottery studio. The conversation was going nowhere. Or, it wasn't going where I wanted it to.

"I'm going to grab a drink," Kane said. He got up. I followed him inside, to the fridge, where he courteously, impersonally, gave me a bottle of beer, from the six-pack I had brought. I drank it by myself, frustrated. Aaron came up and I brushed him off.

In Kane's bedroom, a girl was drunk. The lights were dim and an external monitor was playing an animated video. I remembered the girl from the pottery studio party, a UX designer. "I've done a lot of work on myself," she said, slurring. "Now I tell my boyfriend exactly what I want. Can you believe he had lunch with his ex without telling me the other day—"

Kane sat apart from her. "Listen," he said earnestly, "for guys like me, that makes things harder."

I sat down gingerly on her other side. His bedspread was a paler shade of the absorbent green of his sofa. Whatever he was, Kane had good taste. The closet door, a third of the way open, showed a patch of pink. The hat he'd worn at the beginning of summer. The girl's head suddenly lolled onto my shoulder, a warm, human weight.

"You agree with me, don't you?" she implored, looking at me.

"I agree," I agreed.

"Hey, where have you been all night?" Aaron appeared again, his weight sinking down on the bed next to me as he wrapped a possessive hand around my hip. I flinched, trying to shrug him off. But he kept his hand there, even moved his thumb to caress the curve of the back of my skirt. He rarely touched me like that.

I tried to laugh it off. "What are you doing?"

"That's what I should be asking you. You've been dancing around all evening."

His hand was stubbornly attached to my butt. "Come on, let's go back to your place."

"Stop it." I refused to say his name out loud.

Aaron reeled back. Not so drunk as all that, he was clearly angry. "Hey, let's be clear here. You're the one who wanted me to bring you, I wasn't even originally planning to come, and now you . . ."

How annoying, how embarrassing. We'd put boundaries on our feelings from day one. It had been agreed, I thought, that we would only be passing through each other's lives. I thought he would have vanished by now, as everyone did. It was the end of summer, why was he still stubbornly here?

The UX designer's head was heavy. I looked at Kane. He was looking at the animation playing on the monitor, pretending not to know anything was going on between Aaron and me. Lost in his own world, as usual.

The girl groaned. Her mouth was closed, her beautiful neck clammy.

"Oh god," Kane said.

"She needs water." Me.

"What a mess." Aaron.

"Get her to the bathroom," I ordered, looking directly at Kane. Perhaps it was the first time I had looked at him head-on.

His face showed he didn't want to. But he gestured to Aaron, the two of them gathered the girl up between themselves and hauled her through the door to the bathroom. I was left almost alone with the cool green bedspread. White light spilled out from the bathroom, and retching sounds that made it all too easy to imagine what was going on. I heard Kane's voice, clear, melodic, slow.

I sensed how unreliable he was, how passive. I knew he was not interested in me, only in my reflection of him, and for this I suddenly hated him a little. Even so I wanted to fasten on to that fleeting, ungraspable quality in him, his flippancy, his airiness, his ability to shake off consequences. In the manga he reminded me of, there had been immeasurable distance between the girl and her vanished high school boyfriend, but years and years later, after all the loneliness and loss and pain, they reunited, they were able to return to the summer of their youths, before so much pain intruded.

I wanted Kane to turn back and look at me. One real look and I would tell him everything: about my sealed-off parents, the silent fish tank, my solitary walks, the endless years. I couldn't help it. Even though I knew it was dangerous to take such feelings as signs, even though I knew that this breathless, gut-hollowing feeling of yearning didn't mean he would not be hurtful, or neglectful, or unkind, I couldn't forget the feeling I had had watching him dig his fingers into the clay and the smell of dryer sheets in the laundromat. These are the feelings of someone at sixteen, or eighteen, or even twenty-three, and I wish I could say I was that young, but I was twenty-six, and by that age we have already seen more of the world, it's not so young as all that.

The closet door gaped open, near the bed, near my hand. Quickly, before I thought too hard about it, I reached inside and pulled out the pink bucket hat.

I could put it on the cold head of my mannequin. The pink would go well with the blue dress.

I could wear it myself in London. Bobbing along on cobbled streets.

While Aaron and Kane stood in the bathroom, I stuffed the hat quickly into my bag. It crumpled easily, sliding in like a wadded tissue. I left the party without saying goodbye. Outside, the two girls were still sitting on the stoop, cigarette butts dotting the step. They nodded to me as I walked away, out of that summer, clutching my prize, their eyes glimmering behind me like the eyes of coyotes in the canyons at night.

MESSAGES

FROM EARTH

Early on in her life, Luna had received the indelible message that life was uncertain and not to be trusted. No one said this to her outright; she didn't find it written anywhere. Still, she understood the communication, the way a spy understands the radio signals that might otherwise be a series of cheerful, even musical beeps, in which can be read the direst warnings.

Luna's radio signals were small events that went unexplained and unremarked on, like, for instance, that quiet morning, winter vacation of fifth grade in elementary school, when she came downstairs to find her father sitting on the couch, in the ratty T-shirt from some anticonvulsant manufacturer and the basketball shorts he slept in. He was drinking coffee and reading the paper as though he'd been up for a long time. The next morning she came downstairs (and where *was* her mother, who was usually up first, during those 7:00 a.m. descents?) to find her father there again, as though he had been there all night, as though he had never left downstairs; and the two days became three, became a week, became two, her father always sitting on the couch in the morning as though he had spent the night there, though family dinners and pickups from school continued in wholly ordinary fashion. And then one day, she woke up and came down and he was suddenly not on the couch anymore.

Perhaps her intuition developed from observing that things were not, quite, as happy as they should be—though—*should* things be happy? It seemed to Luna that happiness was around her, in the colorful stars teachers drew on the corners of papers, in movies with red-haired mermaids with button noses, in photographs taken of students standing shoulder to shoulder, holding balloons, smiling. Yet she couldn't be sure that her parents were overly interested in happiness. Birthdays, for instance: Why did they pass so unnoticed, unmarked? For their family there was no cake, no ribbons, maybe an extra meat dish at dinner, but that was all. And what was meat, after all? It was easy to get, here in America, while her parents told her more than once that it had been a rarity, in their childhoods, to have pork. But it wasn't like meat was the point of it all. But then what *was* the point?

So out of a fundamental sense of the precarity of living, Luna looked for differences between the surfaces of things and their undersides. She was like Nancy Drew, collecting clues. Or, no—she was a huntress. Like Artemis, goddess of the moon, who was her favorite goddess. There was the connection between Artemis and her own name, too, Luna, like *lunar* (though, when she asked her parents, they said: "We picked your name because it was a harvest moon on the night you were born").

Luna clung on to the reality of objects, scratching memos of her daily activities into piles of notebooks and hoarding tchotchkes picked up at grocery stores. She hunted for the difference between things that were said and truths that were silently understood, and as for happiness, she understood she must hide it somewhere secret when she found it, lest she not know where to find it again.

*

Some objects collected from her childhood:
— a ten-book set of yellow *Nancy Drew* hardcovers
— purple fountain grass from the cracked trail of the canyon
— a poster of a harvest moon, photo taken by NASA

*

The day Andrew W. McGann put his hand up her shirt for the first time, Luna came home and went straight up to her bedroom, and her mother came in and said she wanted to talk. Immediately Luna felt her heartbeat speed up and she crossed her legs and leaned back against her pillows in what she hoped was a natural-looking position. Her mother dawdled at the threshold, as though uncertain of her own authority; as if this were not a house she had paid for, as if this were a stranger and not her own daughter.

"Vicky is going with you to Shanghai this summer," she said finally.

"What? Why?"

She hadn't seen Vicky in over a year. The last time they'd spoken was a phone call on Christmas, when the families were together but not, for another reason that went unexplained, her cousin. On the phone Vicky had said she was dating someone, and very busy with work.

"We think it'll be good for her to just spend some time away. With you, with family." Her mother spoke vaguely.

"But Vicky's from Harbin."

"She's not close with anyone there, you know she hasn't been back since she was born. It'll be better if she's with you."

"Is she okay?" Luna asked, keeping her tone carefully light and casual. She knew when not to ask for secrets.

"Your aunt is very upset," her mother said. "You two are a different generation. Now that Vicky's an adult, sometimes she does things your aunt doesn't agree with . . ."

But how could that be possible? Vicky was the good one. Where Luna navigated through the world uneasily, groping for obstacles she suspected were in her way, Vicky intuitively grasped how the world worked. Put another way, if Luna experienced life as a maze, Vicky was jogging easily down a straight, well-paved road.

Vicky was not, as many people assumed, actually related to her. On the plane from Shanghai on that first flight to America, their parents had sat across the aisle from one another. Luna's parents had two suitcases and a cord-bound box in cargo, two hundred dollars in cash, a job offer for her father from the Center for Drug Discovery Innovation in San Diego, and the name of someone they could stay with while they got settled. Vicky's parents were hardly better off. The whole long flight the two Chinese couples were silent, each body tense or numb in its own way.

When the plane touched down at LAX, Luna's father reached into the overhead compartment and knocked a duffel bag askew. It half dropped onto the shoulder of the man standing next to him. Her father apologized profusely, slipping into *bu hao yi si*. The other man responded in the same tongue, and the two couples talked as they walked out of the plane and into the terminal, a relieved babble.

Vicky's father insisted on treating all four of them to something— McDonald's. Luna's father knew that even the four dollars it cost to get four burgers was too much, but Vicky's father's pride won out, and he even added two apple pies into the mix. Luna's mother slipped the money (the currency still unfamiliar, so she had to go to the bathroom to count it out, a five and a one, leaving them with $194) into the outer flap of Vicky's mother's purse, who pretended not to notice. So their first encounter in the new country was with a familiar hand, possessed of the rituals of their native one. Her parents grasped at it.

When Vicky was born, Luna's parents dropped in with babysitting help and caretaking duties. Five years later, when Luna came, Vicky's parents returned the favor. In this co-parenting life the children grew up calling each other's parents aunt and uncle.

And Vicky was a filial child. She was the oldest, and had done everything first: mastering English, going to school, learning to drive. She knew how to get the best groceries for cheap, how to fix computers, which products were useful and which were just marketed well. She knew how to mix Gatorade with ginger ale when people were sick, and brought Luna hot milk with honey when her stomach hurt. She could sing and play "Fly Me to the Moon" on the guitar; she was a certified lifeguard and captain of the swim team. While Luna was dreamy, clumsy, too quiet, and too lost in manga and novels, Vicky washed dishes, chopped vegetables, took the car to the shop. She was personable, reliable, and never complained. For this she was gifted with that most approving of Chinese epithets: she "understood things."

*

That Vicky had so much knowledge of the way things worked, so much confidence in her ability to discern what was right and proper, was something Luna was deeply envious of. She herself was so uncertain, she sometimes questioned the very ground she stood on. In the sixth grade, Luna had met Marilyn, blue-eyed and intense. "God sees everything we do," Marilyn explained. "When we die he judges us and decides if we go to heaven or"—she pointed at the ground—"down there."

"What's down there?" Luna crossed her legs nervously.

"It's bad to say the word." Marilyn spelled it out. "*H - E -* double *L.*"

This was a word Luna had heard before, but she had never appreciated the full context of its horror. That night she lay awake thinking of her sins and feeling her soul clench in fear. There was no time to lose; tomorrow was not guaranteed. She scrunched her eyes together, clasped her hands, and prayed, in one long mumble, "Now I lay me down to sleep, I pray the Lord my soul to keep," hoping she was doing it right. Why did Marilyn know these things? How come no one had told Luna? *What would have happened to her if no one had?*

In the summers, Luna's parents sent her on her annual pilgrimage to China. She stayed with one set of grandparents in Anhui, then the other set in Shanghai, braving customs alone with a suitcase stuffed with Costco multivitamins. In Shanghai, she would sleep with her grandmother on a pullout in their small apartment. Every day, after lunch, her grandmother would say, "Aren't you tired? Go lie down." And if Luna had shown the slightest resistance, if she had said she wanted to read, or walk around, or eat candy, or watch TV, her grandmother would have simply been not angry, but astonished. After her nap, she would be escorted to restaurants and department stores. Her Mandarin was dubious; she never responded when spoken to. She was ever shyer than she was in America.

The summer after Marilyn, Luna started reading *Little Women*, which she bought in the English section of a Shanghai bookstore, and got to the episode where Amy almost drowns and Jo is filled with regret. The night before she was to fly home to California, Luna lay on the pullout with an awful sense of guilt that arose from nowhere. Life, she sensed quite clearly, was unknowable and the future full of dreadful possibilities.

In the cramped, hot room, she screwed up her courage. "Grandma, I love you," she whispered in Mandarin in the dark. Her grandmother stirred and said, "Oh, good," and Luna fell asleep with her heart beating more peacefully. At their farewell lunch the next day she heard her grandmother telling the other adults, gleefully, what Luna had said during the night—her grandmother, and the relatives listening, laughed. At the airport she asked her grandmother why they'd laughed, trying to sound as unhurt as possible. The reply was that no one ever just *said* that to their family members. How was she supposed to know?

*

— a branch with dried purple flowers from the jacaranda tree outside the front door

— a copy of *Little Women* with 小妇人 printed below it, on a cover that looked slightly off, like the Walmart version of an expensive shoe

— a purple Tamagotchi without batteries

＊

The years continued to pass, but did not clarify themselves. Vicky's father was transferred to a job in New Mexico, into a bachelor-like existence in a low one-story house where the sunset bathed the desert plants out back red every night. Vicky got a swimming scholarship and went to SF State. Luna's parents moved them to a bigger house in Long Beach and Luna started high school. Now alone, Vicky's mother started fostering dogs, and brought them over sometimes, each time a different dog, along with news of Vicky's life, which came down like echoes through the deep ocean. Luna's parents started sleeping in separate bedrooms, but still they all ate dinner together without mentioning it.

Then it was summer—a summer that was supposed to be significant. The summer after Luna's last year of high school. The summer of unfettered freedom, no studying, no volunteering, no worrying, complete license on the cusp of her transformation to adulthood, which would take place that fall when she flew to New York to start at Barnard. She might study English literature. Or maybe psychology. Maybe even cinema studies.

There was the hot walk across the football field, tossing the hats with the tassels in the air, photographs taken of her with curled hair. In the graduation photos, she stood on the other side from Dake, her partner-in-failure all the way from Algebra II to AP Calc, whom she hadn't spoken to since an unfortunate kiss at prom. The seven friends standing in between them pretended they knew nothing.

And then there was Andrew.

Andrew W. McGann, who had been in her AP English Lit class all year but who had never spoken to her. Who drove a black pickup with fat speakers loaded on the back playing thumping music she never recognized. Who was thin and white, with a pleasingly untidy nest of light brown hair, who had pale eyes and a stern and unsmiling face and a clear voice that could convince you, or at least Luna, of anything. A week after prom, she was walking across the parking lot by herself, alone, feeling sad and confused and excited and a little abandoned, all at once. And maybe it was the new skirt she was wearing, or maybe the essay her English teacher had praised in front of the class that day, or something she wasn't aware of in her own expression, but Andrew called out to her.

"Luna," he said, like he was already used to saying it. "Want a smoke?" He offered her a stick from a blue-and-white box labeled *Parliament*. She watched him inhale first, and tried to copy his motions.

And so in between packing up her room and clearing out old trinkets for Goodwill, Luna listened to Andrew talk. She'd meet him at a smoothie shop a mile away from the high school, where she'd find him in the driver's seat of his black pickup with the windows down (the air conditioner didn't work), or go back to his room in the two-bedroom apartment where he lived with only his mother, who was never there. Andrew had much to say. He talked about more writers she didn't know: Thomas Pynchon, Don DeLillo, Bret Easton Ellis. When he got on the subject of movies he'd name drop David Lynch, Terrence Malick, Quentin Tarantino. "What? How do you not know Lynch?" he'd said one time when she innocently let slip her lack of knowledge. "He shows that film doesn't have to rely on structure or dialogue," he raved. "People talk about *Twin Peaks* a lot, but personally I think *Eraserhead* is one of his strongest works. He's such a visionary. He doesn't just see convention but what's possible."

Luna listened to him hungrily, wanting to get something—an answer, an experience, some knowledge, a way to cut to the heart underneath the surface of things. But the more Andrew talked, the more she felt the vast conspiracy of the world around her, keeping her in the dark and enlightening others. This was the problem, wasn't it? There were so many things she didn't know, but for whatever reason, other people did. They—the people that Andrew W. McGann represented—were intelligent, worldly, and, above all, dangerous. Not dangerous in a violent or even intentional way. But with a single comment they could puncture potentially any thought that she, on her foundation of vast ignorance, might formulate. For they knew things she did not, and she didn't know where the end to her unknowing was.

Finally, the day after graduation, while they were hanging out in his Jeep, Andrew lackadaisically, even absentmindedly, kissed her; he put a hand under her shirt, his cold tongue had flicked into her mouth, and then, for some inexplicable reason, he stopped.

*

— a dark green AP Art History textbook, pencil marks smudged and erased
— an empty Parliament cigarette carton, pressed flat and mounted on white card stock
— a guide to parenting difficult teens, still shrink-wrapped, unopened, found in her parents' closet

*

At LAX, Luna was startled to see how much Vicky had changed. She'd cut her hair short, above her ears, and swapped her wire glasses for contacts. She wore a loose gray hoodie; her calves, poking out of board shorts, were muscled and tan. Still, there was an air of weariness to her, of—Luna searched for the words—slovenliness, neglect. One of the first things Vicky did was call her "cuz," as in, "Hey, cuz," when she leaned down to hug her, a slang term that sounded strange coming from her mouth. "It's been ages. I haven't congratulated you on Barnard yet."

Luna raised her hands up just a second too late.

On the twelve-hour flight to Shanghai, and on the drive from PVG airport after, Luna held herself tightly, afraid she'd come across as strange. Vicky slept, and Luna darted looks at her, feeling shy, wondering who this person, this unknown older girl, her not-cousin cousin, was.

Finally, when they arrived at her grandmother's place, Luna left Vicky on the couch and retreated to the room with the pullout. After lying there for a long time, she couldn't fall asleep, so she turned on the lamp and pulled out a book Andrew had told her to read before she left: Don DeLillo's *Underworld*. She opened to the first page.

He speaks in your voice, American, and there's a shine in his eye that's halfway hopeful. She read the sentence over again. It was a good sentence; it was promising.

But as she turned the pages, the old gnawing, anxious feeling started blooming in her chest again. The whole world of the baseball game, the ticket vendors, the turnstiles, the slang, these, like the new Vicky, passed across her eyes and gave her nothing familiar to grab on to. She couldn't even think whether or not she was enjoying the book, only that she could not formulate any thoughts on it. Why not? Was she stupid?

Luna closed the book, put it on the desk, and looked at the cabinet next to the bed: a beautiful vintage bookshelf, cherry wood with glass panes in the doors. There were old white paperbacks with yellowing spines that her grandfather had written the titles on in shaky, spidery writing. He'd been born to a family later labeled bourgeois. He feared the Communist Party and loved everything Western: Hollywood movies and Häagen-Dazs ice cream and books like *Gone with the Wind*, which Luna had read one summer because it was on this shelf, a bilingual copy with the English in the left column and the Chinese on the right. She'd read *Tess of the D'Urbervilles* and *Rebecca* for the same reason. Luna paged through those old books, feeling comforted by the clean, crisp, scholarly typesetting of the English. On the bottom shelf of the cabinet there were framed photos. Her parents on a date thirty years ago, hands tentatively touching each other like they were actually in love; baby photos of her; a picture from Disney World, Vicky lifting her up onto her shoulders.

She passed her finger lightly over the other books in the cabinet. Those had Chinese titles, characters of which she recognized only a few. One slim volume had the word for *sky*, or *heaven*, and a few characters later, the one everyone knew, *love*. Luna opened to the first page and tried to read the first paragraph. *Zhang something something leaving his office something something.*

She smoothed her palm over the thin paper. Then she put all the books back and turned off the light.

*

On their third day in Shanghai, instead of napping after lunch, she and Vicky went out alone. Shockingly, Vicky had simply said, "I'm not tired, can Luna and I go out instead?"

When her grandmother didn't want to let them go, Vicky turned on her eldest daughter voice. "Nainai," she said sweetly, "I'll take good care of Luna. We won't be home late. We'll stay in the public spaces. And we'll carry our bags like this." She put her backpack over her stomach, and though Luna's grandma clicked her tongue, she had to laugh—and let them leave.

Shanghai had become more pleasant to visit over the years. Rapidly, astonishingly, almost overnight, Luna had seen the buildings become cleaner, apartment complexes mushroom up, nicer cars fill the streets. Piss puddles on the public stairs vanished, along with the children who used to tug on passersby's sleeves and even grab their legs, asking for money. The subways were fast and punctual, with huge glass barriers over the tracks. The bathrooms were cleaner. Some had Western-style toilets. And some, at the nicest places, even had toilet paper.

They spent the first hours sightseeing, Vicky pointing out milk tea and *jianbing* and rice cake stalls with the joy of a tourist. When they ordered, Luna spoke in short syllables, hoping the staff wouldn't catch their foreignness. Vicky had no such compunctions. When she didn't know a word in Mandarin she gestured, or sounded out English words slowly, and the waiters and shop assistants would loosen up and smile, asking them where they were from, making oohing noises at the mention of California.

"Vicky, they're going to cheat us if they know we're American," Luna hissed.

"Chill out," Vicky said. "Why does it matter? It's just a couple of bucks."

They ended up near the sweeping, futuristic glass concoction of the Science and Technology Museum. As evening fell they found a small restaurant on the street and ordered noodles, sitting at a folding table on the edge of the street. It had been hot and muggy all day, and the spicy noodles broke Luna out in more sweat.

Vicky was the one who ordered the two green bottles of Tsingtao. "Cheers," she said, clinking her bottle with Luna's. "My first drink with my cousin."

She polished off two bottles while Luna nursed one. The afternoon noise faded into evening bustle. Gradually, hesitantly, under Vicky's relaxed questions, Luna told her the news of her own life.

"This Andrew guy sounds like a real tool." Vicky rolled her eyes. "Who cares if you don't know all the stuff he knows?"

"But I *want* to know all the stuff he knows."

"What's the point? You know stuff *he* doesn't know, either. Like, you think he's ever been here?" She gestured broadly around her. "You think he knows what pig's blood tastes like?"

"Yeah, but no one *cares* about pig's blood."

"Trust me, pig's blood is way more interesting than—whatever he's telling you. What, Lynch? Any precious little eighteen-year-old kid who wants to think he's smart can talk about Lynch."

Luna was silent, remembering her mother's worry, her aunt's disapproval. How much could she trust Vicky's advice now? When she'd booted her VPN up that morning she'd seen a new email from Andrew in her inbox. He'd written about a concert he'd attended and what he was reading, but hadn't asked her how China was.

And though she half wanted to defend him to Vicky, at the same time, a secret pleasure unfurled inside her. Because maybe it *wasn't* interesting—*Eraserhead, Underworld*, all of it. Andrew's kiss, she admitted to herself, had been damp and unthrilling.

"Vicky," Luna asked. She kept her voice gentle. "I don't know what happened to you."

"Your parents didn't tell you?" Her cousin looked genuinely surprised.

"No. I mean, I heard you were in school, but now you're not?" Luna probed.

"That's messed up. *God*." Vicky exhaled heavily. "Our parents just repress *everything*."

A moped sputtered to a stop on the street next to them, a car honked, but not angrily. Luna held the silence.

"I was dating a girl," Vicky said abruptly. "Up in Oakland." She shook her head and her whole face sagged with weakness. "She . . ."

"What was her name?" Luna asked when Vicky didn't finish the sentence.

"Emily." Vicky suddenly shivered, all over, with a gesture like a dog shaking off water. Her face returned to its usual calm. "Well, we're not together anymore. But when we *were*, I tried to introduce her to my parents, you know? Like . . . we were in a relationship! She was my girlfriend! It did not go well."

"I'm sorry," Luna said softly.

"And my mom . . . we just fought, and fought, and fought after that. And also," she added, with a tone of closing the door on what she had just said, "both of them didn't like that I actually wanted to get a career, you know. I was studying communications. I wanted to switch colleges, study robotics, go work at NOAA. And they were like, that's too much for a girl, you should try to meet a nice boy at

Haas. It was just a snowball effect. One thing after another, and so many big things."

She threw the bottle cap from the Tsingtao bottle onto the sidewalk and ground it under her shoe.

"My parents," she said, "are so controlling. It's fear, you know? They have so much fear. It's just been *years* of me living under that. It's so toxic."

Luna didn't know what to say. "So what are you going to do?" she asked.

"I don't know." Vicky's voice, flat until then, wobbled. Luna darted a look at her, astonished and frightened, for surely Vicky—Vicky, who understood things—was not going to cry.

Vicky was not going to cry. Her nose was a little pink, but she sat up and said, "Let's go walk around."

The street was warm with car exhaust. Girls in white dresses and espadrilles walked by holding ice creams and tiny handbags. A café worker pulled down the blinds in the windows of his shop. An anachronistic cricket-cage seller stood at a stand on the corner, a few lonely chirps breaking into the air. Into the fading light the museum's sleek glass facade unspooled organically, like a ripple.

Vicky walked ahead and Luna couldn't tell whether she was being ignored. She tried to think of something to say.

Vicky paused. "Wait. Do you hear that?"

Behind the museum there was the sound of laughter.

"I think some people are over there," she said.

She sped up, then turned the corner. Luna caught up to her. Behind the museum was a river with signs tacked all over the shoreline in Mandarin: NO SWIMMING. A huddle of figures laughed together in the distance, clearly submerged.

The sunlight was fading fast, the figures were backlit in orange. For the moment, there were no headlights, no cars, not even the ting of a passing bicycle.

Facing the river, her back to Luna, her cousin looked so lost and lonely. A stray ray of light refracted from a museum window and glinted off a silver ring she wore on her index finger.

Luna drew closer. She thought of those years, all those years when Vicky had been running in front of her, but at this moment her so-called cousin was close enough she could put a hand on her shoulder, if she reached out and tried.

There was a sound. A gulp. It came again. And Luna looked—astonished—Vicky *was* crying, even in the half-light she could see her round, dependable face, the wetness under her eyes, the quiver of her chin and throat.

"Vicky," Luna said, "oh no," and reflexively she came up to her and hugged her. It was so different, to be hugging her. When they were young, Vicky had always been the one who comforted her. Who had comforted Vicky, all those years?

"I'm sorry," Luna said, and didn't know what else to say. Her arms felt thin and inadequate, wrapped around Vicky's taller, stronger torso.

But it was a moment, only a moment, when she felt the older girl's ribs trembling through her arms. Then Luna said, "Do you want to go in?"

She felt the shock. Vicky's tears stopped. "*Really?*"

Helplessly, Luna gestured at the people swimming farther out in the water, their dark silhouettes cutting holes into the twilight. They were going to get deported, she thought. They were going to get hepatitis, the industrial pollution would probably kill them in five seconds. Her grandmother would never let her do anything again.

Laughter from the young adults sounded in the night like bells.

"Come on," Luna challenged, more bravely than she felt. She edged closer to the barrier, which was a clear wall, knee-height, right at the edge of the water. She knew she had to keep the momentum going, or they would be stuck here, and go nowhere at all. Without letting herself think further, she kicked off her sneakers and socks and swung a leg over the barrier.

But that was as far as she could bring herself to go. The museum's illumination was ghostly, and the last dregs of sun and maybe something about the water itself, which was more brown than blue and slow-moving, made her tremble. The fear! Luna felt it, the instability she had always known was there, the precarity of the solid world, and she couldn't move.

"Wait," she said, and this time the hesitation was clear. "Maybe we—"

Then there was a shove from behind, then there was the force of wind, the *smack* of her bare feet hitting the riverbed, the shock up her shins—the water—

"*Vicky!*" Luna raised her head and spluttered. Her vision all fractals. Her throat burning.

Her cousin laughed, already in the water next to her.

Luna sunk to her chest. The water was warm and shallow, and when she stood up on her own, her steps squelched into the sucking sand. She wiped water from her eyes, gasping. Her feet felt their way over hard pebbles, the mud and weeds of the riverbed.

"You always take so long to get in!" Vicky crowed. Her dark hair, so short now, clung to her skull.

Vicky waded deeper to the center, ducked in, and moved to chest stroke. Farther away, the other swimmers were staring. Luna leaned her head back. The water had a close, marshy odor. She realized she smelled like noodle sauce. Her tank top and shorts were plastered to her skin.

"Vicky!" she called again. She could see the outline of the other girl's body under the muddy ripples. Vicky cut a confident stroke through the water and resurfaced much farther away, treading water now.

"Slow down," Luna called, but less anxiously. She watched Vicky swim away, more quickly than she could follow. Then, for the first time, a great certainty descended upon her. It was the kind of knowing that would later retreat, that would be tested, would fade as Luna forgot over and over again—but it was a certainty that, once felt, would return again and again.

Luna knew: There would be no final answer to anything. There would be no arbiter of how they should be, no guarantee of how they were going to turn out, who they would become, what lives they would live, what the outcomes of the choices they made would be. However far ahead one ran up the road in life, there was only more uncertainty ahead.

Constantly, they were in the process of becoming.

She waded deeper into the water. Her body cooled, the burning heat of the day floating off from her. She raised her arms out of the water; the air around them felt lighter. She realized she had, very quietly, started humming. "Fly Me to the Moon." There was so much they hadn't spoken of, Vicky's unstable life, her heartbreak, the whole upending of her future. But at that moment, Luna was impressed. She was still Vicky, still the one who had come first, the one who knew best.

Later, after they returned to California, Vicky would tell her she'd decided to enlist in the American Army. If she stayed, they'd pay for her next degree. A semester later, when Luna came back from college for the winter holidays, her aunt was tight-lipped and heartbroken; she had a picture of Vicky in army fatigues, her hair buzzed off, her face blunt and a little shy.

Luna copied it and taped it into the back of a new journal. In the photo, the camouflage pattern of Vicky's fatigues looked like the water of the river they'd swum in—not a river, as she later found out, but the Zhangjiabang Creek, which was the target of a three-year urban restoration project between 2005 and 2008 that cost the equivalent of 157 million dollars. The river in which Luna had watched Vicky swim away, and watched her put her head up, spitting a spout of water into the open night.

*

— A memory:

It was before Vicky left for college. Before Luna went to high school.

That evening, Vicky told Luna they were going out, just the two of them, to see the red tide. It was a sudden expedition, and outside, it was cold. Luna had forgotten to bring a sweater. She usually never came to the beach at night.

The lot at the beach was crowded with cars. From where they had parked, it was a long walk to wherever Vicky wanted to take her. Luna let herself be led by the hand, her feet slipping in the pale, cold sand. The air blew her sleepiness away.

Then they climbed up a slope, the plants all brown and weed-like in the darkness, and Luna caught her breath. Vicky pointed. *Look.*

The waves rolling in were bright and electric blue.

No no, Vicky said, *it's called a red tide, but the plankton—*

But Luna didn't understand the explanation. She watched the waves roll in, dark and subtle, and the edge of the surf flickered with a vivid blue florescence, sometimes fading, always coming back, sometimes stronger, sometimes weaker. Radio signals, she thought—radio signals! The ocean, the world, was sending a message. What was it? She watched the flickers, trying to decode them.

SEAGULL VILLAGE

I went on the road trip alone at the beginning of spring. My plan was to first head north to the three holy mountains clustered by the sea, round the tip of Honshu, and then come down south again by way of the eastern coast. When there was no more frost blinding my car windows in the mornings and the roads were clear of black ice, I packed my Leica into the trunk and left.

Up north, I saw the remains of winter's spectacular frozen trees, the fantastic, monstrous shapes formed by the snow, now slowly melting into the landscape. I saw the enormous crater lake of an ancient volcano, its waters a startling, pure jade green, the sand by its shores dark yellow ochre. In the evening I took the ropeway to the summit of the central mountain, where a five-story temple stood. In the early hours of the dark, still-cold morning, the sun rose, burning through the clouds closer and more radiant than I had ever seen it.

As I started driving south, the rains began. For three days I drove with my wipers working furiously against the lashing downpour, the roads grim and damp, the sky unyielding. Whenever I stepped outside, my hands shook uncontrollably with cold. The expressways were empty. At night I stopped at cheap motels or inns and ate dinner in empty neighborhood bars, where I hunched over my food fiercely, a woman guardedly alone. In the mornings I paced outside what small shops were in business until the owners shuffled over to reluctantly unlock the door and unshutter their windows. I browsed to buy only the occasional magazine or cheap pack of chocolate. For my lunches I ate thick udon in hot broth at roadside stands or packaged sandwiches outside convenience stores, and bought hot coffee for the road.

Then the weather cleared up and I finally saw the sea. It glimmered from my left side as I drove, gradients of twilight blue and steely gray, the sky above scattered with wisps of clouds. I rolled down my windows to breathe the air, fresh and tinged with salt. Occasionally the landscape smoked as farmers lit fires to clear the dead grass from winter. As I went farther south, I saw paddies of water burgeoning with shoots and sweeps of long pastures.

One day I took a small road that zigzagged around several miles of farmland and came out only half a mile from the sea. The gas stand I refueled at was an ancient one-man operation, the owner a leathery-faced scarecrow in a grease-stained jersey, constantly smoking and wordless, whom I paid in crumpled bills and the coins left from my motel jaunts. The houses around me grew smaller and farther apart. In the afternoon a tall hill, covered in burgeoning yellow charlocks and dandelions, rose to my left. As I wound round the hill I saw a small cluster of houses. It looked like any other town. I stopped to rest, parking in a sunny, empty lot by a large wooden building.

I stepped out of my car. The building seemed to be closed. Another building across the street had a faded and tattered sign, rust beginning to edge in on the doors. But there were still irises and pot-ted daisies on some street corners, and the other buildings looked at least clean, if not new. I walked for several minutes before coming to a steep staircase that led down to the sea. It was carved from the dark blue-gray stones that I had seen in the hills, and heavy cracks ran down the middle. I descended, and saw the woman.

She was walking out of the surf, wearing dark cropped trousers and a loose white blouse clinging half-translucent to her belly. Her wind-tossed hair was bluntly cut halfway down her neck. She had a pale face, a fine nose, and a short, strong neck. When she reached the dry sand she stretched her arms, turned her face from the wind, and caught sight of me.

"The weather is wonderful, isn't it?" she called, walking in my direction. I headed toward her, too, my sneakers slipping in the loose sand. A seagull wheeled and cawed far down the beach. As we drew closer I saw her skin was startlingly clear and luminous, almost transparent. Her feet were covered in a golden crust of sand.

"Are you lost?" she asked when she was near. "Can I help you find something?"

"I'm not," I said. "I was just driving through."

Standing in front of me, she wiped her bangs out of her face. Her hand, glistening with damp, was large and strong, with loose knuckles. "Driving through here?" she said curiously. "We don't get a lot of visitors."

When I didn't add anything, the woman asked, "Are you looking for something in particular?"

"Nothing really." I had no reason to be suspicious of her, but her presence was unsettling.

"And who might you be?" she asked, putting a hand under her chin thoughtfully.

"Ames—Aimee," I said, tripping myself up. At my all-girls' school, friends had called me Ames. I carried their backpacks, killed spiders and flies. But in front of this woman, so frank, so self-assured, I felt vulnerable and self-conscious.

"Aimee," she said, slowly feeling the name out in her mouth. My name sounded new as she luxuriated over the syllables. "Are you from around here?"

"No."

"Do you know where you are?"

"No."

"I see." The woman pointed up the stairs. "This is Seagull Village."

"Seagull Village?"

"A long time ago it was some samurai's feudal domain. There was a much longer, grander name. No one uses it now." The woman started walking toward the cracked stone steps. I followed her.

"And you? What do they call you?"

"Miho."

*

She took me to a wooden house with a small, sky-blue pickup truck parked outside and short cloth curtains covering the garage windows. Once, they had been patterned, but the cloth was now mostly a faded beige, the weave of the linen loosening. Inside the garage there were rough beams and bare concrete floors, and a dirty mattress propped against the wall next to a pile of blond wood. There were no light fixtures. It looked like a blown-out bomb shelter.

"*This* is where you live?" I was aghast.

"No," she laughed. "Look." She pushed open a small door with two clear panels at the end of the ruined garage. We emerged into a well-kept garden with an even lawn of thick, soft grass. A tree hung over it, a weeping one with thin leaves dangling and twisting from its branches, clumps of dandelion and clover at its roots. There was a white dog asleep in the sun. "That's Lune," Miho said. She approached the dog and scratched it behind its ears, and it stirred and lazily thumped its tail.

She slid open the door to another, smaller building behind Lune, and I followed her into a one-bedroom apartment. There was a narrow kitchen; a room with a low table, a radio, an outdated tube TV, and a bookshelf; a tiny bathroom with a deep blue bathtub, chipped and sunken into the floor; and a half-open door through which I could see the edge of her futon.

It occurred to me that this woman was remarkably comfortable with taking a complete stranger into her house like this. But then again, even though I was tall, and had played basketball, and held myself like I could handle myself in a fight, I was still a girl, barely above student age, and Miho looked like she was in her late thirties. She had slight crow's-feet edged around her eyes. She looked strong, too, wiry and compact, and while we'd walked here I had struggled to keep up.

She disappeared into the kitchen and came back with cups and a jug of iced tea. "Are you hungry? I can make something."

"No, no, thank you," I said.

"So what's your story?" she asked. "Just driving around? Sightseeing the country?"

"Yes." Though she seemed relaxed, I didn't lose my formality or drop my guard. Briefly I filled her in—how I had been born in Japan, but spent most of the next two decades abroad for school; how I'd worked and traveled in the years following graduation, Latin America, South America, parts of Europe; and how I'd returned only recently, taking a long break to figure out what I would do next, and to spend time with my aging parents. Her eyes, clear and intelligent, never left my face.

"Do you find it strange to be back in Japan?" Miho said at the end. She clasped her bare feet together. I could still smell, I realized, a strong marine odor, water and kelp and salt. But after all, she had walked out from the sea.

"A little bit," I admitted. But I was burning with curiosity about her. "And you? Have you always lived here? There don't seem to be a lot of people."

"You're right about that," Miho said. She laughed, but it was a sad laugh. "No, I'm not from here. Once I was just like you, a stranger wandering into town on my way somewhere else."

*

She was the only one who lived in Seagull Village. That first day, she took me around in her sky-blue pickup, the windows rolled down, our elbows hanging over the sides. We drove past the empty elementary school, rusted, dark-windowed, and haunted-looking; we drove past houses painted in unblemished white, though the grass around them grew up to my knee; we drove past shuttered restaurants and shops in various states of disrepair and neglect. For every few abandoned buildings, though, I saw at least one or two that looked still-maintained, as though their owners had just stepped out and would be coming back for dinner.

"After the earthquake two years ago, a lot of the buildings fell—as I'm sure you remember," Miho explained as she drove. "We were rebuilding. Everyone along the coast was trying to."

I didn't remember, I only knew. I'd been out of the country when the reports of the tsunami came, and my parents' home was too far inland to be affected.

But though other towns along the coast had rebuilt themselves, Seagull Village was simply too small. The population was aging; all the young people had moved to the city, or bigger towns. After the quake, the people left in the village gave up on reconstruction, moving on, rejoining their families elsewhere.

"So they all just left?"

"Yes," Miho said. "One by one, they all left."

She added, as though anxious to make me understand: "It's not just that they had to rebuild the buildings—they had to rebuild their whole lives. Their personal histories and networks, everything that had been broken apart. Eventually it became easier to just remember it from somewhere else."

But why, I didn't ask, *are you staying?*

Miho took me to the outskirts of town, which morphed into grass and unkempt fields. We stopped the car near a narrow bridge with its barriers oxidized copper-green. I followed Miho when she walked onto the deck. On the rails hung simple dolls made of white cloth, with cylindrical bodies and round heads with caps sewn on. Some had closed eyes drawn on, though most were featureless and unseeing. The light was dimming, gray and wild. The dolls fluttered in the breeze, almost as though they were waiting, listening.

"They're left in memory of those who died in the quake," Miho said softly. I turned my head to look at them more closely as we walked past. Their blank, blind faces were unnerving.

The bridge came out onto a slight knoll, and when we reached the top, I looked down and saw the slope was a mile or two from the sea. It was a long run of grass and wildflowers, and appeared better kept than any of the rest of what we had passed through—yet this, too, had an air of lack, of grieving.

Miho stopped walking. Farther down the hill, I saw two rows of short, thin trees. There were a surprising number of them, spaced evenly apart, clearly arranged by human hands.

"Once," Miho said, her face turned into the wind, "this was a long road of cherry trees. The blossoms came together so thickly in the spring that you almost couldn't see the sun. Walking through was like going through a tunnel, an endless whirlwind of flowers." She pointed at the ocean. "And then when you got out—the sea."

I could almost picture it, just as she described, those white and pink petals forming clouds that could have been the seats of gods. A vault of them, leading out to the roar of surf and salt wind.

But it was hard to superimpose that image onto the slope that lay before me. The hill looked like something out of prehistoric earth: a raw, nascent land not fully formed.

"Did you see it yourself?" I asked.

"No. I never saw it." Miho's white blouse blew loosely in the breeze. For a moment the smell of ocean damp, which I had become so used to as to almost forget, intensified. "The others told me about it, when I first came."

I looked at the saplings, and understood she was the one who had planted them.

*

That night Miho put a futon out for me in the living room, and in the morning I woke up to see her practicing some type of ritualized form out in the garden. She moved liquidly from one move to the next as she kicked and flashed her hands, each step perfectly prescribed.

I didn't move on that day. Instead we took Lune and got into Miho's blue pickup and drove to the next town over for lunch and groceries. In the restaurant, I thought the other customers were giving us strange glances. It must have been me, I thought, a newcomer in the tiny town. One gap-toothed, balding old man cackled at me as he left the restaurant, "So you found our ghost of the sea village!"

While we were eating Miho talked about traveling. Many of her travels were for her work as a tournament judge—Miho, it turned out, had been a karate grand master, a black belt of the second dan in the Kyokushin school.

On our way back, she stopped by a low building cluttered with leaves and potted plants. This shopkeeper, dressed in clothes for gardening, knew her, too; she immediately emerged with an armful of young saplings and three bags of fertilizer, which Miho carefully arranged in the back of her truck. Miho introduced her to me, and to my surprise, she got into the truck and the three of us went back to Seagull Village together.

We spent the afternoon on the hill by the bridge, planting the new saplings carefully and weeding, watering, and fertilizing the rest. The sun was hot and I soon retreated to rest in the shade of the truck, but Miho and the gardener kept on. Lune prowled around the hill, and I began to throw an old ball for her to run after and catch.

"So she's roped you in, huh?" the gardener asked when I went back down. Miho toiled away farther down the hill.

"Not roped," I said cautiously. "I chose to help."

"Why is that?" There was genuine curiosity in her voice, warm rather than prying. But what could I say?

I spread my hands. "Did you ever see the tunnel she talks about?"

"I did," the gardener said. "It really was beautiful. And quiet, too. Not like the crowds of tourists you get in parks in the bigger cities." She shook her head. "It's a tragedy it's gone. There was room to breathe."

"Why doesn't anyone help her?" I sounded almost angry, and reined in my voice.

The gardener smiled gently. "Some did, at first," she said. "But there was so much else to do. Houses to build. Or even now, a lot of people are still working on the Buddhist temple across the hill—have you seen it? It's the biggest temple in the area."

I twisted my mouth. Seeing my dark face, the gardener changed the subject. "My grandmother used to love it here. She looked forward to coming all year long."

"At least she'll appreciate it when Miho finishes planting all the trees."

The woman regarded me with something close to, but not quite, amusement. "She won't have a chance, I'm afraid," she said. "She was one of those who passed away in the quake."

Before I could even begin to formulate a jolted apology, she pointed at some of the taller saplings. "Look," she said lightly, "the ones we planted last year will bloom soon." I looked at where she pointed, a cluster of tender and vivid young leaves, and told myself I'd stay to see the first flowers.

*

We fell into a simple rhythm of days. In the mornings I would help weed and water the small garden Miho kept behind her house; we'd cook a meal together, beat and air the futons, then tend to the saplings on the hill. In the late afternoon we might have the radio on in the background while we read. On weekends Miho and I went into town, to buy whatever was necessary for her planting. In the evenings we always took Lune to the beach. Miho seemed to look forward to these walks even more than Lune, anxious to be near the water, to walk in it.

A few days in I took out the camera that had lain unused in the trunk of my car and began to take photos. I'd dabbled in photography for years, but I liked film photography best because it required patience. There was always that element of surprise.

So I began documenting Seagull Village, the setting of Miho's cutoff life. I followed Lune as she meandered around the small garden and chased leaves and bits of debris that blew down the streets. I spent hours at the beach, capturing the sunset, the empty sand, the waves midmorning, the stone steps to the village. The empty hut with old life vests and remnants of fishing tackle and nets. I shot the abandoned houses, the few stoplights that still lit for no one, the rust on windowsills and the cobwebs that accumulated on the bushes. On one walk, I found a lone yellow towel someone had forgotten hanging on a laundry line. I shot the saplings, thinking I'd do a series as they were planted and bloomed. But the more I took photos of the saplings, the more I took photos of Miho tending to them, and soon I was filling my camera roll with photos of her.

Miho as she walked through the village with a watering pot, tending to the dry potted plants left on a street corner or sweeping away a spiderweb. Miho in the mornings pulling open the curtains in the kitchen, dark-figured with dawn light falling through her hair. Miho in an elegant pose in the garden, fingertips pressed together, eyes closed, inhaling. Miho tooling with the engine of the pickup, a slick of grease on her shirt. Miho kneeling on the hill in a nest of greenery. Miho walking by the ocean, tide lapping her feet, with Lune a white spot near her ankle.

My mother called, asking when I was coming home. My father called, asking what I had planned for my future. I fended them off, telling them I was working on a personal project. I didn't tell them about Miho. The images of Seagull Village seeded themselves in my mind, growing, I wondered, into what.

*

Lune didn't warm up to me immediately. She often inserted her body as a barrier between me and her master or wrapped herself protectively around Miho's leg. The only time she forgot her wariness was during our evening walks along the beach. Then she lost herself, yelping at birds scattered along the shore, trying to catch the waves as they drew back, and leaping ecstatically into the water.

One evening the tide was especially high. Miho had gone ahead while I lagged behind. The light was cool-toned but bright, the water a pleasing storm-dark gray, Lune's white fur blending in with the seafoam. I brought the Leica's viewfinder to my face and then lowered it hastily. Lune was in too deep. She yelped, high-pitched, turning back to shore as a wave rose over her. Miho splashed into the water, but I was quicker—running in to snatch Lune by her collar, the wave hitting my back just as I turned.

"Close one!" Miho said, panting slightly as she drew closer. "Silly dog." She gathered Lune up and patted her head; the dog was sodden and cold, and my back was soaked. I realized Lune's collar had come undone in my hand.

I absentmindedly turned the collar around. A gold medallion hung from it with LUNE inscribed on the front, and as I ran my fingers over the pendant, I felt indentations on the back.

I turned it around. There were two characters engraved on the underside. As I stared I realized together they made a name: JINBO. A name that was not Miho's, and this meant that Lune was not her dog.

Suddenly Lune was at my feet, tongue out and barking. She butted her head against me. "She likes you now, Aimee!" Miho teased, closer than I'd expected. Seeing the collar, she held her hand out: "Oh, thank you."

She didn't seem to notice anything wrong. I stared at Miho but couldn't think of what to ask her; about Lune, or Lune's dead owner, or Miho herself.

*

I avoided Miho the next day, not joining her on the hill. I got into my own car for the first time since my arrival and started driving. I was almost at the next town before I decided I didn't want to be there, either, and headed past it onto the expressway.

I was going north again, back the way I'd come, but didn't know where I was headed or where to stop. I drove and drove, and, as though a reminder of my journey on the way down, the sky soon clouded over and began to drizzle. Eventually, I pulled to a stop at the side of the road.

My heart was as tight as a spring. I couldn't unclench the coiled confusion of my feelings. Sitting in my car, I asked myself: What did I want from Miho, really? What was I doing there? Why was I staying?

After the sun had set, I turned on the ignition and turned back to the village in pitch darkness. It was nearly midnight by the time I pulled in to the town hall. Instead of going to Miho's, I parked and descended the stone steps to the beach.

Hints of moonlight shone in the black water. I kicked my sneakers off to wade into the surf until the water reached my knees. The wind picked up, the cold making me shiver. This was finally the antidote to my restless emotions: the rhythm of the tide, the feel of wet sand around my feet, the breeze along my bare arms. I took a deep breath, and another. I felt my urgency dissipating. My mind worked over the events of the day. I thought again: *Why are you hesitating?*

A splash. I turned and saw Miho, standing a little ways behind me with her feet, too, in the water. I felt an internal quiver that I tried to suppress.

"Looking for pearls?" she called from behind, lightly. When I didn't say anything, she drew closer. With an odd, formal catch in her voice, she said, trying to joke, "Are you the prince going back to your capital beneath the waves?"

Her question chilled me. "It's cold out here," I said.

"Then let's go back."

We splashed to the shore.

"What were you thinking about?" Miho asked. "All alone in the dark."

I didn't want to talk about myself.

"Why are you here?" I finally asked.

"I was looking for you," she said, still lightly.

"No, not that. Why are you here, in this village? Why don't you leave?"

She didn't seem surprised by the sudden question. "I thought I already told you. I was just passing through, and I liked it enough that I wanted to stay."

"That's not an answer." I felt the anger rising again. "So you're just a loner? Unattached, untied, wandering from place to place?"

Miho chuckled softly. "I'm a lot older than you, Aimee. I'm used to being by myself." In her words I heard only some sort of secret penance. For what, for whom, was she staying in this ghost town, keeping her white dog? For what, for whom, was she planting the cherry tree road?

"How long are you going to stay here?"

Miho paused at the foot of the stone steps. "Why?"

"You must have had a life before this. You can't live here forever."

Miho started climbing the steps. Her back was to me, a dark cut-out against the night.

"You can't stay here forever, either, Aimee," she said.

Her voice, meant to be kind, suddenly seemed condescending. I began following her up the steps. We lingered uncertainly at the top. For a time there was only the soft and endless roar of the ocean.

"It's so empty here," I burst out. "How can you stand it?" I threw a pebble I'd found on the steps and listened to it clatter below. Above us, clouds had crept over the starless sky. The pebble hit the sand, and its noise was swallowed.

*

The following week Miho and I went to the next town to see the last of the plum blossoms. When we arrived we found the townspeople having a picnic, barbecue smoke wafting sweetly into the air. Miho's friend the gardener waved us over and passed me an iced beer. Taking it, I felt an odd shock—I had been alone with Miho so long, I had almost forgotten what it was like to be in the company of many people at once.

The picnic area was full of life: old couples bickering or holding hands, children sprawled on the grass or running around, one girl crying and being shushed by her mother. A tumble of beer cans in the grass. I half raised my camera, then stopped. The scene was too out of place with the rest of the photos I had taken. The townspeople seemed distant, unconnected to any part of Seagull Village. No one spoke to us. Next to me, Miho and the gardener had their heads dipped in conversation. The three of us stood on the periphery. Life went on outside of us.

Miho wandered to some farther trees, and as I watched her retreating figure, I had a vision of what she would look like as an old woman, white-haired, arms veiny and speckled from sun, still bending over her saplings on the hill. My chest clenched at the thought.

"You really are comfortable with her," the gardener said from my side.

I thought about Lune's dog tag. I muttered bitterly, "I still don't know anything about her."

She didn't reply, examining my face, looking for what, I didn't know. Whatever she saw there, she seemed perturbed by it. Then, as though she'd internally come to a decision, she said, "Remember what I said about my grandma?"

"Yes," I said, startled. "She passed away."

"Well," the gardener said, "I saw her again."

"What—!"

"Listen," the gardener said impatiently. She launched into the story as though she'd told it many times, or had been waiting a long time to tell it.

"One day, a few months after the quake, when we'd just finished repairing the house, the door opened. It was dinnertime. I was cooking, my mother was laying the table. And I heard her say, 'Mother!' I thought I'd misheard, and I turned around. But my mother was standing at the table, looking at the door, and so I looked at the door, and my grandmother was there."

Her grandmother looked just the same. She was wearing the clothes she'd had on the day she died. But she was completely fine. She asked, "Did you chop the tofu properly?"

Though the gardener was surprised, the moment her grandmother entered, she thought, *What's wrong? This is normal. We always eat dinner together.* The three of them sat down. Her mother set out the rice and the soup and the dishes. Her grandmother started lecturing her on what she should have done better—this with the fish, that with the vegetables—just as she'd always done.

After dinner, the gardener started to wash the dishes. Her mother asked, "Mother, would you like some tea?" And her grandmother said yes. So they sat over a pot of tea together before bed, just as they used to do. Then they laid out the futons—three of them. They went to sleep. And in the morning, her grandmother was gone.

I watched her numbly. "And then?"

"When I woke up, I first thought, *Oh, Grandma was here.* And I thought everything, the shaking, the tsunami, the broken houses, all of it, had been a terrible dream. Then I looked around and she was gone. Her bed was empty, the teacup she'd drunk from was still in the sink. But she was nowhere to be found, in the house or outside. Then I knew nothing had changed. But she'd come one last time, for one last totally normal evening."

"It must have been terribly sad to lose her again," I whispered.

But the gardener shook her head. "No," she said, looking up at the plum flowers. "I didn't feel sad at all. Maybe it was then, I felt—better, for the first time."

But she wasn't finished with her story.

The next day a monk from the temple over the hill stopped by their house. Monks were traveling all over the county then. He told them there had been many reports of family members acting strangely—speaking with different voices, or getting on their knees and howling. He was going around helping with spiritual restoration. Or exorcisms. He asked the gardener if she needed anything from him. The gardener almost chose not to, but then she told him she'd seen her grandmother. The monk said she was lucky, because her grandmother's spirit must be at peace.

"But—but surely—" I couldn't say it. *That's just not possible*, I thought. It just couldn't be. It must have been the shock of grief, the aftermath of trauma. But the gardener looked at me as if she knew what I was thinking, and I found I didn't quite believe myself, after all.

"Then, someone in town told him to go to Seagull Village," she said. "He heard what had happened, how so many people had died, and wanted to go see how unsettled it was. But I'd been there. So I stopped him."

"But there's no one over there," I said. "There's only Miho."

The gardener didn't say anything. And then I understood what she was trying to tell me.

"Miho—" I choked. But this was unbelievable. Miho was real. She was as solid as I was. I had seen her eat. I had seen her move, seen her breathe. We had spent hours together, laughing, talking, walking. I had touched her. Hadn't I?

I swirled the beer in my can, all thirst or appetite gone. The strange looks at the restaurant. How, even now, everyone else was ignoring her.

The gardener was silent.

"So you think Miho is—" *Like your grandmother?* I couldn't finish the sentence. I took a gulp of beer. "And Lune?"

She grinned. It had a flash of mischief in it, so surprising I couldn't swallow.

"Lune is a normal dog," she said. "She belonged to a family that left the village. See? Not such a big mystery."

But there's no greater mystery than the truth, I thought.

The rest of the afternoon I drank and forced myself to laugh more loudly than I had in months. In the evening, the atmosphere rose-gold rich, I drew Miho under one of the flowering trees.

"You've got sauce on your chin," she said, amused.

"Let's take a picture," I said forcefully, holding out my camera. "Come on."

"Shouldn't we get someone to take it for us?"

"No, this is fine." I tried to aim the camera lens at our faces. It was at an awkward angle. Miho took it from me, waved with her other hand, and the gardener appeared.

"Will you take a photo of me and Aimee?"

The gardener took the camera and motioned us closer together. My hand suddenly felt naked. She raised the Leica. I wanted to slip my hand behind Miho but, just as I was about to, stopped myself. Instead my hand lingered an inch or two from her back. The cloth of her blouse brushed against my fingers, cool and light, and I thought I could detect again, though here we were farther inland, the salt and kelp smell of the ocean.

"One, two, three," the gardener said, and the flash went off.

We drove back to Miho's house in silence. As I was about to fall asleep, I heard Miho quietly moving about. "After the plum blossoms, it won't be long before the cherry trees bloom, too," she said, as though to herself.

More peaceful, interminable days passed by. The rust on some of the buildings had already increased since my arrival. On the edges of the village the roads were steeped in morning glories and bush clover, and weeds snaked up around the abandoned houses. The trees grew full of green-yellow moss. Bats began to come out in the evenings. On the hill, the saplings were steadily increasing in number. I took photo after photo, a sense of urgency mounting in me, which I stifled.

I remembered the promise I'd made to myself to stay until the first flowers. In the end, I was the one who saw the cherry blossoms first.

*

Miho had gone into town and I drove to the hill alone. I crossed the bridge, brushed dirt off the caps of the dolls as I passed, headed down the slope, and then saw the first buds.

Miho's saplings were dusted in pink, a pink that spoke of revival, of renewal, of peace. There were hundreds of them. The flowers were hauntingly perfect. Below, the grass of the hill was a deep and abundant green.

I let out a harsh laugh. I was alone, no camera, no Miho. All around me was the proof of her labor of love and longing. Against the empty sky the trembling cherry blossoms were the saddest, most beautiful flowers I had ever seen. I suddenly had a feeling that in this vivid, rooted, living landscape, I was the one who was passing through and must seem like a spirit.

I reached out my hand to the branch nearest me and touched one flower. Then I violently plucked it off and let it fall to the ground. I brought my hand to my face. There was a bittersweet aroma on my skin.

When Miho came back that afternoon, I was stretched out on the hill, face curled into my arms, asleep.

"Aimee," she said gently as she approached. "Aimee."

I stirred.

"Look!" She pointed with childish delight at all the trees around her. "They're here! They're really here!"

I sat up groggily, rubbing my eyes, and then she hugged me. For a moment, it was as if I were submerged in a cool, thick mist. The smell of seawater filled my nose and pressed all around me. Then the mist dissipated and my face was digging into the bone of her shoulder. *Is this real?* I thought wildly. *Is she real? Is it really the two of us alone here?*

"Have you been here all day?" Miho set down the things she had brought and whirled, bending close to inspect one tree, then another, then another. "This is amazing. They're so beautiful. Aren't they so beautiful?" She laughed, bright and clear, and repeated herself. "I can't believe it. Aimee, where's your camera? It's what we've been waiting for!" She whirled around the trees again.

"I left my camera at your house," I said slowly.

Something in my voice sobered her. Miho drifted back, idly letting her fingers linger on a trunk here, a branch there. The brilliant green of the leaves looked like a firework under her hand.

"That's all right," she said. She smiled. "It's too good for a picture, anyway."

She came to sit by me. A wind picked up. It was very quiet.

She asked suddenly: "Aren't you leaving soon, Aimee?"

"What?"

She was gazing down at the bottom of the hill. "How long are you planning on staying?"

"Why does it matter?"

"But it's something to think about." Miho plucked a blade of grass and shredded it in two. "You have parents. You have a family. You have your whole life to live still." Now she looked at me, and my reflection in her pupils was startlingly clear. For the first time, I noticed how dark and dilated her pupils were. "You're so young. This isn't the place for you."

"And it is for you?"

"Yes. I've chosen it."

I stood up. I was angry—shaking. The outside world crashed into the dream between the saplings.

"And how long do you plan to stay here? Until the trees grow up to rebuild your tunnel? How many years will that take? If you ever even finish." I started talking faster. "It's an impossible task. How can you stay here? Why don't you leave?"

I stopped. I repeated it. "Why don't you leave with me?"

"But Aimee," Miho said softly, "you know there is something for me here."

"One woman can't bring a village back to life," I said bitterly. "This is a ghost town."

The air seemed to turn cold with the word *ghost*.

Miho looked at me with her gentle, tired eyes. She said, "A tree will stay where you've rooted it."

I shook my head. Miho placed a hand on the bark of one of the taller saplings.

"Every winter, it will die. Every spring, it will flower. Growing all the while." She turned to face the ocean. "And the people you love," she said, "won't always stay. You should know that best."

"Why?" My frustration was leaking away even though I wanted to hold on to it.

"You're always leaving, aren't you? Always going somewhere new." When she smiled, her eyes were moons. Lune came bounding to her ankle and Miho put her hand on her ears. "Let me ask you. Have you ever gone to the same place twice?"

She reached out and, very lightly, brushed a piece of grass off my shoulder.

I turned to look at the shoreline with Miho. The water was a stormy palette of innumerable shades, cut into by the coarse, rocky sand. In front of me were all the blossoms she'd promised. They were almost like tiny clouds on top of that vast, gray sea, which now seemed like it belonged to a completely other world—one I couldn't reach.

CREDITS

Thank you to the following publications, which initially gave homes to these pieces (in earlier forms): "Monitor World" in *Shenandoah*, "We Were There" in *Witness*, "The Virtuoso" in *Hyphen*, "Zeroes:Ones" in *The Adroit Journal*, and "Seagull Village" in *Pleiades*. Thank you to Ling Ma, who selected "Chicken. Film. Youth." for 2nd place in the *Zoetrope* 2022 Short Fiction Competition.

NOTES

"Zeroes:Ones" references an *otome* game, *Hakuōki ~Shinsengumi Kitan~, Demon of the Fleeting Blossom: The Tale of the Shinsengumi*, first released in 2008 by Idea Factory, and *Ef: A Fairy Tale of the Two*, an adult visual novel released in 2006 by Minori.

"LET'S GO LET'S GO LET'S GO" was inspired by the 2019 Japan Society exhibit *Radicalism in the Wilderness: Japanese Artists in the Global 1960s* and Reiko Tomii's book *Radicalism in the Wilderness: International Contemporaneity and 1960s Art in Japan*. This story is heavily indebted to conceptual artist Yutaka Matsuzawa and his piece *Banner of Vanishing* (1966), a long pink silkscreen banner upon which is written, in massive words, in Japanese, "Humans, Let's Vanish, Let's Go, Let's Go, Gate, Gate–Anti-Civilization Committee." The title of the story, and this collection, are taken from this piece. I was also inspired by Group Ultra Niigata (GUN) and their painting performance *Event to Change the Image of Snow* (1970), in which members blasted colorful pigment on a snowy day onto the landscape, which was quickly covered by more falling snow.

"Power and Control" depicts an emotionally abusive relationship. The title refers to the Power and Control Wheel, developed by the Domestic Abuse Intervention Programs (DAIP), which depicts some of the methods and tactics an abuser may use to control an intimate partner. You can reach the National Domestic Violence Hotline at 1-800-799-7233, or text START to 88788.

"We Were There" references Yūki Obata's manga *Bokura Ga Ita*, which ran from 2002 to 2012.

Some of the elements of "Seagull Village" were inspired by Richard Lloyd Parry's *Ghosts of the Tsunami* (2017), a reported account of the aftermath of the 2011 Tōhoku tsunami and includes accounts of spirits, ghosts, and supernatural possessions experienced on a wide scale after the massive loss of life of the tsunami. Miho's comment about the prince with the capital beneath the waves refers to Prince Antoku's death from *The Tale of the Heike*.

ACKNOWLEDGMENTS

Thank you, first and foremost, to Alyssa Ogi, who picked my book out of the slush pile and made my lifelong dream come true. Thank you for being a most probing editor and gentle human.

Thank you to the vibrant Tin House team for their scrappiness and enthusiasm, including Masie Cochran, Beth Steidle, Nanci McCloskey, Becky Kraemer, Meg Storey, Craig Popelars, and Lisa Dusenbery.

Thank you to Annie Hwang of the 626, who stepped in with poise and assurance at the critical moment and handled the chaos with grace.

Thank you to Jean Chen Ho, Ling Ma, Yan Ge, Raven Leilani, and Kyle Dillon Hertz for their generous praise.

Thank you to my teachers, especially: Rachel DeWoskin, Vu Tran, Brian Keaney, John Freeman, Emily Barton, Nathan Englander, Hari Kunzru, and Katie Kitamura. And to Mrs. Jane Chambers, once of Aviara Oaks Middle School—I hope this book finds you. You were the very first teacher to encourage my writing.

Than you to my friends in writing who read drafts and provided the richest intellectual companionship: Raven Leilani, Katie Barasch, Elizabeth Nicholas, Silvia Park, Nadine Browne, Kyle Dillon Hertz, Jenzo DuQue-French (you should really get your own motivational speech book, my friend), Willa Zhang, and Claire Jia.

Thank you so much to Egocircus, our rowdy bunch, and its reluctant leaders, Anne and Currie, for reminding me how to play.

The stories in this book span years. For their generous friendship, humor, and comfort during hard times, I would like to thank Michelle Sit, who has carried me through the hilliest terrains; Wendy Wei; David Huang; Sophie Son; Gautam Srikishan; Janine Chow; Ashley Tran; K Liu; my beloved brother Angus; and my therapist Anthony, who helped me live. Thank you to Joshua McDowell and Sean May, who were safe havens in Tokyo. Thank you to Casper Yen for the photos and laughs. My cat Merlin also deserves a place here.

Thank you to the Hefei family for memories of long summers of warmth. My grandfather, Qian Feng, 钱峰, was the original Qian family writer. Here I would like to pay my respects to him and my grandmother, Shi Zhengwei, 石征玮. 天堂安息.

I did a lot of this alone, and it was hard. Thank you, also, to myself.

© Casper Yen

CLEO QIAN has published work in *Pleiades*, *The Guardian*, *Shenandoah*, *The Margins*, *The Common*, and elsewhere. Originally from southern California, she lives in New York City.